Winter Dreams

Trana Mae Simmons

JOVE BOOKS, NEW YORK

If you purchased this book without a cover, you should be aware that this book is stolen property. It was reported as "unsold and destroyed" to the publisher, and neither the author nor the publisher has received any payment for this "stripped book."

WINTER DREAMS

A Jove Book / published by arrangement with
the author

PRINTING HISTORY
Jove edition / October 1997

All rights reserved.
Copyright © 1997 by Trana Mae Simmons.
This book may not be reproduced in whole or in part,
by mimeograph or any other means, without permission.
For information address: The Berkley Publishing Group,
a member of Penguin Putnam Inc.,
200 Madison Avenue, New York, New York 10016.

The Putnam Berkley World Wide Web site address is
http://www.berkley.com

ISBN: 0-515-12164-9

A JOVE BOOK®
Jove Books are published by The Berkley Publishing Group,
a member of Penguin Putnam Inc.,
200 Madison Avenue, New York, New York 10016.
JOVE and the "J" design are trademarks
belonging to Jove Publications, Inc.

PRINTED IN THE UNITED STATES OF AMERICA

10 9 8 7 6 5 4 3 2 1

HIGHEST PRAISE FOR JOVE HOMESPUN ROMANCES

"In all of the Homespuns I've read and reviewed I've been very taken with the loving renderings of colorful small-town people doing small-town things and bringing 5 STAR and GOLD 5 STAR rankings to the readers. This series should be selling off the bookshelves within hours! Never have I given a series an overall review, but I feel this one, thus far, deserves it! Continue the excellent choices in authors and editors! It's working for this reviewer!"
—*Heartland Critiques*

We at Jove Books are thrilled by the enthusiastic critical acclaim that the Homespun Romances are receiving. We would like to thank you, the readers and fans of this wonderful series, for making it the success that it is. It is our pleasure to bring you the highest quality of romance writing in these breathtaking tales of love and family in the heartland of America.

And now, sit back and enjoy this delightful new Homespun Romance . . .

WINTER DREAMS
by Trana Mae Simmons

Jove Titles by Trana Mae Simmons

TOWN SOCIAL
WINTER DREAMS

To Leslie, Anthony and Zoey Megahey, and Shirley Ferdinand.
You're all I could ever want
for both friends and fellow authors.
Smintch and MOT!

To Jessica Faust,
who knows Grand Marais, too.
Thanks for being the sort of editor
an author dreams of finding.

And never last or least,
once again to Rob Cohen,
who knows I'll follow her anywhere!

1

Grand Marais, Minnesota
October 1909

SANDY GLARED ACROSS the polished desk as Tom Goodman leaned back in his chair, steepling his fingers beneath his chin. Feeling like a wolf snared in a wilderness trail trap, Sandy damned Goodman for lying to him. For not letting him in on the whole deal.

But Goodman didn't know how broke he was, and Sandy had enough pride left to not want his potential employer to realize he had him over a barrel. He also needed to be sure Goodman didn't probe into the reason he'd left Alaska and hightailed it to a town in Minnesota few Alaskans even knew existed. By necessity, he had made the trip in record time, even with the stop to pick up his sister, Cristy.

The problem was, he couldn't swallow the new information—the information Goodman had conveniently failed to disclose until after Sandy arrived.

"Let me get this straight," Sandy said. "I knew from your

telegrams that the position in your shipping company wouldn't open up until next spring, so I agreed to train your sled dogs over the winter. But you forgot to mention two things to me. One, your dogs aren't the malamutes I'm used to—they're this new breed, the husky, that's been invading both Alaska and the States. And two–the 'musher' I'm supposed to train to run in an Alaskan race four months from now is your *daughter?*"

Goodman pursed his lips and nodded, a twinkle fleeting through his eyes and a corner of his lips quirking. "That appears to be about it. We've already discussed most of the other arrangements. You'll have living quarters at our home, Ladyslipper Landing, which is just a little northwest of town." His voice grew sterner. "And make no mistake, Sandy, the kennels are for the most part my daughter Laura's responsibility, but I keep a sharp eye on what she's doing. She's my only child."

Sandy leaned back in his chair, a disbelieving whoosh of breath escaping. If the man was so damned protective of his daughter, what the hell was he doing agreeing to the ridiculous idea of her competing in an Alaskan race?

"Mr. Goodman. . . ."

"Tom, please," the older man broke in. "After all, we'll be in contact quit a bit down through the coming months. This is a very small town, with only a population of a little over three hundred people, and most of us are on a first-name basis. Besides, when you call me 'mister,' I think of my father."

"Fine," Sandy conceded. "But listen, Tom. Do you have any idea how dangerous it could be for a woman to run in one of these Alaskan races? Good lord, man! We're talking a week on the trail, solely accountable for yourself and your dogs!"

"I understand they have checkpoints and overnight accommodations set up at periodic spots. Besides, you'll be running with her, with me paying all your expenses. Laura has her heart set on this. In fact, she won't agree to set a wedding date with her fiancé, David, until she makes an attempt at this race."

Sandy stared at the man, incredulous. Tom Goodman didn't look like a fool. Somewhere around his mid-forties, he was still fit and could probably handle his own team in the Alaska race. Gray had infiltrated his hair, liberally sprinkled in his sideburns and prevalent enough in the rest of it to lighten what must once have been a dark auburn color. Yet along with his confident demeanor, the signs of aging seemed to bespeak experience and knowledge, not a weakening or physical laxity.

Knowing from his friend, Ted, in Alaska that Tom Goodman was filthy rich—having even more money than Sandy's former father-in-law—Sandy had expected to find a man dressed in an expensive suit with condescending manners. Instead Tom Goodman wore a pair of wool trousers and a red plaid shirt similar to those favored by lumberjacks. A heavy parka hung on the coat rack in the corner of the office. As in Alaska, the fall evenings in Minnesota could be extremely chilly, the nights, biting cold.

Sandy started to speak, but thought better of it when he realized he was on the verge of calling the man an utter idiot. He couldn't afford to antagonize Goodman. Blowing out a breath instead of the ill-advised words, he gazed around the office, playing for a little time. Instinct told him that Goodman saw through his ploy when the other man pursed his lips and nodded his head slightly, yet Tom allowed Sandy time to think over his decision.

Unlike Tom's practical appearance, the office reflected wealth. Floor-to-ceiling windows opened the view to the grandeur of the Lake Superior Harbor and the rugged shoreline north of them. Sandy had also seen the Goodman name on several of the gray-planked, weathered warehouses beside the docks when they arrived by ship that morning.

According to Ted, Tom owned a shipping company, a logging and lumber company, and even employed some commercial fishermen. He had his finger in every successful pie in Grand Marais. Now he seemed to want to spend some of his excess money on his daughter and her sled dogs, since it was a fairly expensive undertaking to ship an entire team clear across the States, then north to Alaska and back here—two teams, with Sandy accompanying her. He should have an idea of the cost, since he'd just completed a one-way journey of that type with his own dogs.

And Sandy's having to return to Alaska as part of the job he so sorely needed had been the other thing Tom forgot to mention. *That* couldn't happen, but if he admitted as much to Goodman right now, he might as well give up any chance of landing the position.

"Why me?" Sandy asked.

"You come highly recommended by Ted Erickson," Tom replied without hesitation. "Ted did a fine job for me as my right hand man in my shipping company, before he got itchy feet and headed up to Alaska. I sent him an inquiry, and it was a real stroke of luck when Ted told me that you had the qualifications for both the dog trainer and shipping management positions I need to fill."

"I can handle your shipping position," Sandy agreed. "It's the same type of job I had in Alaska, and I kept things organized enough to give me time to train and race my dogs. But my dogs were beaten in the last race I ran—by a team of huskies."

"Ah, those huskies," Tom said with a chuckle. "I've heard there's some resentment directed at the breed, mostly from established mushers—the ones who've used malamutes and Eskimo dogs from the beginning."

"Some?" Sandy muttered. "I'd call that an understatement."

"Laura's been working with her huskies for several years now. She was one of the first breeders to import a couple pair after they were discovered in Siberia, and we saw some skepticism here, too. But I think you'll find she's put together a hell of a team."

Sandy stood, prepared to leave. "I'll have to consider this turn of events. Can I get back to you tomorrow?"

"Of course." Rounding the desk, Tom walked beside him to the door, where he extended his hand for a leave-taking. "I'll be in my office here by eight tomorrow morning."

Briefly, Sandy shook Tom's hand, then left the office,

closing the door behind him carefully rather than with the sharp *thud* his emotions dictated. No sense burning any bridges by flagrant discourteousness to Goodman. He'd sort all this information out overnight and be sure he made the best decision by tomorrow.

What sort of woman could Tom's daughter be? He visualized a somewhat homely tomboy, whose fiancé was probably content to postpone their wedding. Money had bought more than one less-than-comely female a husband. But women like his late wife, Colleen, drew men with their beauty as well as their trust funds.

Colleen had been lovely with her auburn hair and sparkling green eyes. Despite her snooty parents, she had also been one of the most loving and giving women Sandy had ever met. It still hurt him almost beyond bearing whenever he remembered Colleen's dim, pain-filled eyes and ravaged body as she slipped away from him. She'd left him their wonderful six-year-old daughter, Tracie, however, and Tracie was already showing signs of the same beauty as her mother—both in her face and in her bubbly personality.

He looked for Tracie now, scanning the snow-covered street filled with dog paw and sled runner tracks, as well as deeper impressions of horses' hooves and wagon wheels. Up the street he saw a team of huge draft horses pulling a wagon of freshly-cut logs. Virgin pine, some of the trees were too large even for four men standing in a circle to reach around. As soon as a little more snow covered the ground, the wagons would be exchanged for lumber sleds in order to continue the work as long as possible into the winter months. Most of the other transportation waiting at the various storefronts was either dogsleds or smaller wagons. None of those horseless carriages had made it this far north—less than a hundred miles from Canada—although he'd seen a few of them in Duluth.

He didn't see Tracie up that way. When she had asked permission to wait outside while he reported to Tom Goodman, his daughter had assured him that she would remain within seeing distance. An obedient child, she would keep her promise.

His sister, Cristy, had remained down on the docks while Sandy and Tracie walked on into town, insisting she would verify that all of the dogs were unloaded and every piece of their baggage taken from the ship's hold. He assumed she was just as interested in making sure none of her art supplies were left on board. He smiled when he saw her still down on the shore, standing beside a wind-weathered warehouse. Staring out over the water, she was probably mentally setting up her easel, her artist's eye panning the distance and transferring the sights to the canvas square in her mind.

Though he was supposedly now responsible for her, since their parents had died shortly before Sandy left Alaska, he had no idea how he would have handled Tracie on the trip without his newly-matured younger sister's help. Even though he and Tracie had to make allowances for Cristy's propensity to daydream when her muse visited, for the most part he and his sister had bonded in a deep friendship, which strengthened their blood relationship.

Ah, there was Tracie. Red braids bobbing on her back and green muffler dragging, she skipped down the walkway on the other side of the street. One mitten dropped out of her coat pocket as Sandy watched, kept from being lost because Cristy had sewn a sturdy ribbon between the pair. Just as Sandy was about to call to her a wagon pulled by draft horses rumbled up the street and he was forced to wait for it to pass before he could be heard.

As soon as he could see Tracie again, he caught sight of the snow-white sled dog not twenty feet from her. One of those damned huskies, it bounded to its feet in a confrontational stance, which Sandy recognized all too well from his years of dealing with dogs. The sled it was hitched to, tilted on its side and secured with a snow anchor, kept it in place, but Tracie continued walking closer as she wandered on down the steps at the end of the walkway. A gull flying overhead snared his daughter's attention, and she lifted an arm, probably chirping to the bird, though he couldn't hear her from this distance. Her meandering steps led her closer to the dog.

"Little girl, stop!"

Sandy barely noticed the woman who emerged from a store near the other end of the street. Her shout blended with his own yell at Tracie as he pounded across the rutted ground to rescue his daughter, but from the corner of his eye he saw the woman drop her armload of packages and race in the same direction. At his charging approach, the white sled dog growled viciously, jumping and straining against its harness. Any other time Sandy would have dominated the dog into submission, but not when it was his daughter in danger.

Tracie froze, her teal blue eyes wide with trepidation as she stared back and forth between the two people racing toward her. The woman, closer from the beginning, reached her first and scooped Tracie into her arms. Sandy's booted feet slid on the frozen earth, and he barely kept from sending all three of them crashing to the ground when he gathered his daughter—along with the woman who held her—into his arms and swung them around to place himself between them and the snarling dog.

"Heavens," the woman said as she gazed up at him, her mouth right in line for him to kiss if he would have bent his head, "I do apologize for Blancheur."

"That's your damned dog?" Sandy snarled.

She nodded, a touch of fear in her green eyes. Damn, she looked more than a little bit like his dead wife with that auburn hair and sea-green eyes. He hoped Tracie didn't notice that. It was bad enough that Tracie had overheard him discuss with Cristy the fact that this was the one-year anniversary of Colleen's death on the trip up from Duluth this morning.

When she tried to step away from him, he realized he still had his arm around her in a firm grip. A stab of consternation went through him when he felt a reluctance to remove it, and he counteracted that by jerking it free and almost snatching Tracie from the woman's arms. Then she spoke a sharp word to the husky, which quieted immediately.

Politeness demanded he introduce himself, but Sandy didn't give a damn about that at the moment. His heartbeat needed to calm and his senses stabilize while his brain took a moment to translate the fact that his daughter hadn't been mauled. He clutched Tracie tight, and against his will, studied the woman without apology for his examination, since she didn't appear to be in a hurry to move away.

He could see calling her a woman might be stretching it. She appeared to be barely out of her teens, if that. She couldn't have been over five foot two, a couple inches shorter than his wife had been.

The greenish color of her eyes reminded him of the summer sea off the Alaskan coast, and she met his gaze expectantly now, her fear of him evidently gone and replaced by the anticipation of an introduction. When a cloud shifted and uncovered the sun, he finally realized her hair was a much darker red than he'd thought at first—darker than Colleen's and Tracie's.

She'd opened her blue-gray, full-length cloak, although she still wore her mittens. The dark emerald gown beneath the cloak appeared to be made of wool, the hem of her skirt caught on the top of one of her boots, which were of a rather mannish style. What curves she had were less than voluptuous, and she didn't appear to have any false padding on her figure, such as extra petticoats.

Tracie shifted in his hold, hugging one arm around his neck and settling her tiny rump on his bent arm.

"I'm sorry I got too close to your doggie," Tracie said to the woman. "Daddy's told me not to go close to strange doggies, but I was watchin' the birdie and didn't see him."

"I'm just glad you weren't hurt," the woman replied with a relieved smile. "I'm Laura Goodman, but please, call me Laura, not Miss Goodman. And you are?"

"Tracie." She patted Sandy on the cheek. "And my last name's same as my daddy's—Montdulac. This is my daddy, Sandy Montdulac."

"Oh!" Laura pulled a mitten off and held out her hand. "You're my new trainer. I'm very glad to meet you. We have your quarters all ready for you out at Ladyslipper Landing."

Sandy reluctantly shook her hand, taking note of the fragile bones and diminutive size. But his most prominent thought was that this woman had never had the word "homely" connected to her in her life. Frowning, he pushed that thought aside and concentrated on wondering at the incongruity of her wearing her mittens when she evidently didn't think it chilly enough to keep her cloak buttoned. His face must have given away his second thought, or maybe he stared a second too long at her hands. She dropped her grasp, laughing gaily and pulling off her other mitten.

"If you're wondering about the mittens on this pretty day, it's because my hands chill very easily, as do my feet," she said. "I've found that as long as I keep those four things warm, the rest of my body is fine. From late fall, like this, until the ice melts in the late spring, I seldom bare my hands outside."

Glancing down, she noticed her skirt hem and tugged it free. Sandy's eyes widened when he caught a glimpse of trousers beneath the hem. She giggled once again, tilting her head coquettishly as she waited for his reaction.

"I can't very well travel behind a dog sled in a skirt, now, can I?" she asked airily.

Ignoring her levity, Sandy very abruptly stated his case. "There were a few things your father kept from me when he telegraphed me about this position. For one thing, he didn't tell me that I'd be training dogs for a *woman* to drive in an Alaskan race."

In a quicksilver change of expression, Laura gazed at him arrogantly from those sea-green eyes, lifting a feathery auburn brow. "I assure you, Mr. Montdulac, I can handle a team. I've been driving sled dogs since I could walk. And if your rather denigrating reference to my gender means what I think it does, I can also assure you that I'm definitely a woman. In fact, I attained the age of majority—twenty-one—last January. I'll be twenty-two by the time I participate in the race."

Sandy clenched his throat muscles, stemming the retort fighting for freedom from his beleaguered mind. Hell, he could do the job. That was the least of his worries. Not wanting to was the problem.

Not wanting to do the job, though, wasn't a valid reason to allow his sister and daughter to starve to death while he looked for another position—something more suited to his damned excess of pride. Being responsible for a family was about the most humbling situation he could imagine. And if it meant teaching this slip of femininity some of the tricks of racing, he could gulp down a huge dash of pride with the best of men. She didn't need to know that his focus would be on showing her how totally ridiculous her idea of competing in that race was, should he accept the position her father offered.

Besides the weather, which could in itself be a death threat, her other rivals would be a dangerous throng of cutthroat men. They would all be determined to win the race not only for the huge purse, but also to prove the superiority of their teams. A beautiful woman in their midst would further complicate matters, he thought, even while he chastised himself for admitting he'd noticed her beauty himself.

He forced his thoughts away from the way she looked. She damned sure didn't need the money. She probably only wanted to have a high old time talking to her grandchildren some day about how she'd been the first woman in history to run in an Alaskan race.

"When I take on a position as a trainer," he said in a rough voice, "I'm the boss. My word is law. The first time a driver I'm training defies my orders, I'm gone."

"Agreed," Laura responded immediately.

"I told your father I'd let him know in a day or two."

"Just what is it you have to think over, Mr. Montdulac? Both my father and my fiancé support me in this venture, and they're the only men in my life whom I have to opt to please. You'll be paid more than adequately for your services, you know."

"Yeah," Sandy growled. "But your safety is a little more important than money, wouldn't you think?"

"I see," Laura mused. "I believe my father has chosen well then, since you feel that way."

"Hell, it wouldn't do my reputation as a trainer any good if you got hurt, now, would it?" Sandy snarled. He expected Laura to snap back at him, but instead her face creased with concern. Whatever she was thinking, though, she kept to herself.

"You'll need somewhere to stay while you're making your decision," Laura said. "And Father said you were bringing your own dogs with you, so they'll need a kennel. Everything is ready for you at Ladyslipper Landing, if you'd like to stay there. And you can look over the facilities, which I believe you'll find more than adequate."

"The dogs will be fine in their cages on the dock, and I saw a place called the Lake Side Hotel as the ship pulled in. I very much doubt it's full, since the ship's captain told me that he seldom gets passengers for up here this late in the season."

"Suit yourself, I guess. We'll wait to hear from you."

Over Laura's shoulder Sandy caught a glimpse of a man crouched behind a bush. Enough dry leaves remained stuck on the branches to camouflage him somewhat, but his red-plaid shirt gave him away. He dropped to his knees and inched toward Laura's sled dog, tied right behind her.

Grabbing Laura, Sandy swung her away from the dog and thrust Tracie into her arms. He ordered Laura to stay—as he would have a sled dog under his control—swiveled, and launched himself at the skulking man. The next thing he knew, he was flat on the ground beneath the white husky, a set of snarling teeth in his face and one brown, one blue eye, glaring at him. A vicious growl sounded in his ears.

"Blancheur! No!" Laura yelled. "Buck, pull Blancheur off!"

A red-plaid-sleeved arm reached for the dog's harness, and Sandy jerked his gaze away from the husky, centering on the skulking man's rummy brown eyes. The man's lips pouted in his tobacco-stained beard, and he sniffed as though he had a cold. Astonished, Sandy realized the man was on the verge of crying.

"Here Blancheur, old boy," he said. "Get offa that there man a'fore you get me in more trouble."

"Trouble's right, Buck!" Leading Tracie by the hand, Laura stomped over beside the dog as Sandy rose to his feet. "Look, I know you like Blancheur, but I've told you before to ask permission from me when you want to say hello to him."

Buck hung his head. Thin and wiry, he wasn't much taller than Laura. His hips were almost nonexistent, and Sandy figured if he hadn't worn a pair of bedraggled suspenders, Buck's trousers would have been down around his feet.

"I know, Miss Laura," Buck said with a whimper. "But—"

Laura took a step back. "You've been drinking, haven't you, Buck? I can smell it."

"Yes, ma'am," Buck whispered. "And I knowed you wouldn't let me 'round Blancheur like that. Like you said, I just wanted to say hello to him."

The dog made his own decision. He sidled up to Buck, whining and begging for attention. Buck knelt and laid an arm around the white neck, scratching behind a pointed ear with his other hand.

"Hi, boy," he murmured.

Laura heaved an exasperated sigh, then glanced at Sandy. "He used to work at my kennels. But he got drunk one afternoon, and I came out and found him asleep, with the dogs unfed and unwatered on a hot summer day. I've since hired Pete Tallwolf, who'll be your assistant."

"I haven't agreed to take the job yet," Sandy reminded her. But though she couldn't have known it, his ending up beneath that snarling husky had given Sandy another reason to accept the position rather than walk away from it. As he strived to hide his humiliation that a rummy drunk could approach the husky with no problem, while it turned vicious on him, he vowed silently to dominate that animal if it was the last thing he did.

"I prefer malamutes to huskies," he informed Laura.

"I used to myself. But be assured, I'm well aware a team of huskies won the last Alaskan race."

"Yeah," Tracie unfortunately put in. "Daddy was in that race. He only got second."

Ignoring his daughter's comment, which threatened to bring on another spurt of humiliation, he abruptly motioned his head at Laura's sled dog. "That animal will have to be taught obedience around me if I come to work for your kennel."

"Blancheur will learn who you are fairly quickly," Laura assured him. "Whether or not he learns to like you will be up to how you handle him. But he will obey you. I'll see to that."

"No," Sandy corrected her. "*If* I take the job, *I'll* see to that."

"Agreed," Laura said, yet again defusing his antagonism by simply refusing to rise to the bait. She told Buck she was leaving, and the little man rose, nodding to her and shuffling off. Pulling her snow anchor free, Laura up-tilted the sled. Before she stepped onto the runners, she replaced her mittens, then gathered her skirts around her waist and tied them into a knot, exposing her trousered legs.

"I will be hearing from you shortly, I assume," she said, and Sandy responded with a curt nod. She slipped Tracie a wink. "Good-bye, Tracie, honey."

"Bye-bye." Tracie lifted a hand, waving it back and forth.

A soft "mush" was all it took for Laura to get Blancheur moving. She stopped and retrieved her scattered packages on the walkway and quickly stacked them on the sled. With another quick wave back at them, she remounted the runners.

Sandy's expert eye told him that she handled the sled well, but driving one dog for a short distance was a world away from handling a full team of sled dogs day in and day out on a trail. Efficient functioning of the team could even depend on the personalities of the dogs harnessed as partners. He'd withhold his opinion until he saw her in action on a trail run.

And see her in action he would, given the fact he already knew he had no choice right now other than to accept the position Tom Goodman offered. He'd also fallen more under the spell of this area of the States the further north he came, since it reminded him a lot of his beloved Alaska. He might be able to make it as far back south as Duluth if he were extremely careful with the money he had left, but he'd be safer from discovery up here. He'd make Laura and her father wait at least until tomorrow, but then he'd give them his affirmative answer. By the day after that, he'd probably be harnessing up his own team and making a run with her.

She still had no damned business even thinking about participating in one of those dangerous Alaskan runs, but he very much doubted her father would let that happen. Surely Tom Goodman was just humoring his daughter, since he had plenty of money to be able to afford to do that. Surely.

2

A<small>FTER A BRIEF</small> stop at her father's office, Laura headed Blancheur up the snow-covered trail from Grand Marais to Ladyslipper Landing.

"What an arrogant—*sad*—man," she told the dog, whose ears swiveled to catch her words as he padded along silently.

She'd lost track of how many conversations she'd had with her various dogs over the years. Her childhood girlfriends had confided in their dolls, while Laura had shared confidences with her favorite dog or puppy of the moment. She frequently had a dog or puppy in her room overnight—sometimes an entire litter of puppies, if necessary, due to some problem with the bitch.

She had hand-fed at least a dozen puppies over the years, a few of which the vet told her were hopeless cases. One by one, she'd proven him wrong, but Dr. Erik Sawbill still stubbornly thought he knew more about veterinary medicine than Laura did. A cozy warmth stole over her at the memory of the bantering spit-spats she and the crusty old vet had engaged in over the years, and Laura smiled at the rambling turn her thoughts had taken. She supposed one of the first people for Sandy Montdulac to meet after Pete Tallwolf should be Dr. Erik.

If Sandy even accepted the position, she reminded herself.

She didn't quite understand why on earth she focused on calling him Sandy in her mind, rather than Mr. Montdulac as she did to his face. It was a nice face. He wasn't quite six feet, but since she'd stopped growing at five foot one—one and a half if she stretched it—she had to crane her neck to look up at most people except children.

He was definitely old enough to command the respect of the title before his name, since her father had told her Sandy was thirty and a widower. What her father couldn't have known, or probably hadn't even noticed when he met with Sandy, was what a rugged, handsome thirty the man was. Or how his blond hair, a little too long, curled and shone even in muted sunlight. How his teal eyes, twins of his darling daughter's, held shadows of pain and secrets better left untold.

He carried a reserve around him like a polar ice pack. Still, she'd managed a glimpse of his pain, deciding to overlook his surliness at least for now. Later might be a different story, because she had an instinctive feeling she would be seeing more of Sandy Montdulac. She wasn't a person to exercise her authority over her employees, preferring to develop a working-together relationship with them, but she might have to shake this man up a little. She didn't like the idea of all the time they would be spending alone, with only each other for company, being filled with tense altercations—unlike the give-and-take she and Erik, and even Pete, shared.

Fifteen minutes out of town, Blancheur headed through the line of sheltering blue spruce planted to protect Lady-slipper Landing from the winds off Lake Superior. All too soon what the locals called the Gales of November would hit, making shipping on the lake a deadly business, and the spruce would be a welcome shield. Later the pines would serve as a buffer against the blizzards moving in, as would another line planted north of the kennels. Here and there, however, a few open spots allowed them to enjoy the view of the lake, which was unsurpassed in good weather.

Windy and snowy weather didn't much bother the sled dogs who, being insulated by their winter coats, actually preferred winter to the summer heat. Each animal had a wooden doghouse of its own, but they likely as not curled up outside the doorway, where snow covered them during the storms. Many winter nights Laura lay awake listening to the howling winds and forcing herself to remember that the dogs wouldn't appreciate her protective feelings. She always found such concern useless, anyway. When she headed out to the kennels following a storm, sometimes after as long as two days of blowing winds, the dogs rose from snowy beds, yapping and barking their welcome.

By habit Blancheur bypassed the rambling two-story log structure that was Laura's home and headed for the kennels around back. She "gee'd" him to the right, pausing at the rear steps to unload her packages, then mushing on to the kennels two hundred yards behind the house. A chorus of howls and yaps from two dozen dogs staked here and there welcomed her. The large log kennel building, with dog runs and cages inside of it, seldom held any animals until spring, when she planned her litters—unless a dog became injured. One side of it contained her office, which Pete Tallwolf shared.

Tall and looking very Ojibwa Indian, as he was, Pete wandered out of the kennel office door. She very much doubted the frown on his face came from his being sorry to see her, and she giggled under her breath, trying to keep her amusement from showing. Pete must have been at the books again.

They constantly disagreed about whose job the books were, as well as how they should be kept. Laura did a slap-dash, hurry-up job, assuming her father's accounting clerk would straighten out the mess. Pete was more meticulous, and many times she found her own figures erased and penciled in more carefully. Yet they continued to share the job, each respecting the other's unspoken desire to be out on the trail instead, but knowing the dirty deed had to be done to Tom Goodman's satisfaction.

"Thought you might be bringing back our new trainer," Pete said as Laura "whoa'ed" Blancheur. "Your father said he was gonna get here today. That's why he took the wagon in this morning instead of riding his horse."

"He's here," Laura replied. "But it seems Father neglected to inform him that *I* was the musher he was hired to train. He's holed up in the Lake Side Hotel pondering the matter."

Planting his large hands on his hips, Pete laughed uproariously, his black hair shining in the sun as guffaws erupted from his broad chest. Laura's giggles joined his laughter, more subdued, since she couldn't shake the lingering recollection of Sandy Montdulac's shadowed eyes.

When his laughter died, Pete asked, "You want me to go in and talk to him? I can tell him what a little hellion you really are, despite looking like a bit of fluff that could blow away in the wind when you ride on those sled runners. You can bet your snowshoes your being so tiny was as big a concern to him as your being a female."

"You can if you want," Laura said with an easy shrug. "But he didn't look like the type of man who would be swayed by anything anyone else told him. I think he's the sort who makes up his own mind. And as far as I'm concerned, I really don't want a trainer who isn't totally dedicated to working with me, even if I am a woman."

"Yeah, I agree with you there. So I think I'll just take a couple of the young dogs out for a training run. We can sort of wander on into town, and I'll have my dinner at Mrs. Sterling's restaurant in the Lake Side. Never know who you might run into there. I'll take a change of clothes and switch at my brother's house."

"I'll tell Katie you won't be here for dinner. I won't be here, either, since David's picking me up so we can eat at Mrs. Sterling's too. After I talk to Katie, I'll get the new linens I picked up at the general store on the beds in the guest house."

"Why bother if you aren't gonna need the house open right now?" Pete asked logically. "Knowing how you hate housework, you could wait till Katie's granddaughter comes up to help with the weekly heavy work in a couple days."

"I suppose," Laura agreed. "But I don't have anything else planned this afternoon, since I thought I'd be showing Mr. Montdulac and his family around. The linens were supposed to be in last week, so the beds could be made up then, but they weren't in that order. Just in case Sandy and his family *do* show up, I ought to have them ready. And Katie's arthritis is bothering her, although she'd die before admitting it."

Pete lifted an inquiring black brow. "Sandy?"

"Uh . . . umm . . . that's Mr. Montdulac's first name. I assumed you'd figured out from what I've said so far that I actually did meet him this afternoon—and his beautiful little daughter, Tracie. His telegraph said he was bringing his sister, Cristy, with him, too, but I didn't see her. And he didn't mention where she was."

"Sandy," Pete repeated with a smile that told her he didn't buy her attempt to switch the focus of their conversation to her prospective trainer's sister. "All right. I'm heading out." Smiling slyly and whistling a jaunty tune, Pete quickly walked away.

Laura shook her head at how easily Pete saw through her at times. Unhitching Blancheur, she led him to his chain, stroking his head briefly before she headed back to the house. She found Katie, their elderly housekeeper, in the kitchen cradling a cup of hot chocolate at the table. The spicy smell of cinnamon intermingled with the chocolate aroma made Laura's mouth water. Cinnamon-laced hot chocolate was her favorite, as well as Katie's.

"There's some left in the pan on the stove," Katie told her. "What happened to your trainer and his family?"

As she hung up her cloak and unbuttoned her gown, which she removed and placed on an adjacent hook until she could take it upstairs to her room, Laura once again repeated her tale of Sandy Montdulac. Dressed in the trousers she'd had her dressmaker sew for her, much more comfortable to work around the kennels in, she poured some chocolate. Sipping it, she sighed in appreciation.

Katie motioned to a chair, but Laura shook her head and remained on her feet, making innocuous conversation as to the other acquaintances she had seen in town whom she and Katie had in common. Finished, she rinsed her cup in the sink and set it with a few other dishes waiting to be washed and headed out of the kitchen.

"You already know I'll be having dinner with David in town this evening," she reminded Katie. "And Pete asked me to let you know he'll be eating at Mrs. Sterling's tonight, too."

"You off to doing my job again for me, Missy?" Katie demanded astutely. "I saw them packages on the back porch. Looked to me like that order of bed linens came in."

With a sigh, Laura turned to face her. "Katie, I wish you'd let Father hire you some permanent help. Land sakes, you've taken care of us since before I was born. I know Meg doesn't want to work full time, since she has her own young ones at home, but. . . ."

"The day I can't handle my duties," Katie broke in softly, "is the day I'll go live with one of my sisters. I don't need no charity."

"It's not charity," Laura said in exasperation, then instantly give up. She and Katie had had this discussion already—several times in the last couple years. Walking over to the woman she loved almost as much as her father, she dropped a kiss on Katie's forehead.

"I'm going out to the guest house and make up the beds," Laura admitted. "And I'm doing it because I know your hands are bothering you today from your arthritis. It won't hurt me one bit to do a little housework around here."

Running a gnarled finger down Laura's cheek, Katie chuckled tolerantly. "You're a little love, Laura darlin'. Go on with you. Maybe I'll reward you by makin' some butterscotch pecan rolls for breakfast tomorrow morning."

"Yum! But only if your hands feel like kneading the dough."

"Get on with you."

* * *

In deference to the expectation that evening diners at the restaurant would dress, and because she truly did enjoy being completely feminine sometimes, Laura bathed and donned a stylish gown before David arrived that evening. When he yelled up the stairwell, she called back just as loudly, "I'll be down in a minute."

"Yeah," David replied. "Make sure it's a real minute and not a Laura minute!"

Deciding to surprise him, she gave her hair a final adjustment and left the room. When she descended the stairs, he looked up from beside the fireplace where he was conversing with her father.

"I don't believe it," he said, and she mouthed the words right along with him. Chuckling, he continued, "There might be hope for you being able to tell time yet, Laurie, honey."

She resisted the urge to stick her tongue out. Instead she tipped her nose up just a tad and walked toward him, then circled him. His dark suit and a snow-white shirt set off his hair, slicked back and nearly as black as Pete's. One renegade lock fell across his forehead, though. Stopping in front of him, she flicked a nonexistent piece of lint from his lapel, then brushed the curl back into place. It immediately fell forward again.

"Evening, Davie," she murmured.

Brown eyes sparkling with mischief, he dropped a brief kiss on her lips. "Evening, Laurie. I'm hungry. Let's get going."

Tom Goodman laughed at them, shaking his head. "You two sound more like brother and sister than an engaged couple. But I'll have to admit, friendship is a stable building ground for a good marriage. Why, Alice and I were childhood sweethearts—"

"—from the time our nannies changed our nappies together," Laura and David chorused along with him. All three of them burst out laughing, and Tom waved them away.

"Get on with you both. Katie and I are eating in the kitchen tonight. She's cooking moose steaks for us."

"Moose?" Laura curled her lip. "I'm glad we're going out."

"Well, if I'd known what Katie had planned," David contradicted, "I'd have found some way to get invited here this evening instead of going to the trouble of taking Laura out."

Laura whapped him on the arm. "You just remember that if you want moose or venison or any of those other wild meats you like so darned well after we get married, you'll have to find someone else to cook them. All I can see when I look at that sort of meat are those beautiful animals' eyes."

"Good thing you don't think of cows that way," David mused. "I've seen you dive into your steaks. And as far as asking you to cook anything at all for me—wild or tame—no way! The first thing on my agenda when we set a firm wedding date is hiring a cook, so I can train her in the things I prefer before you start living with me."

"You better," Laura agreed. "And get a housekeeper, too, who'll wash your dirty socks. It's the nineteen hundreds, Davie, and women can be more than some man's chattel. What do you want to bet we'll have the vote before long?"

David gave a mock shudder and slipped Tom a wink. "Can you imagine what sort of shape the country will get into then?"

That comment earned him another rap on the arm. Then Laura swept over to the front door, reached inside the closet and took out her more dressy cloak. A few minutes later, she and David were warmly ensconced beneath the wool blankets in his buggy. He picked up the reins and clicked his tongue at the horse, setting it in motion.

Stars scattered across an ebony sky above them. Whenever they passed an opening where they could see the lake on their right, she spied a half moon hanging low in the far horizon, spilling a creamy light across the water's surface. Only a faint breeze soughed through the towering pines lining most of the trail, and the snow from last night had already melted. Soon the pines would be covered with a snowy icing until spring, their branches bending with the weight of the pretty decoration.

She and David didn't need to perpetually carry on a conversation. There weren't many things they didn't already know about one another—from the past or even from day to day—since hardly a day went by they didn't see each other. She enjoyed their easy camaraderie and looked forward to the same stability down through the years.

But first, she wanted her one chance at excitement—the Alaskan race.

The trip into town took only a little more time than it had taken her and Blancheur earlier this afternoon. The downhill trail descended gradually, and even the uphill return trip would be fairly easy on the horse—at least until the heavy winter snows hit. Then most of the transportation in the area would be by dogsled, snowshoes, or sleighs pulled by the stronger draft horses.

Laura loved winter and the jangle of sleigh bells. And fall, with the cool days and beautiful colors on the leaves. And spring, with the awakening of the forest around her and return of the loons and geese. And summer, with its brilliant days of sunshine and the picnics and socializing the townspeople organized so they'd have memories to carry them through the long, snowbound winter season. She heaved a huge sigh as David pulled the buggy up beside the restaurant.

"What is it?" he asked.

"I was just thinking how much I enjoy each different season," she replied. "Every one of them has something wonderful about it."

Climbing down, David tied the horse to a hitching post before returning to the buggy and holding out his arms to her. "Well," he said, helping her down, "all you've ever had to do is enjoy yourself. And I'll make sure I keep your life that way."

"You make me sound rather useless," Laura grumbled as they walked up the pathway. "Maybe that's why I want to go to Alaska. At least I'll have accomplished something on my own, instead of just spending my life as an ornament on your arm and a hostess for you at your business parties."

Just before they opened the door, David dropped another kiss on her face, this time on her nose. "Don't forget being a mother to all the children we'll have. Remember, we both decided we wanted a full half dozen."

Laura smiled up at him. "That's one thing I really am looking forward to. I missed having any brothers or sisters myself, and I'm going to teach the girls to drive a sled right alongside me."

"I don't know if Cook County is ready for a bunch of little Lauras tearing all around in miniature dogsleds." David rolled his eyes. "But I guess it will have to put up with it."

"Yep," Laura agreed saucily.

David held the door for her. As usual when they dined here, their regular table beside a far window waited for them. Knowing every person in the room, though, it took them a while to get to it. While they chatted, Laura caught herself looking for the Montdulacs and spied Pete instead. He winked at her, then nodded at the table along the wall just past hers and David's.

Tracie spotted her first. "Miss Laura!" the little girl cried. "Come eat with us!"

Sandy put an admonishing hand on his daughter's shoulder, and Laura smiled to herself. That must be Sandy's sister on the other side of Tracie, since the young woman definitely resembled him. Laura glanced at David, who had halted abruptly, his gaze on the Montdulac table.

"Can we say hello to them, David?" she asked. "That's the man Father offered the job as my trainer to."

"Huh?" David gave a start. "Oh. Yeah. Yeah, sure. Go ahead."

Frowning, she took his arm. "I asked if *we* could say hello. It would be extremely rude of you not to welcome them to town, since you'll be seeing a lot of them if Sa . . . uh . . . Mr. Montdulac takes the job."

"Oh. Yeah. Yeah, sure," David repeated, then swallowed hard.

"Are you all right, David?" she questioned.

"Of course. Come on. Let's go on over."

Sandy rose at their approach, greeting Laura politely. As soon as she introduced David, Sandy presented his sister, Cristy, who studied them with interest while she nodded hello. Tracie fidgeted in her chair until her father smiled tolerantly and introduced her to David.

"Are you gonna eat with us, Miss Laura?" she asked. "We's got plenty of room at our table."

Laura laughed at her enthusiasm, but shook her head. "No, but we have the table right next to yours, honey. That will be almost like eating with you."

"All right," Tracie agreed, quickly firing another volley of questions at her. "Did your doggie bring you to town? Is his name Bl . . . Blancheur? I thought that's what I heard you call him when you told that man to get him off Daddy. What's Blancheur mean? Is it somethin' only huskies get called? I never heard of a malamute named that, but I've heard lots of them called Brutus or Lady or Prince."

"Tracie," Sandy said in an exasperated voice, "Miss Goodman's here to have dinner, like us. You can ask her all this stuff another time."

Tracie tilted her head at her father. "But you tol' Aunt Cristy we mights not be stayin', and. . . ."

"It's all right, Mr. Montdulac," Laura said with a laugh. "No, honey, we came to town in a buggy. And yes, the dog's name is Blancheur. It's a French word meaning whiteness, and it probably wouldn't fit a malamute. Most of them are black and white, although I've seen a few pretty gray ones."

"The Eskimo doggies are white. They's different than malamutes, you know."

"I've heard of them," Laura said. "In fact, a few years back I was debating whether to buy them or the huskies."

"They's strong," Tracie managed to say, then heeded her father's stern look. "Uh-oh."

"Well, I thoroughly enjoy talking with you, Tracie," Laura said. "And if you're around long enough, maybe you and I can make a run with Blancheur one day."

"I'm afraid," Sandy said in a controlled voice, "that I'd rather not have that dog around Tracie."

"Whatever you say," Laura acquiesced. He was Tracie's father, after all. "Well, it was nice seeing you again. And meeting you, Miss Montdulac."

Cristy glanced up with a hint of a smile, then busied herself straightening the collar of Tracie's dress. Laura turned away to their own table, then stood beside her chair for a long moment, waiting for David to pull it out for her as he had begun doing the past few months. Before their engagement, he always told her that she had two good arms of her own. When she finally glanced over her shoulder, she didn't see David, and just then he walked past her and took his own seat. Shaking her head in confusion, she pulled her own chair out and sat.

Completely out of character for him, David picked up a menu, holding it in front of his face to study. They already knew every selection listed, and this was lake trout night. They *always* ordered that. Trying to puzzle out her fiancé's strange actions, she realized he hadn't said one word to the Montdulacs, only nodding in polite acknowledgment of the introductions.

Since they were sitting in close enough proximity to the family to be overheard if she discussed them with David, she searched her mind for another topic of conversation for right now. Her gaze wandered to the nearby window. The darkness outside made the window into a mirror, reflecting the room back at her. Her eyes caught on Sandy, his blond head bent over his plate, and at that moment he raised his head and stared right at her reflected image in the glass.

Laura jerked her attention back to the table, but not before a tiny prickle ran up her spine—the same sort of prickle she'd experienced when she first saw Sandy a few minutes ago. The same sort as that afternoon, when he raced across the street toward her.

Ridiculous! She picked up her own menu and studied it.

"Why are you looking at the menu?" David asked. "We always have lake trout when it's the special."

Laying down the menu, Laura stared at him in surprise.

He'd placed his menu aside, and he lifted his eyebrows in inquiry.

"Maybe I'll have something different," she snapped. "We don't always have to stay in a rut, do we?"

"Laura, is something wrong?" he asked gently.

Releasing a sigh, she placed a hand over his. "No. No, I'm sorry, David. Everything is fine. I just had an out-of-sorts second."

David opened his mouth to say something, and she pinched the back of his hand between her thumb and forefinger. "Don't you dare!" she whispered furiously. "If you make some comment like I know you've got in mind, David Hudson, I'll leave you sitting here to eat alone!"

"Why, Laurie, honey," David whispered back with a chuckle. "I wouldn't think of saying anything about your periodic 'out-of-sorts' seconds—"

"David!" Noticing the mischievous sparkle in his eyes, she pinched him again, a little harder, then broke into smothered laughter.

"Sometimes I wish you didn't know me so well," she said at last. "The women in the books I read are always mysterious, and it takes the men the entire book to figure them out. You know everything about me from how much I weighed when I was born to how much I weigh now. And even husbands and wives don't talk about what you were getting ready to say about me!"

"Mysterious might not be that bad," David mused. "But then, what would happen if we got to know one another and decided we really didn't like each other? There would go all our plans."

Sternly controlling the urge to peruse the window beside them again, Laura agreed with him. Rosalyn, their usual energetic waitress, approached and set two glasses of water down, leaving her order pad in her apron pocket.

"Be bringing your plates out in a few minutes," she told David, giving Laura a smile to include her.

Laura bit her lip to keep from saying she'd decided to have something other than lake trout. What in the world was wrong with her this evening? She looked forward to the special at the restaurant all week. Sandy had lake trout in front of him, also, and she wondered if he enjoyed it as much as she did. Instantly she chastised herself for even noticing what the other man was eating. She was here with David.

A while later, when she and David were halfway through their meal, Cristy led Tracie past their table. Both of them voiced goodnight, and as they walked on, Sandy paused beside Laura.

"I'd like to come out and look at your kennels in the morning," he said. "Would ten o'clock be a good time?"

"Fine," she agreed, studying his hooded eyes and trying to determine if he had come to any decision yet. "Will Cristy and Tracie be accompanying you?"

"Not this time. Perhaps later tomorrow, if things work out."

"I see. Father can give you directions to Ladyslipper Landing, and you can come on out yourself with your dogs or drive Father's wagon out. It seems a shame your sister will have to fend for herself for lunch tomorrow, though, since it will take you some time to see our facilities. I've even got some training trails laid out, which I'd like your opinion on if you have time." She turned to David. "Why don't you see that Cristy and Tracie have an escort for lunch, David? You wouldn't mind, would you?"

"Uh . . . no, of course not," he replied. He clumsily grabbed his water glass, barely managing to keep from overturning it and drenching the tablecloth.

"I'm sure my sister will appreciate it," Sandy told David courteously, ignoring the bumbling. "I'll see you tomorrow morning, Miss Goodman."

He made his way across the room and stopped at the cashier's desk outside the dining room door, and Laura noticed several women's gazes following him. Even two women whom she knew were married till-death-do-they-part regarded him in an appreciative manner.

Huh. David's just as good looking as Sandy, she mused. But she'd never noticed women in town giving David looks saying they might be interested in getting to know him a lot better. But then, she and David had been a couple for simply forever. The women could have felt they were wasting their time.

Sandy reached into his back pocket for his wallet, his actions snugging the white shirt tighter on his chest. A lot of men who spent hours on their sleds had better developed lower bodies than upper. Their leg muscles got the better workout when they sometimes ran alongside the sleds, both to expend some energy and lighten the loads for their dogs. But Sandy Montdulac's chest and flat stomach appeared in perfect condition.

He retrieved his change from the cashier and looked straight into her face. Her cheeks heated immediately at being caught studying him, and she grabbed her water glass. Land sakes, she wondered if any of the other women in the room had noticed her watching Sandy as closely as they were? But if she looked up now, he might still be standing there.

Before she could decide what to do, Rosalyn hurried over to their table. "Is something wrong with your trout, Miss Goodman?" she asked in a worried voice. "And yours, Mr. Hudson? Oh, my, I hope not. Cook said it was an especially fine mess of fish this time."

From the corner of her eye, Laura noticed David jerk his head around from staring out the window. His own half-eaten trout was also growing cold on his plate.

"Everything is fine," David assured Rosalyn. He picked up his fork, and Laura followed suit, giving the waitress a huge smile.

Laura added her hearty praise for the meal. "Tell Cook it's perfect." Cutting off a chunk of fillet, she popped it in her mouth.

3

ANOTHER DUSTING OF snow fell overnight, less than two inches but enough to make it possible for Sandy to give his malamutes a run the next morning. After their lengthy confinement, they itched to keep moving, but each and every one of them obeyed his command when he ordered them to "whoa" as soon as they broke through a line of blue spruce.

Hardly any wind blew this morning, and what little there was blew toward him, touching his face, which was warm from his exertion of the uphill run. The Ladyslipper Landing dogs didn't catch his and his dogs' scents at first, and Sandy remained on the sled runners, studying what he would soon accept as his new home.

The two-story log house just ahead of him, with a porch along the front, was evidently the Goodmans' residence. On past it, on the left, he saw Laura's dogs and their wooden doghouses. Off to the right were several unoccupied doghouses, evidently recently built since their white paint glowed in the sunlight. He assumed they had been readied for his dogs after Tom Goodman learned he'd be bringing at least part of his team along. He'd only been able to afford to bring eleven dogs, enough for a full team, and he counted at least that many doghouses.

The kennel building must be hidden behind the house. He saw a log cabin set back behind the empty doghouses on the edge of the cleared area. A lot smaller than the main house and only one story, he decided it was probably his quarters. It looked big enough to have at least three bedrooms, and he'd be willing to bet Cristy would enjoy the multitude of windows, especially the two large ones in the front of the house. His sister could set her easel up right there and have plenty of light. He didn't know much about Cristy's painting, but he recalled her complaining many times about either the lack of light or a change in it.

Smoke feathered from the chimney of the smaller cabin— from both chimneys, he realized. There were obviously two fireplaces, another fact to delight his sister, who didn't tolerate the cold all that well.

He remembered Laura Goodman mentioning her own lack of endurance for cold, and her tiny hands. It stuck in his mind both from their first meeting yesterday and last night's dream. Her small hands looked extremely delicate on the reins of the dog harness in his dream, but were more than adequate on his bare skin when the dream shifted, as dreams are wont to do.

That was another reason he ought to get the hell out of town and settle somewhere else—a damned critical reason. The woman stirred his desire for the first time since Colleen had died.

He'd figured his sexual urges would return some day, but not this soon. He hadn't even had an inkling of the slumbering sensations stirring to life until they slam-banged him last night. Way too much worry prowled his mind this past year to fret about how long that part of his life— granted, an important one—would remain in abeyance. It took him an hour's walk in the falling snow at two A.M.

before he could even attempt to return to his room and fall back asleep.

Funny, he thought as he saw Laura round the corner of the two-story house and shade her eyes, as though watching for his approach. As much as Laura resembled Colleen, it hadn't been a case of mistaken identity in the dream. That he knew for sure. Laura Goodman's hands had trailed fire across his skin and down to. . . .

Laura raised that same hand just then and waved at him. Still Sandy didn't start his team moving. He'd met Laura barely twenty-four hours ago, and she'd already crowded into his thoughts—and his dreams—slam-banged into his life. She wasn't one of those voluptuous women men talked about among each other after a few drinks, yet there was an obvious sensuality packed into her tiny frame. Mostly what attracted him, though, was her self-confident demeanor.

He'd never met a woman who had such grandiose plans. And even while he scoffed at her, worried about her safety, which he would be responsible for, Sandy admired her. He wondered if the man with her last night appreciated what he had? He hadn't seemed to. David and she hadn't appeared to be a pair of lovers dining together. Hudson had stared out the window instead of acting like a man besotted with his fiancée.

He called a curt halt to his musings, but not before a thankfulness for Laura being safely engaged flashed across his mind. He never trespassed on another man's domain. Among other reasons, her engagement put a firm halt to contemplation of anything further with her besides teaching her how to handle a racing team—an entirely different situation from a team on the trail solely for transportation or pleasure.

He growled a low word of disgust, both at himself for his thoughts and the cacophony of sound, which broke out just then. That darned white husky trotted around the side of the house, ears perked to sharp points and tail curling aggressively over its back as soon as it looked up the rise toward him and his dogs. Immediately, the husky roared a confrontational bark.

Laura's other huskies picked it up and joined in. Sandy's own lead dog, Keever, returned the less-than-welcoming greeting, backed up without delay by his teammates.

Hardly ever did Sandy resort to the twenty-five foot whip every sled dog driver carried, but his hand fell on it now. Why the hell did Laura have that dog running loose this morning, when she expected him to arrive for their appointment? Maybe she assumed he would drive out in the wagon Tom Goodman had offered him, but any musher worth his salt knew fresh snow called for a run with his dogs.

Her salt and her dogs, Sandy's mind corrected. He thinned his lips.

Blancheur headed out to confront the violators of his territory, getting several yards from Laura before she called him back. After only a brief hesitation, the husky obeyed, and Laura disappeared around the house, Blancheur obediently trailing after her. The noise level, however, stayed steady.

"Quiet!" Sandy picked up the whip, but his dogs whined and calmed down in response to the verbal command. The most the whip would do anyway was get their attention when he cracked it over their heads. Not one of his dogs feared it, knowing from experience he would sooner use it on himself than them. It did come in handy to direct the dogs in severe weather if the wind blew too hard for his words to reach Keever. A pop on the ground on one side or the other of his lead malamute would make Keever swerve in that direction, leading the team with him.

"Kra!" he ordered, using the Inuit word to mush, which each member of his team responded to. The dogs surged forward. By the time Laura returned to the front of her house without Blancheur, he had anchored his sled and knelt beside Keever.

"Good morning, and I'm sorry," Laura said breathlessly. "I got busy and forgot the time, or I'd have had Blancheur tied back up."

That same darned breeze carried a scent of wildflowers to him, out of place in this cold weather. He savored it for a few seconds before realizing she probably thought him rude for not rising in her presence. A glance at her face showed her frown, but she didn't voice a reason for the scowl. He got to his feet.

"My dogs won't attack you, like yours did me yesterday," he said. "So don't worry about them."

She rolled those sea-green eyes skyward. "Welcome to Ladyslipper Landing, Mr. Montdulac. And thank you for your good morning to me, too. Yes, yes, I do believe it's a fine day. Would you like to come in and have something warm to drink before we start our inspection?"

At her sarcastic comment on his lack of manners, the corner of his mouth twitched wryly and a heat of embarrassment flushed his cheeks. Darn her, she could make him feel small enough to track a snake's trail in the dark. Still it would be best if he didn't let her know she'd gotten to him.

As if his being on the run and her being engaged weren't enough, one look at the huge home in which she lived had reinforced his judgment. By the time he made back even a portion of the money he'd been cheated out of in Alaska, Laura would be walking with a cane. Besides, he had about as much chance to rebuild any financial security in his position now as of it not snowing in Alaska for an entire winter. He'd be lucky to take care of Tracie and Cristy on the wages he earned, which were probably less than Laura Goodman's monthly spending allowance.

He took the dream last night as a warning. He intended to start off their association on a strictly business-type basis and keep it that way the entire term they worked together. Given his attraction to her, even a slight friendship wasn't possible, and he aimed to keep the barriers firm between them.

"In a race, where there's a pile of money waiting at the end," he informed Laura, "you won't find a lot of amenities among the entrants. If they tell you something as simple as 'hello,' you better check your sled after they walk away. They probably sabotaged it in some way while you had your attention elsewhere."

"We're not in a race right now, Mr. Montdulac."

Laura's dark auburn brows lowered even more as she

deepened her frown and set her hands on slim hips. She'd tamed her hair today in one long braid, which hung down her back over a heavy green-plaid shirt. The color enhanced her eyes. She wore those darned trousers again, and he could tell they'd been made especially for her, since they didn't bag or hang. They followed the lines of her legs—and rear, he saw as she turned sideways and stared away from him for a second.

Damn, he'd always thought himself more of a breast man!

Laura gave an irritated sigh and brushed a loose tendril of hair from her cheek. "Come on," she said over her shoulder, walking away from him. "You can at least meet Katie, our housekeeper, before we go look at your quarters. She made butterscotch pecan rolls this morning and kept a couple back for you when I told her you'd be out this morning. I don't think even you can be impolite enough to hurt Katie's feelings by not accepting the rolls, especially since you'll know how hard it was for her to knead the dough when you see her hands."

Hell, there she went again—so easily stirring his guilt. Sandy shook his head and followed. She'd managed to prick his conscience twice already. Given her obvious distaste for him, he truly couldn't figure out why she didn't send him packing and find someone else stupid enough to take on the job of training her, along with that pack of new-breed animals overrunning the race scene these days.

Maybe that was what he was trying to do, he pondered honestly, although he usually never analyzed his actions. If she fired him before he formally accepted the position, he would have to find something else—hopefully somewhere there wouldn't be a slip of femininity forcing him to keep probing his barriers for any sign of weakness.

As Laura implied, Katie Larsen proved too much for Sandy's aloofness, and he didn't even try once he saw her knotted knuckles. His own mother suffered the same problem for years.

"My mother swore by red cherry juice to help the pain in her hands," he blurted to Katie barely five minutes after they met. "She drank a glass every day."

"Why thank you, Mr. Montdulac." Katie beamed a smile. "We had a bumper crop of wild cherries this past summer, and I put up dozens of jars. I'll give that a try."

"Please call me Sandy," he murmured, taking a huge bite of the butterscotch-pecan roll and unable to quell a grunt of satisfaction as he savored it.

"You mentioned your mother as though she's passed on, Sandy," Katie said. "Is it a recent bereavement?"

"Yes. She and my father both died a little over a month ago. My sister Cristy lives with me now."

"I'm sorry. But you'll have someone to keep house and cook for you then. Laura tells me you have a little one, too, and I'm truly looking forward to having her around."

Sandy chuckled and replied, "My sister Cristy's not much good at the stove. Well, she is when she pays attention, but if something catches her eye, we're as likely to have burnt meals as edible ones. Cristy's an artist, and she does beautiful work. But she goes off into her own world periodically—at times right in the middle of a conversation. And I'm sure you'll like my daughter, Tracie. Everyone falls in love with her."

"I was planning on baking a batch of molasses cookies today," Katie told him. "Does your Tracie like molasses cookies?"

"Like all children, she loves anything sweet," Sandy admitted, willing to trust his daughter to this motherly woman.

Laura toyed with her coffee cup, trying to remain inconspicuous. Normally she would have been right in the middle of any conversation in the kitchen, but she was finding out quite a bit more about Sandy by letting Katie draw him out. Given his reticence so far with her, she'd be willing to bet he didn't realize how much he revealed of another side to him. Katie was good at eliciting facts from their guests. It must be her motherly characteristics—both physically and in her attitude.

From her chair on the opposite side of the table, Laura surreptitiously studied Sandy's face through her eyelashes as he talked with Katie. The blue of his eyes softened to a lighter hue whenever he mentioned his daughter or sister. The dark teal color in his eyes yesterday had been as cold as ice, but sparkled with energy in Tracie's. Sandy's voice even grew a little huskier when he spoke of his family, and a person would have had to be a stone pillar not to hear his love for them.

By the time he finished his pastry and a second cup of coffee, Katie had pulled an abundance of new information from Sandy. Laura knew his parents and Cristy had lived in Washington State, and that Cristy was twenty, almost a year younger than her. That, as Tracie had said yesterday, his wife had been dead a year. That they had no close family other than Tracie's grandparents, who still lived in Juneau, Alaska. Even Katie, however, couldn't draw any information about Sandy's in-laws from him. In fact, he abruptly told her they had severed ties with his dead wife's parents and refused to elaborate, changing the subject when Katie pressed him.

Other than that, he and Katie chatted like old friends, with the housekeeper following them to the door when he and Laura finally left for the guest quarters. As soon as they exited the house, though, Sandy's chilly withdrawal stole through Laura almost as though he physically built a wall between them. She wasn't used to having her attempts at friendship rebuffed, by either males or females. Sighing in frustration, she led the way to the cabin, boot steps nearly silent on the new snow.

She showed him around inside, his sparse conversation a direct contrast to his careful inspection of the rooms. She'd hoped he would at least be impressed with this part of their offering as a bonus to his employment, since she'd assisted Katie and Meg in their efforts to make sure the house possessed a welcoming atmosphere for its new occupants. She would have thought it was rational for him to bring Cristy for a determination on the house, but perhaps what he admitted about his sister a few minutes ago explained why the burden of ascertaining what would make adequate living quarters for them fell on him.

The cabin had been the first home of her mother and father, and her father built onto it before he finally constructed the large two-story residence. Since then the cabin had remained vacant, but as soon as Laura received her father's permission to participate in the Alaskan race, she brought up the possibility of using the cabin for living quarters for her dog trainer. Having always had a soft spot for the cabin, her father easily agreed.

Katie had directed updating the kitchen, and both she and her father had also decided to take advantage of the opportunity to make things less difficult for Katie. They ordered two of any of the modern conveniences Katie suggested—like a new gasoline-powered washing machine. They didn't overlook one thing, and Dick Berglind, the proprietor of the general store, fell all over himself filling their requests. He even ordered a new Montgomery Ward catalog when the one they used became tattered from their zealous examinations.

The rest of the house merely needed a good cleaning and the dustcovers removed from the furniture. She had replaced some of the faded curtains and rugs, and hired one of Pete's brothers to refinish the oak floor in the large living room. One of Pete's sisters had made new braided rugs. A feminine talent Laura did possess was an eye for colors, and she chose earthy tones, brightened here and there with fall maple reds and birch yellows.

There was a bedroom for each of the Montdulacs. The master bedroom was more subdued, but the middle room was decorated in peaches and greens. Recalling her own childhood bedroom, Laura had used eyelet-lace-trimmed curtains and pillow cases in the smallest bedroom. She was extremely proud of how the house had turned out, but Sandy didn't comment on it, frustrating her once more.

After touring the cabin, Sandy stopped by the large front windows a second time, staring at the view of Lake Superior. With a clear, brilliant blue sky today, they could see a freighting ship disappearing over the far horizon.

"I love watching the lake," Laura murmured. "There's

just something about it that relaxes me, except when a storm comes up. Then it's different—a wild and fierce beauty."

He grunted an acknowledgment, then rather bluntly pronounced the house adequate for his needs. Turning away from the window, he asked, "Shall we go look at your kennels now?"

He strode to the door without waiting for her to precede him. Instead, he opened the door and pivoted around to wait for her, nearly catching her as she mocked his last sentence with silent lips. Cut off in the middle of the word "kennel," she realized her top lip was drawn back in a sneer, and she quickly widened her eyes and covered her mouth, forcing out the most believable cough she could manage. However, it ended up sounding like a half-strangled giggle as she comprehended the silly picture she must have made.

"Uh . . . I guess we missed a little dust in here," she said when she could speak.

He very deliberately slid a finger across a small table beside the door, then examined the end of it. "Looks clean to me."

Losing control, Laura bit the side of her cheek to keep from laughing. Instead of arguing with him, she tilted her nose up just a tad and walked by him. Too bad she hadn't worn a skirt this morning. Sweeping it aside as she passed would have been the perfect accompaniment to her haughty comportment. She thought of giving a disdainful sniff, but quelled the urge since he'd already caught her mimicking him a few seconds ago. Besides, he'd probably take it as a slight, instead of the joshing she meant it as.

If Sandy Montdulac had ever had a funnybone, it must have gotten broken somehow.

At that thought, she stifled another giggle, hurrying faster so she could stay far enough ahead of him to hide her facial expression. The problem with that was she also kept her nose tilted upward, and the peg pins for the dog chains were set in the ground in front of each of the new doghouses. Catching her toe on one of them, she sprawled facedown before she could catch herself.

Immediately she felt his touch on her shoulder and knew he'd knelt beside her.

"Are you all right?" he asked.

Giggling wildly, she flipped over onto her back and stared up at him. "Ever make a snow angel?" she asked around her laughter.

Sticking her arms out, she moved them up and down, while she spread her legs back in forth in the opposite direction. He quickly stood, and she reached out a hand to him.

"Help me up so I don't ruin my angel," she demanded.

Rather reluctantly, he took her hand, and she heaved to her feet, stumbling against him when he released her. Stepping back to catch her balance, she shook her head at him.

"Do you *ever* have any fun, Mr. Montdulac?"

He drew a hand down his face, then quickly averted his head. "Are those the kennels?"

"Yes," she said in a resigned voice. "Come on. I'll introduce you to Pete, and let him show you around there."

"I can introduce myself to him!" Without apologizing for his snarling tone, Sandy strode off.

She followed more slowly, wanting to actually see how he got along with her dogs. She also pondered why she didn't just tell this cantankerous man she'd decided he would be inappropriate for her needs and to go on back to Alaska. One reason, she admitted, was they might not find anyone else her father would approve of in enough time for her to train for the race. And she very much doubted David would tolerate her postponing their wedding date for another twelve months, so she could make a try at the race the following year.

David hadn't resisted the lengthy engagement thus far, but it would humiliate him in front of the townspeople if it went on too long. In David's mind, keeping up a measure of propriety was necessary for him to attract sufficient clients from the town and the surrounding county. And if she did go ahead and get married this coming summer, she'd probably be with child by that winter, from what she'd seen of most of her friends' marriages. David darned well wouldn't let her participate in a race while carrying one of their children. Of course, she would never think of taking a chance like that anyway.

There was something else about Sandy Montdulac, however, which made her a little more patient with his uncommunicative behavior than she would normally tolerate. She responded to some sort of unspoken challenge to at least make him chuckle, as he had once with Katie. Next on the agenda would be a full-fledged guffaw, and then maybe a rib-tickling bout of falling-down hilarity.

She had no earthly idea why she felt like she should plug away at his hostility. Perhaps it was the stubborn streak her father and David took every opportunity to remind her of that prodded her. Or perhaps it was just because she'd never run up against such a blatant disregard of her attempts at friendship before, and her self-esteem was taking a beating.

She marched on, determined to breach the impediments. Sandy and Pete were already deep in discussion when they exited the kennel door. She walked up to them, and Sandy sidled around Pete, placing Pete between her and him. She held her peace, but when they approached one of her breeding bitches and Sandy knelt to examine the dog, Laura started to lean over his shoulder to pet it. Seeming to sense her intent, Sandy stood and walked around the dog, only barely brushing her shoulder.

He didn't appear ready to approach Blancheur yet, but Sandy looked over all her other dogs—all the while maintaining as much distance between her and him as he could. She allowed Pete to explain the attributes of the various dogs and the harness positions for the ones she used on her team. Pete even talked about the timing of when the bitches would come into season, not tempering his wording at all, since he had to have those discussions with her at times. Sandy, however, gave her a fleeting glance, then turned a bright red. He hurried over to another dog, this time a male, smoothly moving to the far side of the dog when she came up.

"I'll bet he dances well," Laura murmured to Pete.

Sandy's eyes flew to her. "What?"

"Oh, I was just commenting on how good my pants felt on my legs in the chill this morning," she said.

His gaze flickered to her trousers and immediately away. Pete fell into a violent coughing fit, and she smiled at him enigmatically when he finally controlled himself.

"You better take care of that," she told Pete. "Do you want me to ask Katie to make you up some thyme tea with honey?"

"Sounds like a good idea," Pete surprised her by saying. "I could use some right now."

He jerked his head toward the house, and Laura read the message in his eyes. He and Sandy would get a lot more accomplished if she'd leave them alone. Agreeable for the moment, she wandered toward the house without excusing herself. At the back door, she turned. The men were walking back toward the kennel.

She didn't see how on earth Sandy Montdulac would be able to handle the hours on end they'd have to be alone together out on the trails. Why, he'd be a jumpy mess of nerves by the end of the first day if he kept trying so hard to keep his distance from her.

Whatever was his problem? He related fine to Katie, and her father had admitted last night to being impressed with the man. She knew Pete had taken to Sandy right away, otherwise he would have been standoffish. She'd seen Pete snub men before. It must be her, but she couldn't think of anything she might have done to alienate the man before he even arrived. Since their first meeting his attitude toward her had been distant.

Well, she mused, maybe there were a couple things Sandy couldn't accept about her. One, she was a woman who had the audacity to breach the masculine stronghold of sled dog racing. Two, she was a woman who ignored his cautions about the dangers of the race, and most men expected a woman to heed every word they uttered.

All right. Maybe there were more than a couple things. Three, she was a woman who would in effect be his boss and on whom he would depend for approval for his wages to be paid. Four, she was a woman who didn't accept his taciturnity and kept trying to make him laugh. Five, she was a woman who. . . .

Land sakes! Maybe it was just that she was a woman. Or, since he got along fine with Katie, a *young* woman.

She delivered Pete's request for a cough remedy to Katie, then headed back to the kennels. She and Sandy Montdulac had to get a couple things straight if they were going to work together.

4

$\mathcal{W}$HILE PETE GAVE the dogs fresh water, Sandy sat at the office desk to study the huskies' breeding records. Pete had made it a point to assure him that Laura made the decisions as to which dog covered which bitch during her season, and Laura's face intruded between him and the pages of records. He couldn't imagine casually discussing things like that with a woman—Laura, especially.

He leaned back in the chair, completely distracted from the records. My God! Did she have any idea what she looked like sprawled on the ground while making that snow angel? She'd laid at his feet, legs wide open on their outward sweep as though to beckon him and accept him into her! Her arm movements verified to him that, even though her breasts were small, they mounded deliciously and perked to delicate points. She darned sure wasn't wearing any undergarments on her upper half!

"I see you're looking over the records," her voice said beside his ear as a delicate touch landed on his shoulder.

Sandy flew from the chair, and it skittered backward, crashing against the wall. Instantly he controlled his emotions. This had to stop! If they were going to work together, he couldn't let her know how much it bothered him when she got close to him. After passing a hand down his face, he turned to her.

"I thought you'd gone into the house."

Her green eyes twinkled mischievously. "I did, but it didn't take long to ask Katie to mix up a cough remedy for Pete. And I knew you'd need me out here when you finally got around to becoming better acquainted with Blancheur."

"I'd rather approach that dog on my own. He and I need to set up the standards of our relationship right from the start."

"Speaking of setting up relationship standards . . ." Laura pursed her lips in thought, then nodded as though coming to a decision. "We need to work on our relationship, too, Mr. Montdulac. And the first thing I'd like is your permission to call you Sandy, and to ask you to call me Laura."

When Sandy hesitated, she continued, "Unless you've decided to turn down this position. And I'll be completely honest with you—I hope that's not the case. I was impressed with your examination of my dogs, and I could tell you knew exactly what you were talking about. You also saw the good points of the husky breed, even if you do feel a certain loyalty to your malamutes. I believe we could work well together, if we can iron out the one problem you appear to have with me."

"And what is that?"

"Um . . . I believe I could show you better than tell you—and start working on solving the problem at the same time."

He lifted an eyebrow, and she said, "The first thing I want you to do is say 'Laura.'"

After a second he grudgingly repeated, "Laura."

"Great!" She clapped her hands together and beamed at him. "Now, give me your hand."

Unable to stop himself, he pulled back, then gritted his

teeth and held out his hand. She took it in her small fingers and placed it on her shoulder.

The wool of her shirt was soft beneath his touch, draping across the rounded point where her arm connected to her shoulder. His thumb instinctively moved back and forth, but he halted its movement after one stroke. She reached for his other hand and settled it on her waist. Then she laid her hands on his chest, palms outward.

"There," she said in a satisfied tone. "That doesn't hurt a bit, does it, Sandy?"

"Hurt? Hell, I never expected touching you to hurt," he muttered truthfully.

A quizzical expression crossed her face. "Then what *did* you expect? Why do you jump like a startled deer whenever I get near you?"

"Does it matter?" he asked, pulling his hands free.

"Well, yes, it does," she shot back at him, clenching her fingers in his shirt so he couldn't move away. "We're going to be spending lots of time together out on the trail, with only each other to depend upon. I'd hate to think if I got dumped off my sled or, heaven forbid, fell through some thin ice, you wouldn't help me because it meant touching me!"

"Don't be ridiculous." He stared into her upturned face, his gaze drawn to her lips, which were pouting in reaction to her obstinate comments. "Touching you in order to save you from danger wouldn't be a problem. But . . ." He fought it, but his head dropped toward her mouth. "But you need to remember, touching between a man and woman can *cause* some types of danger, and quit deliberately placing yourself in the direct path of the hazard!"

She gasped and pulled her hands back. This time he grabbed her before she could move away.

"Tell me, *Laura*," he murmured. "Didn't your courtship prior to your engagement give you an idea of what those dangers could be? Why a man and woman have to be careful not to spend too much time with each other until they've been wed—and have the right to examine those dangers together?"

Very slowly he drew her palms back to his chest, covering her hands with his to hold them in place. His head dropped a little further, and she drew in her breath, eyes as wide and wary as a mesmerized deer. He kept waiting for her to jerk free, slap his face, something, yet when she spoke, it took him completely off guard.

"I . . . I started this, so I can't blame you for reacting in a typically masculine manner, Sandy," she said cautiously. "And yes, Katie has discussed these dangers you refer to with me. I act without thinking sometimes, though. So I hope you'll take that into consideration and forget about this."

She twisted her hand beneath his hold, and something hard prodded the side of his palm. Glancing down, he saw her engagement ring, which glowed even in the dim office light, warning him away. He moved almost as fast as the chair had, stepping back and rubbing his palms against his trouser legs. Laura clasped her hands together, hiding the ring from both their sights.

"I apologize," he said. "I overreacted and acted like an ass. I'm sorry."

"It's my fault, too. I hope this doesn't tip the scales against our offer to you during your decision-making process."

"Not really," Sandy admitted. "I do intend to accept this job, if you still want me."

Relief at having the forced acceptance out of the way filled him. During his after-midnight walk, he'd mentally listed each and every barrier keeping him from stepping over the line drawn between him and Laura. He woke this morning assured of the lengthy account being adequate for him to keep his distance. Laura's comments now reinforced his certainty he could handle things. She was at least mature enough to realize they needed to keep their relationship on a business level.

Still, rather than immediately accept his decision, Laura hesitated as she toyed with her engagement ring. He read doubt on her face, but it flickered only briefly in her green eyes, creasing the lovely skin on her forehead. Without asking her, however, he couldn't find out whether she was doubting his experience as a trainer or how their working together would turn out.

Then the determination he was fast coming to know was a primary characteristic of this tiny woman's personality settled into place.

"I want you," Laura said. She gasped, then blushed furiously, appearing to catch the double entendre the same moment Sandy did. "For my trainer, I mean."

She exhaled, which chased a tendril of auburn hair from her forehead, then picked up one of the files on the desk. "Do you have any suggestions for improvements to my breeding program?" she asked in a quick change of subject.

Hell, as far as he was concerned, that topic wasn't any safer to discuss right now. Sandy waved away her question.

"I haven't had enough time to really look it over. I'm going on out to have a chat with your lead dog. After that, I better get back to town and pick up Cristy and Tracie. They'd probably like some time before nightfall to start settling in here."

"Katie was planning on your staying for lunch," Laura informed him. "I told her David would look after your sister and Tracie, so we assumed you'd eat with us."

"Thank her for me, will you? But I have some other things to do in town too—like picking up a few groceries."

"We have an account at the general store, if you need it."

"I don't," he said curtly. Walking out of the office, he turned back to face her when he heard her follow. "Remember, I'm going up to Blancheur on my own this time."

Rather reluctantly, she nodded. "I'll wait outside the kennel and watch."

He started to warn her to do just that, but bit back the admonition. So far he hadn't seen anything about her to suggest untruthfulness; he'd trust her until he had a reason not to. He held the kennel door open, and she walked through, obediently stepping to the side and leaning against the building. Sandy walked on past, toward the white husky.

The moment he realized Sandy was approaching him and not one of the other dogs, Blancheur came to attention.

Sandy had noticed the difference between the malamutes' and huskies' tails right from the first time he'd seen a husky. Malamutes carried their tails over their backs as a matter of course. The huskies' tails trailed downward when they were at rest, but curled over their backs when running or alert to something. Blancheur's tail swept up and curled tightly over his rear haunches, as it had when he growled a confrontation at Sandy's arrival.

Sandy walked steadily onward, concentrating on recalling the physical differences in the two breeds instead of the bruised pride he suffered on his previous encounter with the husky. Their dispositions were as far apart as their physical attributes. Every malamute had similar eyes—almond shaped and dark brown. Huskies' eyes varied, and he'd seen them with both brown eyes and both blue eyes. He'd also seen some with one brown and one blue eye, like the eyes that bored into his own constant gaze right now.

In Alaska he'd heard husky owners discuss what good team dogs the breed made and how docile these animals were. He knew for a fact malamutes needed careful handling to prevent them from becoming too aggressive. Descended from boreal wolf, malamutes carried a wild strain in their breeding.

After he checked out the background of the huskies, he'd assumed their more gentle nature came from having been domesticated for so many years in Siberia, the pureness of the breed maintained because they'd been cut off from the rest of the world. Only in recent years had the breed even been discovered. From what he understood, they were working dogs for the Siberian Inuit families, used to pull sleds and herd reindeer. But they were also very much a part of the family life, due to their importance in the Inuit lifestyle.

Anyone could tell, however, that huskies, too, descended from wolves. Now and then, despite selective breeding, a dog like Blancheur would crop up—one with more belligerent traits.

One of them would break and bow to the domination of the other—either him or the dog. Just like in wolf packs, there could only be one alpha male. Sandy was determined to be the alpha in this situation. For his dominion over the animals to be complete, and their obedience unquestioning, there could be no other way. Lives depended upon their teamwork and the dogs' submission on the trail.

Blancheur growled and curled his upper lip, exposing sharp white fangs, but Sandy kept on walking. The husky crouched as though to spring. Sandy never hesitated—and Blancheur didn't leap. Sandy stopped right in front of Blancheur and the husky broke contact with his gaze. However, Blancheur didn't roll over and expose his stomach, as a lesser male would have done to complete his submission to Sandy's authority. Instead the husky laid his head on his paws and stared past Sandy. The growl died in his throat.

Kneeling, Sandy reached out a hand. He didn't make his motions slow or cautious—he didn't hurry them. He scratched behind one of Blancheur's ears, then ran his hand down the dog's back.

"Up," he ordered, and Blancheur glanced at him, then rose. Sandy examined the dog's musculature, then picked up each foot and checked for any cuts or sores. The pads were thick and callused, with a hint of webbing between the toes. Each one was perfectly healthy, but he would have leather protective gear made for him and every other dog on both his and Laura's team anyway.

Satisfied with the animal's health, Sandy stood and turned his back on Blancheur. Tension filled the air, and he could almost read the husky's mind. Nothing happened, and Sandy slowly turned back around. Blancheur met his gaze for an instant, then looked away.

He guessed that would have to do for now. Forcing any further confrontation would jeopardize the progress they had made thus far. After laying a hand on Blancheur's head one more time, he headed back toward Laura.

When he got to her, he said truthfully, "He's a fine dog. I like his spirit, though he and I will have some things to work out yet. However, he'll be a good, dependable dog on the trail."

"You can tell that just from those few minutes with him?"

"For as long as you've been around dogs, you should be able to tell that, too."

She bristled, and he held up a hand to forestall her defensiveness. "Your not having that ability is understandable, but it's something you need to admit and work on. So far, you've only travelled your safe, less risky trails around here. You've had dozens of people available to come out after you if you're overdue from a run, and there's a damned good chance they'd get to you in time to keep you from any real harm."

"I . . ."

Sandy talked right over her attempt to interrupt. "If you're out there alone overnight—or against competition for a week or more—with only your team to depend upon, you need to know every one of your dogs inside and out. You need to know lots more than whether or not they'll lick your hand or try to bite you—whether they prefer fish or moose meat to eat."

He lowered his voice and watched her face carefully. "And you need to know which one of your dogs you could bring yourself to eat first, if you were lost somewhere and starving to death."

She gasped and grew rigid. Slowly she turned her head and gazed out over her dogs, her eyes pausing fleetingly on each one. Finally she said, "That's not something I have to decide right now, is it?"

"No," he agreed. "But it's something you have to keep in the back of your mind. It's happened more than once in Alaska—and probably around here, if anyone would ever tell you about it. It's not usually a story they'd pass on to a woman, though."

Her eyes flashed. "You keep harping on my gender!"

"Because it's important," he said through gritted teeth. "That's one fact you better get locked tight into that pretty head of yours. You, yourself, have to make allowances for your being a woman. If you don't, you're making it that much more dangerous for yourself—and for anyone saddled with the responsibility of looking out for your safety."

She nodded slowly, the spark in her eyes dying, a musing contemplation replacing it. "I guess I understand. If I swallow my pride and admit my gender is a hindrance, I'll be much further ahead. I'll have contingencies planned to compensate for my lack of physical power—my lesser callous traits."

A measure of respect for her took root in Sandy's mind right then. He'd expected a prissy just-as-good-as-any-man attitude, since she was determined to take part in a man's race. Instead, when pointed out to her, she faced the reality of the drawbacks her gender presented.

Still he didn't expect her to ever be able to make a race driver. Sure, she had determination a lot of men lacked, but it took more than determination to accomplish seemingly impossible feats.

For some reason a picture of a horseless carriage he'd seen flashed in his mind. That, too, must have seemed an impossibility at one time, but now they were becoming commonplace. One thing was certain, though. They'd never find any sort of transportation other than a dog and sled across the snow. Hell, those drifts in the winter were sometimes roof high. And there would always be things that women just couldn't do as well as men.

Laura snapped her fingers in front of his face.

"What?" Sandy asked.

"You were off somewhere," she said with a laugh. "I thought your sister Cristy would be the daydreamer, given that you said she was an artist. But I called your name three times before I snapped my fingers."

"Sorry. What were you talking about?"

"I was wondering if there were some other things you wanted to discuss with me—things that my being a woman might cause problems about. Since we're on this subject anyway."

Sandy studied her, then took a breath and forged on. "How does your fiancé feel about you spending nights with another man?"

"David?" Her voice rose in a squeak. "Why, I—I'd

n—never *think* of doing such a thing," she sputtered. "What on earth does that have to do with anything?"

He chuckled at her outrage. "Sometime before you leave for Alaska, you and I will be spending several nights together out on the trail." Her eyes widened. "I need to know what your strengths are out there—and your weaknesses."

"We can take Pete with us," she said in a decisive voice. "Or David."

"No. We can't. Neither Pete nor David will be with us if we make it as far as the race you're training for, so they have no place in that part of our training. Besides, I doubt it would do your reputation any less harm for you to spend all night—several nights—on the trail with two men rather than one."

She remained quiet for a moment, and he heard her deep-gulp swallow.

"I'll explain things to David," she said finally. Then she slipped him a mischievous glance. "*You* can tell my father!"

He shook his head and chuckled along with her. "Deal," he agreed. "Now I better head back to town."

Moving away, he halted and turned back toward her when she called his name.

"I have a suggestion of my own," she said with a teasing smile. "I think you should confine your comments about my weaknesses to what you feel you need to work on as my trainer."

"I thought that's what I was doing," he replied, perplexed at her words.

"Well, I don't see what my head being pretty has to do with how well my mind can retain your instructions and learn from them. That doesn't come into it at all, in my opinion."

He gave a resigned sigh. "You're wrong. If you were old-maid ugly, your being a woman would still be a problem in the race. Your being pretty complicates things even more."

This time he left her without being called back. Seeing

him approach, his dogs rose and stretched, eager to hit the trail again.

"We'll start getting a lot longer runs tomorrow," he promised them.

Releasing his snow anchor, he climbed onto the runners and called "kra," then "gee" to turn them back the way they'd come. Thoughts of Laura followed him down the trail, and he could have kicked himself for discussing the nights they'd have to spend together with her. The nights were necessary, of course, but he could have waited a while to bring that up. Now he had weeks to fight the worry of how he would handle those looming nights alone with her.

5

SEVERAL WEEKS LATER, Laura and Sandy had worked out a training routine. Sandy's method of teaching her involved having her do every bit of work from feeding and caring for her own team, to harnessing and unharnessing them each day and maintaining the dogs' harness in tiptop shape. He was able to instruct her verbally, with absolutely no "hands-on" interaction between them. She respected his wishes, and not only because she recalled his initial threat of terminating his employment with anyone who defied his orders. In addition, she couldn't quite completely erase the scene in the kennel from her mind, when she'd so foolishly played a different sort of "hands-on" game with him. That closeness to him had shown her that an engagement ring didn't protect her from being attracted to another man. Lucky for her she'd learned her lesson with a man who had some honor and who didn't take advantage of her immaturity.

The weather into November had held perfectly for her training. Temperatures dipped below freezing, typical for this time of year, but the blizzards that sometimes hit didn't materialize. Instead, light snows laid several inches at a time over the land, and one day Laura had jokingly told Sandy it was perfect, doggie heaven weather for sled dogs.

Today, Laura laughed gaily and "whoa'ed" her team on the edge of a wilderness lake. The lakes were freezing over quickly, but she and Sandy hadn't checked the thickness of the ice on this one yet to see whether it was safe for the teams to cross. Barely half a minute later, Sandy pulled up beside her, his sled swerving to a halt and spraying a shower of snow over her.

"Hey!" she cried. "Don't be a sore loser!"

Shaking his head, Sandy tossed the snow anchor out and stepped from the runners. "You don't have to keep proving your team is faster than mine. Besides, I could have beaten you if I'd taken the shortcut across the marsh. You made way too wide a turn when you changed direction at that huge pine, too. You're going to have to work with your dogs on that. There are times in a race where every foot of distance you cut off counts, especially if you manage to get close to the finish line and one or two other teams are racing you to it."

"I didn't realize the marsh was on our route," Laura replied with a frown.

"Laura, you haven't been listening to me again. The Alaskan races aren't over well-marked, seasoned trails. They give you the starting point, the checkpoints you have to pass through, and the ending point. You figure out how to follow the vague route and get to the end in the least amount of time. Whoever does it the fastest, wins."

"In other words, cheating is fine."

"It's not considered cheating! That's your femininity talking again. A man understands the main rule is that there are no rules."

She must have still looked confused because Sandy said, "Look, it's like a poker game. It's not cheating for a man to act like he's got a royal flush in his hand, when he actually doesn't even have so much as a single pair—or even an ace high. He might end up bluffing out someone who holds four aces, and that's fine with the rest of the players. The player with the most skill won, and they accept that."

"They don't usually let women play poker," Laura reminded him, then broke into giggles at the consternation on his face when he thought she didn't understand his analogy. With a wink, she said, "But Buck taught *me* how. I had to promise him that I wouldn't tattle to Father, though. And come to think of it, Buck owes me fifty cents yet."

He smiled, then gazed over the frozen lake. "There's something else you need to learn," he said, tilting his head in an indicative gesture. "See out there where the wind's swept that ice clear of snow?"

"You mean where it's sort of a different color?"

"Yes. That's probably soft ice. You don't want to get close enough to investigate, though. By the time you found out whether or not it really was soft, your lead dog could already be floundering in the water."

He glanced at her and then at Blancheur, who was sitting on his haunches, fidgeting to get going again. "How's that new pup doing?"

"He's got quite a ways to go," she said. "I'll turn him over to Pete to train after this run, like you said earlier. I just wanted to get a feel for him first."

"As you should," Sandy responded. "Your dogs are your partners out here. Another thing is, never, never force your dogs down a path they're reluctant to take—or to cross an area of a lake that seems safe to you but they shy away from. Dogs can sense unsafe conditions, while we have to depend on our eyes to show them to us."

"Yes, sir," Laura said.

He gazed at her steadily for a full half minute, his teal eyes unreadable but not as stern as they were at other times. His red knit hat balanced precariously on his blond hair, which was badly in need of cutting. She'd heard Katie ask him just last night if she could do the honors of shortening his hair, but he evaded giving her a firm answer. He had, however, agreed to try to work out some suitable appointment time.

They'd traveled a good ten miles this morning, and both

of them had opened their coats to cool down from their exertions. She, as well as Sandy, ran beside the sleds as often as riding on them. Sandy was adamant about that, saying she had to develop her leg muscles for the race.

His jacket was made from dark gray wolfskin, and she'd noticed the first time she saw him in it how the color complemented his eyes. The few times he forced her to follow behind his sled rather than let her race ahead of him, she'd seen that his legs didn't appear to be in need of any further development at all!

Now he grinned at her, exposing even white teeth. Despite trying strenuously, she hadn't gotten him beyond smiles and infrequent chuckles yet, but she didn't have any idea what was amusing him at the moment. He willingly told her.

"Repeat everything you're learned today," he said. "I don't want you forgetting, like you did with the information about not having to follow an exact path with your team."

Laura agreeably repeated the facts he had told her, her upper body moving back and forth in time to the sing-song cadence of her voice. "You don't have to follow the easiest route, if you can get there faster another way. Watch out for different colored ice. It can be dangerous. Listen to your dogs. They're smarter than you are."

He did it! He actually threw back his head and laughed! A frisson of pleasure shot through her, and a huge grin split her face. His laugh was deep and throaty, and he'd closed his eyes. Weathered and tanned from spending so much time outdoors, tiny wrinkles fanned out from the corners.

And heavens. He had the cutest dimple in his left cheek. There might be one in the other cheek, too, if she could see, but his head was turned in profile. She stepped off the sled and sidled around to the far side of him.

He opened his eyes, chuckles still rumbling in his wide chest. "What are you doing?"

"Seeing if you have another dimple on this side of your face," she replied honestly.

"I guess I do," he said with a slight shrug. "At least, Colleen always said I did. I've never watched myself in the mirror while I laughed, though."

"Yep, your wife was right." Briefly, his admonition for them to keep their distance because of his being male and her female crossed Laura's mind. But surely they'd spent enough time together now to prove they could be strictly friends.

Wanting to hear his laugh again, she curled her fingers inside her mittens, stuck her thumb out and punched it into his cheek. "It's right there. At least, I think that's where I saw it. Laugh again and let me see if that's the place."

Shaking his head, Sandy turned away. "Come on. We need to start back."

Without any further forethought, Laura reached out and curved both sets of her mittened fingers into his ribs, tickling him fiercely. Sandy jerked away from her with a shout, and she followed him. He hit his boot heel on his sled anchor and tripped, sprawling onto his back. She stood over him, fingers arched.

"Laugh!" she ordered. "All work and no play makes Sandy a dull boy."

He laughed. Propping her hands on her hips, she stood there and watched, deep satisfaction flowing through her. They'd been working hard for weeks, and he'd been totally serious virtually the entire period. It was time the man learned hard work and fun could go hand in hand.

Hadn't he ever laughed with his wife?

When Sandy sat up and stared at her, she realized she'd spoken aloud. For a moment she didn't think he would answer her. Then he did.

"Yes, Colleen and I laughed," he said in a quiet voice. "A lot. We had our serious times, but we also had fun together. And we enjoyed every minute of our time with each other."

Covering up a stab of something she didn't recognize in her emotions, Laura backed away a little and propped herself against her sled. "I suppose it's really none of my business, but I have been curious about your marriage."

He remained sitting, bending his legs and resting his forearms on his knees. For a second she wondered if he would think her too forward. She'd always been allowed freedom to ask questions and talk about anything that came to mind with her father and David. Looking back on it, she guessed her father may have been concerned about being both mother and father to her, since her mother died when Laura was only two. She was fully aware, though, that not everyone—especially the other women she knew—was allowed the freedom she had. Hopefully, Sandy would take her inquiry as natural curiosity, a trait shared by almost all the rest of the world's female population.

Sandy's eyes deepened to that lovely teal color as he contemplated her comments, and she waited for him to speak—or tell her that he didn't want to discuss his marriage, at least not with her. With all the time they spent together, she saw no need to be standoffish. He'd also made it clear they had to develop a close, dependable partnership if they were to run the Alaskan race together. That, with a strong partnership between the two of them, they could protect each other from danger.

And she'd never have to face looking at one of her dogs as an entrée!

"They say everyone has a twin somewhere in the world," Sandy said at last. "And I noticed the day we met in Grand Marais that you looked quite a bit like Colleen. But the more time I spend with you, the more I realize how different you are from my wife." He chuckled and shook his head. "I couldn't imagine Colleen deciding she wanted to go with me when I ran in a race, although I could definitely imagine Tracie demanding that. Tracie looks like her mother, too, and I'd be willing to bet she's going to be her mother's twin some day. But she's very different—a combination of my traits and Colleen's, I guess."

"You never said how your wife died, and I've never asked Tracie. I was afraid it would upset her to talk about it."

Sandy rose to his feet, dusting the snow from the back of his trousers. "Colleen died of pneumonia. It started out as a simple cold, but by the next day, she was down in bed. She died the day after that. I guess the saying about time healing is true, because Tracie and I are coming to grips with it now. We've started to talk about her between ourselves—and with Cristy. So if Tracie wants to talk to you about her mother, I have no objections."

"I'll remember that. And much as I hate to be the one to call a halt to our training today, we did both promise Father we'd attend the Commissioner's meeting this evening. I'll need time to get ready. Father expects me to look like a woman rather than a man in training when he puts me on display at those things."

Chuckling at her parallel, Sandy yanked at his sled anchor, but it refused to pull free. "Yeah, I remember. Did he say why he wanted me there? I'm not really a part of this town yet."

"He's very mysterious about what the meeting tonight entails," Laura said. "Usually I can tease a secret out of him, but all my wiles were useless this time. The only thing I can figure is that it's something he's sure I'll really like, and he's drawing out his pleasure at anticipating my reaction."

When he yanked on his sled anchor again, Laura smirked at Sandy's back. She hadn't anchored her own sled, depending on her dogs to obey her command to stay until she ordered them on. Suddenly she leapt onto her sled runners and cried "Mush!"

"Hey!" Sandy yelled after her.

"I'm just taking advantage of a situation that's to my benefit!" she yelled back at him. "Like I would in a real race! Catch me if you can!"

Remembering his mention of the marsh, she guided her team in that direction. Her dogs, fresh once again after their rest, pulled her behind them effortlessly, and she laughed joyously, enjoying the ride. She couldn't imagine anything more fun than racing across the snow, the noise of her dogs' excited barks the only sounds making it past the rest of the wind in her ears.

She saw the large brown animal on the other side of the marsh when she topped a slight ridge. The moose raised its huge, antlered head, but she'd encountered plenty of moose on her runs, and her dogs knew to avoid them. She didn't slow the team.

This time, though, she forgot she was training the yearling pup with the team. She always harnessed the new dogs right behind Blancheur, trusting her lead dog to provide an example of expected behavior. Blancheur justified her trust. He swerved the team's path to give the moose a wide berth without Laura even shouting a change of direction. Unfortunately, the pup went berserk.

She'd dubbed the pup Trouble, and he lived up to the name. Lunging against his harness, he stumbled and rolled when the rest of the team didn't follow. The unexpected action pulled Blancheur into a misstep, and he turned on Trouble with a growl. Screaming at the dogs, Laura grabbed her sled anchor and threw it out, then reached for the whip she hardly ever touched.

Blancheur was already tangled with Trouble, and Trouble's harness-mate jumped into the melee. The two dogs behind the fighting bunch twisted backward, tangling their own harness as they tried to avoid getting pulled into the fray. The rest of the team howled and barked, half of them straining to join the fight and the other wanting out of there before they got bitten.

Busy worrying about the dogs, Laura missed the moose's charge. When she glanced up, it was within a hundred yards of her, head down and five-foot-wide span of antlers sweeping the ground with deadly intent.

The moose weighed well over a thousand pounds, hooves as large as the iron skillet Katie used for fried chicken pounding the ground. Those antlers could cause severe damage—or death—to whatever they encountered. Vicious eyes glared, and Laura heard its snorts and grunts of rage even over the dogs' growls and yaps.

Oh, God! Sandy didn't carry a rifle and neither did she. Laura looked at her whip, realizing at once how ineffective it would be against the huge animal. Hoping prayer would work better, because that seemed the only thing left, she uttered the first one coming to mind: The Lord's Prayer.

A rifle shot *did* ring out, and a bullet plowed into the ground in front of the moose, showering up snow. The moose slid to a halt, head lifting and another bellow of rage coming from its throat. It glared to the side, and even the dogs quieted. When Laura saw Buck with his rifle still on his shoulder, standing beneath a pine tree, she breathed a sigh of relief. The moose turned and trotted away, and Laura grabbed the skinning knife from her pack on the sled, hurrying up to the dogs.

"Be careful with that knife," Sandy called as he halted his team a ways back, so as not to antagonize her dogs again. Anchoring the sled, he walked toward her.

"This harness is in too big a mess to untangle," she told him when he was closer. "I'm going to cut it, and have Pete fix it when we get back."

She didn't glance at him for approval, but he muttered something she didn't hear clearly. She sliced Trouble's harness first, and the pup bounded away before either she or Sandy got a firm hold on him. He headed after the moose, his growls interspersed with the howling bay of the hunt. The moose turned to confront its pursuer.

"Oh my God, no!" Laura yelled. "Trouble! Whoa!"

"Damn it, I told you to hold onto him," Sandy growled, more clearly this time. "Get back here, Trouble!"

The stupid dog ignored them, racing right up to the huge animal and snapping at its nose. The moose swept its antlers in an arc, catching the dog and flinging it aside as easily as a leaf. Trouble ki-yied in pain when he landed, then leapt up and rushed back at the moose, skidding to a stop when the animal lowered its head again. Turning, Trouble headed back for the safety of the team, the moose on his heels.

Sandy shoved Laura toward his sled. "Get on my sled and get the hell out of here!"

Instead she evaded his grasp and reached down with her skinning knife, cutting the traces on her dogs' harness to free them. With the moose only about fifty yards off, they leapt away from the sled. The rifle cracked again, and the moose dropped, the ground trembling beneath its huge weight.

Blancheur swerved, heading for the smell of fresh blood. Only the tangled harness kept him from speedily reaching the moose. Laura shouted at him to lie down, and he stopped, then complied reluctantly, his teammates effectively halted, also. Not unexpectedly, Trouble ignored her. He bounded atop the moose's carcass with a howl of victory.

Buck shouted at Laura, and she turned. He tossed his rifle

on his sled and mushed his dogs forward, "whoa'ing" them well clear of the snarled mess of Laura's dogs. Racing over to Sandy's sled, rifle once again in his hands, he asked, "Are you all right, Miss Laura?"

"I'm fine, Buck," she said, noticing that her voice shook in contradiction to her words. "I can't thank you enough."

Buck glanced at the moose, then back at Laura. "I was trackin' that moose, but I never thought it would—" His eyes rolled back in his head, and he fainted dead away at her feet.

Gritting his teeth, Sandy held back a mixture of lingering fear and the burgeoning anger quickly replacing it. He'd never had any problems making decisions, but now he couldn't decide whether to check on Buck, make sure the moose was indeed dead, discipline that half-baked pup Laura had hitched to her sled prior to their run—or grab Laura and alternately shake and kiss some sense into her!

A vision of what Laura's tiny body would have looked like had the moose not been stopped pushed all other thought aside. And for once he didn't give a damn about his responsibility for her safety being part of his job. He cared that she still stood there unharmed and untrampled—unbroken and unbloodied. That she was still able to look at him with those wonderfully eloquent green eyes. That she could still make him laugh and tickle him with those delicate but expressive hands, should she ever want to again.

Those eloquent eyes met his gaze just then, filled with the lingering traces of her terror. Sandy grabbed her and pulled her into his arms. Striving to chase the picture of what-could-have-been from his mind, he buried his face on her neck, desperately whispering her name. She wrapped herself around him, clinging tightly, and he caught the sound of a muffled sob.

Lifting his head, he cupped her face and gazed into tear-misted eyes, which reminded him of leaves after a brief spring shower. His stomach hollowed, and he would have done anything to take the fear from her face.

"Laura, are you going to be all right? My God, you kept

your head so well I almost can't believe you're crying now."

"I'm not crying," Laura denied even while a shiny tear slithered down one stark-white cheek. "I . . . oh, Sandy. That moose was so huge. And I could feel the ground shaking under my feet while it charged."

His thumb flicked the tear away from where it landed, at the corner of her mouth. "It's over," he whispered, barely managing to get the words past his clogged throat when her tongue tip appeared for a brief instant in the spot where his thumb had just been. He could imagine the salty taste she captured from the tear, and it took everything in him not to cover her mouth with his own and share that taste.

Her arms remained around his neck, and a shudder ran through her. There wasn't even a breath of space between them, yet somehow she snuggled closer.

"I'm all right," she murmured. "I know I am. Yet my legs feel like unset jelly."

"It's the aftereffect of your fear."

She gave a half-strangled giggle. "Too bad I'm not Tracie. You could kiss it and make it go awa—"

His lips cut off her words and his mouth swallowed her gasp of astonishment. For a negligible moment, she stiffened in his embrace, then answered the kiss as she had in the dreams he had no control over during the night. With no restraint. With no further hesitation. With all the ardor and fervor he had come to associate with Laura Goodman—a woman who embraced life with the same intensity as she returned his kiss.

For a long time nothing else mattered to Sandy beyond the confines the two of them occupied. He held her and kissed her, satisfying the yearning he had felt ever since the first day he laid eyes on her in Grand Marais. Most definitely ever since the dream that had stirred his long-dormant desires that night in the hotel.

Then Buck moaned and the sound penetrated his mind. He couldn't let Buck wake and see him kissing Laura. But he couldn't break free, either. Just one more second. One more second to last the rest of eternity, while she was married to another man.

Laura was the one who broke the kiss, and Sandy found the willpower somewhere to let her. Desire rather than fear misted her eyes now, and her kiss-swollen lips pouted temptingly before she quickly covered them with her mittened hand.

"I'm . . . sorry," Sandy choked out. "I lost my common sense due my own fear, I guess. I won't let it happen again."

"I asked you to—"

"No! You didn't mean for me to kiss you literally. You just needed a little comfort to get over the shakiness. I shouldn't have done any more than hold you until that passed."

She straightened her shoulders, the determination he so admired in her flowing back into her face.

"We were both rather shook up," she said, nodding her head as though emphasizing her words. "Let's don't talk about it again. Forget it happened."

Buck moaned once more, and Laura fell to her knees beside him. Sandy clenched his fists and closed his eyes briefly, gathering his decision to not reach for her once more into a firm resolve. Then he swiped Buck's rifle from the snow, heading off to check on the moose.

Warily he eyed the moose as he approached, his concentration an ineffective barrier to the lingering feel of Laura in his arms. Up closer, he saw the hole leaking bright red blood in the middle of the beast's forehead. Buck's drinking evidently hadn't spoiled his aim. He walked on over to it, confident the animal would never rise. No doubt the reason it attacked in the first place was the rut being in full swing. The animal hadn't taken kindly to a bunch of people invading what it had staked off as its mating territory. The troublemaking dog had just sparked the situation into further fury.

Sandy grabbed Trouble by the harness. The pup curled its top lip and snapped at his arm, missing—lucky for it. Sandy yanked the pup from the moose and forced it belly down on the ground. It took only one glance at Sandy's face to break the pup's antagonism. It whimpered and pressed its belly tighter into the snow, and Sandy spoke to it, his tone of voice getting his point across even if the animal didn't understand his words.

"You came damned close to getting Laura killed, you

sorry little son of a bitch. From now on, I'll work you with my team instead of letting Laura or Pete handle you. You'll either turn into a sled dog or you'll spend your life on a pack team instead of a race team!"

Grabbing a piece of rope from his coat pocket, he looped it through Trouble's collar and led the dog back to the sleds. Buck was sitting up now, and Laura murmured soothingly to him, her arm around Buck's puny shoulders. They both looked up as Sandy tied Trouble to the side of Laura's sled.

Buck's presence reminded him sharply that it had been the other man who saved Laura, not him. His near lethal failure to protect her crashed back into his consciousness, and he told himself he needed to drive home to Laura the mistakes she had made. Emphasize the need for her to learn from what had just happened, in order to keep other similar errors from posing a threat in the future. There might not be a drunk to depend on to rescue her the next time a danger he was unprepared for threatened her.

"The moose is stone dead," he informed them in a low growl. "And we've got you, Buck, to thank for the fact we're both alive to tell the tale of what happened here."

Laura straightened and faced him. Her expressive face told him that she was aware his thoughts had gone from wanting to comfort her to wanting to lambaste her from Monday to Sunday for her inappropriate actions. Composed now and over her fear, she waited for his criticism, willing, just like the Laura he was coming to know so well, to take her medicine.

"There's no need for you to say it," she said. "I know I caused this mess. I broke one of your most important rules and several other ones besides. First, I forgot to always be aware of what dogs I have in my team. I forgot I was training Trouble and he wouldn't respond like a seasoned teammate to a threat of danger."

Sandy's respect mounted for the tiny slip of a woman, who made no excuses for herself. But he didn't dare let himself think there might be something over and above the respect creeping into his heart.

"What else did you forget?" he asked.

"I forgot the dogs always have to be made submissive to me. That it's not being mean to them when I force them to obey—it's thinking of both their safety and mine. I should have had a good hold on Trouble before I cut him out of the traces."

"And?"

She chewed her bottom lip, her frown tugging at his heartstrings. His heart would cry a lot louder if someone carried her cold, dead body in from a snowy trail someday, though. He stared steadily at her.

"I . . . forgot that a race is business, not fun?" she asked with a lift of a feathery brow.

He dropped his head and shook it. "Trying to get you to treat a run with your dogs as only business—" He raised his head again and gazed into her green eyes. "—Is like telling a child it's too old to play, when it still enjoys its toys. I blame myself as much as you for this mess. I knew the rut was starting, and I should've been armed."

"Well," Laura said in a dismissing tone. "Everything turned out all right this time, thanks to Buck. And we'll bring our rifles tomorrow."

"Our?" he questioned.

"Of course. I have my own rifles and pistols in Father's study—and a few trophies from some of the competitions at the Gun Club."

He should have known. There wasn't anything usual at all about Miss Laura Goodman. Just then Buck stumbled to his feet, and Laura held a steadying hand out to him.

"Are you sure you're all right, Buck?"

"Yes'm, Miss Laura," he said emphatically. "And I'm a gonna be a lot more all right when I get that there meat back to town. Why, I can make a lot selling that there meat to Mrs. Sterling's restaurant. And what with working for you again, like we discussed while Mr. Montdulac checked on the moose, why, I'll have enough money to enter your pa's race."

"My father's race?" Laura said. "What are you talking about, Buck?"

6

BY THE TIME David pulled the sleigh up at the village hall, it looked like everyone else in Grand Marais was already there for the Commissioners' meeting. Excitement filled the air, but Buck had admitted that all he'd heard was a rumor, and David insisted he didn't know any more either.

David helped Laura to the ground, then reached for Tracie, who rode in the rear seat of the sled with Cristy and Sandy.

"Thank you, Davie," Tracie said, patting David on the face.

Laura smiled tolerantly. David seemed enraptured with the child. More than once she and Sandy had returned from an overlong run to find David with Cristy and Tracie, Cristy at her easel. She'd been meaning to ask Sandy's sister to paint David's portrait for a wedding present and made a note to ask about that the next day.

Even arriving somewhat late, since they had helped Buck

with the moose, Laura found seats waiting for her and her party in the front row. Having a father as one of the commissioners had its advantages. She wouldn't have to strain to hear and miss part of the announcement. Tom frowned a little at her tardiness, but she took it in stride. When he found out what caused her lateness, she'd probably end up with a lecture, but only until his anger changed to thankfulness that she hadn't been hurt. She'd handle that when it happened.

After the disruption from Laura's arrival quieted, Tom spoke to the men seated at the front table with him. "So. Is everyone in agreement to us going ahead and checking on the cost of getting wireless service to Grand Marais? Ayes?"

A chorus of affirmative votes came from the rest of the Board of Commissioners, and not one negative vote sounded when Tom asked. The clerk made a notation in the records, and Tom leaned back in his chair.

"Since what I have to say now isn't commissioners' business, I'll entertain a motion to adjourn this meeting."

The motion passed and was duly recorded, and Tom rose from his chair. "Most of you already heard at least hints of what my idea is. This is a small town and not much is kept secret."

Laura stood to face him. "I've been busy training, and I only heard a rumor today about something you planned, Father. I'd very much appreciate hearing everything from the beginning."

"I'll tell you if you give me a chance, Laura," Tom said with a tolerant wink. She blushed and sat as he continued, "It's much like the rumors say. I plan to finance a dogsled race from Grand Marais to Duluth in mid-January. I believe it will give our town a nice boost of publicity and perhaps draw some interest to us. We could use a few more business enterprises in Grand Marais."

He picked up a stack of papers from the table. "It will be good for the Ladyslipper Landing breeding business, too, as well as the other kennels in the area."

"What's the prizes gonna be?" someone in the audience called. "Tell us the important stuff!"

Shaking his head, Tom handed the stack of papers to the clerk, who read the top one, eyes widening. He scurried to the first row and started passing out the flyers, and immediately the buzz in the room grew louder. Catching the excited vibes, people in the back surged from their seats to snag a flyer before it was their turn.

Tom motioned Laura to him, pulling another flyer from his inside coat pocket. She tugged on Sandy's sleeve, and he followed her behind the table, peering over her shoulder as she read.

"A thousand dollars?!" Laura gasped. "Father, you'll have mushers from all the way up in Canada coming down here for this race."

"That's the idea," Tom admitted. "We want a professional race—a race with a prize that will make the entrants serious about their intents. I want you to get a taste of what's in store for you up in Alaska before you get there."

"This should do it." Laura handed the flyer to Sandy and stared at the crowd in the village hall. "Look at those people. They're already planning what they can do with that prize money. Even the second and third prizes are substantial enough to make a huge difference in their lives."

"We'll call it the Northshore Race, like it says on the flyer," Tom said. "I've already talked to Pete Tallwolf—told him to get with John Beargrease and lay out a route, maybe along the old mail route John ran between here and Duluth. I've decided to have a mandatory overnight layover halfway between here and Duluth, to make it more interesting. It won't be nearly as long a race as the Alaskan ones, but the money should make the competition fierce."

Laura looked up at her father. "The money isn't important to me, Father."

"No, but I know what is important to you," Tom told her. "Winning."

Winning.

A cup of coffee in his hand, Sandy stood in front of the huge windows in his living room the next morning, staring out over Lake Superior as the eastern sky lightened. Ever since his first morning in this cabin, he got up in time to catch the sunrise. The panorama over the huge lake was always awe-inspiring, yet different each morning. He never tired of it.

Blue-black clouds interspersed the red and violet colors today—clouds which darkened with the sure sign of snow after the sun crept over the horizon.

Red sky in the morning, sailors take warning. Red sky at night, sailor's delight.

The adage ran through his mind while he made a mental note to pay close attention to the other warning signs prior to heading out on the trail with Laura today. Squirrels feeding long past their usual morning hours would indicate they were storing food in their nests for a snowy siege. Birds huddled in trees indicated the storm wasn't far off. Of course, there was every possibility during the Alaskan race that Laura would not only get caught in a freak snowstorm, but also encounter a full-blown blizzard. He still hadn't spent any overnights on the trail with her to prepare her for that or judge her capabilities for survival.

Hell, he couldn't trust himself on an overnight with her—not the way he felt. Not after that devastating kiss yesterday. It wasn't an excuse for kissing her at all, but he'd lost a dozen years off his life when the moose charged yesterday. Two dozen years, with that second charge. The animal could have snuffed out Laura's vibrancy without a break in stride. Thanks to that goddamned little runt Buck, they had both lived through it.

It was no excuse at all, either, that he'd been overwrought with relief when Laura made it through that harrowing charge all in once piece. No excuse that he'd been dreaming of her, wanting her, yearning to kiss her every time he forgot and gazed into her face instead of keeping a distance from her.

She was engaged, and even if she weren't, he had absolutely nothing to offer her. It was as simple—and as complicated—as that. He had the solution to all his problems. He only had to win the Northshore Race. With careful, astute handling, even the five hundred dollar second prize could give him a start on his own business. He could leave Grand Marais and settle elsewhere, maybe even further north, where sled dogs were still an important part of the transportation business. He'd made sure most of the dogs he brought from Alaska were breeding-age bitches, so he had a good start on a kennel of his own.

He couldn't stay here. And he had to leave before he was forced to tell Tom Goodman there was no way he could return to Alaska. No way he could take a chance on being jailed and kept there until he sent for Tracie and delivered her into her grandparents' clutches, never to see her again.

His strong attraction to Laura had no future, either. She was another man's property. She was beyond his reach, even if he had any sort of faint desire to change her mind.

Faint desire? Hell, his desire for Laura was a raging beast! His feelings went far beyond physical attraction. He admired her spunk and determination. When she laughed at herself or some amusing situation, the sound cut right into his chest, settling around his heart and warming it. So tiny, yet she handled her dogs with a strength of her will.

Spoiled? Oh, a little. How could she help it, being the only child of the richest man in the area? She expected her desires to be met, but she didn't pout and throw tantrums to get her way when they weren't. She lent a hand when needed, then took the respect and gratitude she received in stride.

Once the sun cleared the horizon, Sandy started a pot of oatmeal for breakfast. Tracie could live on that stuff as long as she had maple syrup to stir into it, he thought to himself with a smile. For him and Cristy, he cut off several thick slabs of bacon and set the pan of biscuits Katie had sent over yesterday in the oven to warm. Cristy would huff and puff, as she did every morning he beat her into the kitchen, insisting she could prepare breakfast. But he still preferred his bacon crisp, not burned.

Despite her late night, Tracie stumbled into the kitchen at the same time as usual this morning—about the time the water boiled for the oatmeal. He picked her up for a morning hug, and she snuggled into his shoulder, all warm and mussed and smelling of sleep and little girl.

"G'morning, Daddy," she murmured.

"Morning, sweetheart. What are your plans for today?" he asked as usual.

She sat up in his arms and stifled a yawn with a small fist, then said, "Davie said we could come into Gan' Mary and eat lunch today. Then Aunt Cristy can start lookin' at the lake for his picture."

"Gan' . . . oh, you mean Grand Marais," Sandy corrected. "And what picture? Has David commissioned Cristy to do a painting for him?"

"Huh uh," Tracie denied. "He's gonna pay her to do one for him. It's a s'prise for Laura, and he wants this special rock in it. It's where he asted Laura to marry him."

"Asked, not asted," Sandy murmured. Hell, now he'd be looking at every rock on the damned shoreline when he went into town, trying to guess which one it was! And he had no right at all feeling this tormenting stab of jealousy!

"We can't's tell Laura, Daddy. You 'member that."

"I'll 'member," Sandy promised.

The water boiled on the stove, and he set Tracie in a chair at the table. After adding the oatmeal to the water and bacon to the skillet, he stepped away. Several minutes later, Tracie tugged on his trouser leg, startling him.

"Daddy," she said urgently. "You's burnin' the bacon just like Aunt Cristy does sometimes."

"Oh, sh . . . uh, dang it!" he muttered. He rescued the bacon just this side of inedible and stirred the oatmeal. Cristy wandered in just then, sniffing the air. He gave her a glare, but she didn't need to say a word. Her sparkling eyes teased him with the silent message she could cook every bit as well as he was managing that morning.

He controlled his thoughts of Laura and got breakfast on the table. Once Tracie finished her meal and left the table, he and Cristy shared a final cup of coffee while he hesitantly spoke to his sister.

"Tracie said you were going into town with David Hudson again today."

"Uh huh. He's asked me to do a painting for him."

"I suppose it's all right, if it's strictly business," Sandy mused.

Cristy set her coffee cup down and met his gaze with a bristling, defensive look. "You mean I'm spending way too much time with another woman's fiancé, don't you, Sandy? You can rest assured it's strictly business—and some friendship—between David and me. Besides, Laura's the one who keeps asking David to entertain me, and vice versa, while she spends her time out on the trail with you. I really like Laura, Sandy, but if David were my fiancé, I don't think I'd leave him all that free time to fill. Or ask another woman to help fill it for him."

"She's got to be in shape for that race. One little misstep in a race the caliber of the Alaskan one can mean a bad injury. Even death."

Cristy's face creased in concern. "Yes, I understand Alaska is a dangerous place in winter." She hesitated, picked up her coffee for a sip, then continued, "Sandy, can I ask you something?"

Her tone of voice sparked an alertness in Sandy. "You can ask," he said grudgingly. "I'm not promising to answer."

Setting her cup down, she leaned her elbows on the table, studying him with eyes an expressive mirror of his daughter's. He could tell the instant she decided to chance her inquiry.

"You've kept an awful lot of secrets from me since I came to live with you," she began hesitantly. "I've managed to pick up on a few things, though."

When he glared at her, she held up one hand in a shielding gesture. "Look, I'm not the scatterbrain you appear to believe I am. Granted, I get lost in my muse at times, but for the most part I'm well aware what's going on around me. So is Tracie. She doesn't understand a lot of what happened in Alaska, but I think I've figured out part of it from some things Tracie asked me."

"It's nothing to concern you, Cristy." Sandy rose, but Cristy's penetrating stare changed his mind about stalking away from the table.

"Have you drawn up guardianship papers for me to use if

it ever becomes necessary for me to take over caring for Tracie?" she asked.

Legs weak, Sandy plopped back down into his seat. "What do you mean?"

"I mean, in case you get arrested when you return to Alaska with Laura. You know as well as I do the names of the race entrants are plastered all over every newspaper in Alaska, and also down into the States. If what I've concluded is true, you can't go back to Alaska without risking losing Tracie."

Sandy leaned his head forward, cupping it in his hands. For so long he had carried the burden of what happened after Colleen's death alone. He hadn't realized it when he first fled Alaska, but he left it for life on the run. He had no choice. It was either that or obey the Alaskan Territorial Court Order his influential in-laws had arranged—possibly by bribing a high-ranking judge. It directed him to give up custody of Tracie to her grandmother and grandfather, an unthinkable surrender.

George Dyer also carefully manipulated the accounts and loans at the bank he owned, stripping Sandy of his financial security. He couldn't fight the man without money.

He hadn't realized how much strain constantly looking over his shoulder would be, though, even thousands of miles away in Minnesota. How every time he glimpsed someone who faintly resembled either George or Elvina Dyer, his heart would pound nearly out of his chest until he confirmed it wasn't either of Tracie's grandparents.

He had also forgotten during the last few years of financial stability how hard counting every penny was. How stressful it could be wondering if his money would last until the next payday—stretch far enough to buy his daughter a winter jacket and keep her tummy full.

He'd been single and carefree during his pinch-penny days, with a home he could return to if things didn't pan out. He'd waited to marry until prospects allowed him to offer a wife and family a secure future. Then it had all been stripped away from him within a matter of weeks.

The urge to share his fear and burden with the little sister, who had suddenly grown up without his noticing, was so great tears stung Sandy's eyes. He didn't know how Cristy had found out the details, or even if she only suspected them. Since she already knew part of it, a compelling need for her to know—and share—the rest of it gripped him.

"You could talk to David about it," Cristy murmured when Sandy looked at her again.

"No. No, I can't," he denied. "Hell, he's engaged to Laura, and he might feel bound to tell Tom Goodman. Then where would we be? Tom might figure since I can't live up to the agreement, firing me is the next alternative. We wouldn't have a place to stay."

"I doubt very much that would happen, Sandy. The Goodmans are wonderful people. I'll bet they'd understand, and even help."

"Can you bet our lives on that?"

Cristy hesitated, then sadly shook her head.

"Let me tell you just how serious this is, Cristy. You can't help, but at least you'll know what the situation is if Tracie needs your care more than just as her aunt."

7

CRISTY CONTEMPLATED THE information Sandy had told her over and over. At least it kept her mind off her growing attraction for David Hudson, the fiancé Laura took for granted. Not that David didn't appear just as blasé about his end of the relationship, she reminded herself as she stood in Tom Goodman's office, studying the shoreline through the huge windows.

She sketched a preliminary drawing for the painting David wanted in the pad propped on her easel. Insisting it was way too cold to do her initial charcoal drawings on the shore, Tom and David had gone to David's office to handle their business, leaving Cristy in semi-privacy. Tracie, never a bother at this point in Cristy's work, sat on a rug in front of the window, playing with a set of paper dolls David had given her.

Cristy had a perfect view of the rock David wanted for his picture. Over time waves had carved a smooth shelf into the boulder, the right height for a woman to sit on. With changes in the shoreline, the boulder was now far enough back from the water to escape the spray from the waves, although ice edged the shoreline now. David assured her this huge lake never froze completely, but the harbor would be inaccessible by Christmas, barely four weeks away. By then she would be ready to paint the surrounding landscape into the picture appropriately. David told her that he proposed to Laura on Christmas Day last year, right after they enjoyed a holiday dinner at Mrs. Sterling's restaurant.

Cristy sighed as she blended a too-sharp line on the boulder with her fingertip. If she were ever lucky enough to find a man half as wonderful as David, she would never allow him more than a year after his proposal to change his mind. Her mother had once told her that she and her father got married within a month of meeting. Cristy had never seen a more suited—or loving—marriage.

"Aunt Cristy?" Tracie asked.

"Hmmmm, darling?"

"Am I bothering you?"

"No. Not right now, Tracie." Cristy turned to a clean page in her pad and began a new sketch from a different angle. "It's only when I start putting colors on canvas that I'll get distracted and involved so deeply I might forget where I am. I promised you could go stay with Katie when it comes time for me to actually paint."

"Katie's nice." Tracie discarded the paper dress she held up to her cardboard doll in favor of another one. "And she's fixin' punkin pie for Thanksgiving tomorrow. I gets to go over when we get home and help her do that."

"Pumpkin's your favorite, isn't it?"

"Uh huh. 'Cept for blueberry." She paused for a moment, and Cristy glanced at her to see a contemplative frown on her face. "And maybe shock-o-lat."

Cristy laughed and shook her head. "Chocolate," she corrected. "You know, Tracie, honey, your daddy and I haven't even talked about getting you into school here. I understand the classes close down pretty soon, though, until spring. You and I could set aside some time each day for lessons. Would you like that?"

"Yeah. Mama taught me to count and say my A-B-C's. I can read words, too, 'long as they aren't real long. I'd like to learn some more, but I thought maybe Daddy wasn't gonna put me back in school 'till he figured out if we was gonna stay here or not."

She gave a dramatic sigh and smoothed yet another dress on her doll. "I hope we does stay here. I don't like leavin' everythin' and going off. 'Specially when it worries Daddy so bad."

Concerned over Tracie's unusual melancholy, Cristy left her sketch pad on the easel and settled on the floor beside her niece. Sunbeams streamed through the window, warming them in addition to the heat from a huge pot-bellied stove in the corner of the room. She held her arms out to Tracie, and the little girl crawled into her lap.

"Your daddy wouldn't want you to worry about stuff, Tracie. He's the daddy, and that's his job. But we women do worry sometimes, don't we?"

"Uh-huh. I think Daddy's afraid Gramma might's come after us and try to make me come live with her. When I stayed at Miss Vickie's that day right a'fore me and Daddy left Alaska, her nasty little brother tol' me that's what was goin' on. He said Daddy had to go see some man called a ju . . . judge, who might take me 'way from Daddy."

"How did you get out of town?" Cristy regretted the question the moment she asked Tracie, feeling a stab of guilt and disloyalty to Sandy. But she also believed she should know, and after all, Sandy had told her some of the story this morning.

"All's I know is we was on one of the ships when I woke up the next mornin'." Tracie shrugged her small shoulders. "We came to get you, then got on the train."

"Sandy must have had some friends to help him," Cristy mused.

"Daddy used to have lots of friends." Tracie's voice grew softer. "Him and Mama both. But he don't got none's here. He's 'lone lots, 'cept for Miss Laura."

"We'll have to see what we can do about that."

The office door opened and Tom Goodman walked in,

followed by David. For a moment it appeared they didn't see the two figures on the floor, and David's face grew concerned. When he came around the desk and spotted them, his eyes lit up.

"Hey, I should commission you to paint that picture for me, Cristy," he said. "Look, Tom. Isn't that a great sight, the two of them in front of that window, looking like a couple of flowers in the spring?"

Tracie giggled. "It's winter, Davie. Not spring."

"Yeah, Davie, it's winter," Cristy said, embarrassed at being caught on the floor and attempting to rise. David hurried over and held out a hand to assist her. It would have been rude to ignore him, but she dropped his hand the instant she got to her feet.

"We're going to quit work early today," Tom said. "That is, if you're done here, Cristy. Katie gave me a list of things to pick up at the store for her, so she can prepare the food for dinner tomorrow. I don't know how she thinks we'll eat all that stuff, but we always manage to put a big dent in it."

"Just let me gather up my things. And Tracie, put your dolls in their box, please."

"I already did, Aunt Cristy. Can I go to the store with Mr. Tom? Katie told me to make sure he gets stick cinnamon for the punkin pies and not that there kind they's puttin' in them tin boxes already ground up."

"Please let her go with me." Tom gave a mock shiver when Cristy hesitated. "I sure as darn tootin' wouldn't want to get the wrong type of cinnamon and have Katie not make her pies. *Punkin's* my favorite."

"Mine, too!" Tracie said excitedly. "I won't let you get the wrong kind, Mr. Tom. Katie showed me what she wants."

"Go on," Cristy said with a tolerant laugh. "I'll meet you at the store as soon as I gather my things."

She was aware—very aware—that David stayed behind when Tom hefted Tracie into his arms and strode from the office. Though she didn't normally allow anyone to see her work in progress, she handed him the sketch pad in order to have something to talk about.

"Uh . . . you probably won't get much of an idea of what I have in mind from these, but it's how I work."

"I'm sure the final painting will be wonderful," David assured her. "I've seen some of your other work, remember? And I'd like you to look at my office when you have time. See what you could come up with for it. The other day one of my women clients said my office had less character than the general store. I have no idea why my office should have *character*, but if it makes my clients more comfortable, I'm willing to work on it. Or have you work on it, if you will. It seems more and more women these days are taking an interest in things like wills and owning their own property, and it's to my benefit for my clients to want to return to my office."

When Cristy only nodded and picked up her box of charcoals, he continued, "I'll pay you for your input. And of course for the additional paintings I hope you'll do. In fact, I saw a couple paintings in among those you brought with you that would be perfect—at least in my mind. You might have some different ideas."

"Don't you think Laura should be the one to help you redecorate your office?"

David laughed that deep, playful sound, which always warmed her heart. "Laura did re-do the cabin you and your brother live in, but she had several people's opinions to give her input. She'd probably bring in pictures of her dogs from days gone by for my place. I'd much prefer something different."

An idea flickered in Cristy's mind, but first she had to confirm something. "When people come to you for legal help, it's confidential, right?"

"I can't even tell a woman's husband what she talks to me about without her permission."

"What if she talks to you about someone else's situation?"

"Same thing, as long as she doesn't want me telling anyone what we discuss behind closed doors. It's called attorney-client privilege."

"Then maybe we can work something out about the paintings and decorating," Cristy mused.

On Thanksgiving Day, Laura wandered out onto the back porch of her house, snugging her cloak around her against the cold. The temperatures continued to fool them, dropping well below zero when the winds blew in off the huge lake, but hovering at tolerable levels on days the wind died.

She recalled a visit from one of her friend's cousins during the past holiday season, when the snows had been especially heavy and the wind at times vicious. Living in a southern state, the cousin had never experienced that type of sometimes violent weather, and at first, tried to huddle inside. However, she soon learned that these sturdy northern people didn't hibernate with the animals in the winter time. They accepted the weather and dressed for it. They made the best of the transportation they had in the way of sleighs and dogsleds. They dug out from the storms and continued to celebrate the season—visit friends and exchange presents— dance into the wee hours at parties and bundle up well to face the bitter-cold rides home.

They co-existed with nature and her fury in the winter, respecting her, but not submitting to her.

In the kitchen behind Laura, Tracie giggled wildly at something Katie said. Laura had been not-very-subtly ousted from there a few minutes ago, when she almost dropped the canister of salt into the pan of stuffing Katie was preparing. Katie and her granddaughter, Meg, who had arrived early this morning to help, not only tolerated but also enthused over Tracie's bumbling efforts to learn to cook. Laura *had* lasted five minutes longer than Cristy, she thought a little smugly. Cristy had dropped one of Katie's pie crusts when she started to lay it over a preparation of blueberries, and Katie shooed her into the dining room to polish silver.

She wished Cristy had been banished outside, however. The men were in one of their man-thing discussions, standing outside the kennel door in a group, their faces looking as though they pondered the problems of the world.

She didn't imagine her father, Pete, David, Buck and Sandy would appreciate a mere female adding her opinion. Just then they all strode over to one of the bitch sled dogs and studied her. She hoped they didn't get any ideas about having input into her breeding program. That was her sole domain.

She really felt left out of things, rare for her. She probably could sneak around the house and tap on a window. Get Cristy's attention and ask her to come on out for some "girl" talk. Instead she closed her eyes, allowing the surrounding sounds to wash over her.

The chattering and murmurs from the kitchen intermingled with the clunk of pots and pans. A splash of water, the snick of a knife being sharpened. Someone opened the window near her slightly, and spice and roasting turkey smells drifted to her. She'd barely touched her breakfast in anticipation of one of Katie's feasts, and she'd be starved by mealtime.

Men's boots crunched across the snow in the yard. It sounded like they were heading over to Sandy's dogs now. She'd considered cross-breeding a careful litter or two of the different breeds herself, so she didn't care that the idea had occurred to the men also. They'd have to get her permission, however, for any of her dogs to be part of it.

Where would she be next Thanksgiving, she wondered? What sounds would she hear then, and who would be making them? David's family home was in town, and he only lived on the first level at the moment. Less than two years ago, his parents had died within a week of each other during a virulent influenza epidemic. She and David both knew Laura would never be happy in town, but they'd put off deciding to place the Hudson house on the market. Her father once casually mentioned there was plenty of land in the Ladyslipper Landing tract to build another house, and she supposed they could get something built over the summer.

She wanted a house like her present home—huge windows, lots of light and an airy feel of freedom about it.

Private, yet near enough to people for companionship when she desired it.

Her children should have lots of playmates nearby, and she tried to envision her and David's children in her mind. With her auburn hair and David's black hair, they would surely have dark locks, perhaps with reddish highlights. Maybe their eyes would be hazel, a mixture of her green and David's brown.

Suddenly she opened her eyes so fast and so wide she almost became dizzy. The curly-headed moppet in her mind had grinned at her, teal blue eyes sparkling in the urchin's face! The child could have been Tracie as a baby.

She definitely needed to find Cristy—occupy her mind with something besides thoughts of Sandy. Before she could act on the thought, a horrible series of growls and howls of pain rent the air.

Laura's hand flew to her neck and she stared out into the yard. The men already raced toward Blancheur, their shouts lost amidst the clamor of dozens of other sled dogs, who'd caught the tension of the fight in progress and responded accordingly. Laura couldn't tell what dog had broken loose and attacked Blancheur, but the faint traces of logic lingering in her panic told her it had to be one of Sandy's dogs. The two teams had never gotten along.

When she raced from the porch, her foot slipped in a patch of ice on the step, wrenching her back and nearly sending her to the ground. Regaining her balance, she ignored the slice of pain and headed for the brawling dogs. Before she reached them, David and her father grabbed her, easily holding her between them when she tried to break away.

"Let me go!" she shouted. "I need to handle Blancheur!"

"Sandy and Buck will take care of it," Tom soothed. "With Pete helping them. You'll only end up getting bit."

Helpless to do anything else, she stared at the melee. Sandy sidled close to the two animals and his arm flicked out. He hauled back on one of the animals, and Laura recognized Sandy's lead dog, Keever. Buck leapt forward to grab Blancheur, but before he reached the dog, Blancheur tumbled over on his side. Laura gasped in horror at the red splotches spreading on his white coat.

"Oh, my God!" Tom and David's hold on her slackened, and Laura shook them off. As Buck dropped to the ground beside Blancheur, sobbing and reaching for the dog, she raced forward. Tom and David followed her, and when she knelt beside Buck, Sandy ordered Pete to tie Keever back up.

Beside her in an instant, Sandy stayed her hand when her trembling fingers sought to touch Blancheur's head. The dog's different-colored eyes pleaded with her, and his tail flopped weakly once.

"Let me carry him into the kennel," Sandy said. "We can examine him there."

She nodded slightly, and Sandy scooped Blancheur up in his arms. With Buck walking beside her, sniffling in misery, she hurried after Sandy's long strides. He paused at the kennel door, and she opened it for him, rushing inside and grabbing blankets from the supply cupboards to arrange in one of the wooden boxes they used for dog beds.

Sandy tenderly laid Blancheur down. The dog feebly licked Sandy's hand as he withdrew it.

Without looking at Buck, Laura said, "Buck, go get Dr. Erik."

"Yes, Miss Laura."

Buck stumbled away, and Tom moved to the other side of the dog bed. "I sent David to the house to tell the women and Tracie what happened, and ask them not to come out here," he told Laura. "They heard the disturbance and were on the back porch."

"Maybe you should let your father take you into the house," Sandy said. "I'll . . ." Laura gave him a scathing look, and he shrugged. "No, I guess that's not a viable idea. You won't leave your dog. Will you at least fetch some warm water and bandages?"

"Father knows where everything is," Laura replied. Steeling herself, she parted Blancheur's blood-soaked fur, examining the deep wounds. One of them was deep on his neck.

"Get padding to staunch the bleeding first, Father," she said.

They cleaned Blancheur up the best they could, slowing the bleeding but not completely stopping it over the deep neck wound. "Erik will have to stitch this," Laura said at one point, and Sandy nodded agreement.

When everything was done except enduring the wait until the vet showed up, Sandy rose to his feet. Laura glanced around to see that her father had left sometime during the last fifteen minutes.

Retrieving another blanket from the supply cabinet, Sandy spread it on the floor beside Laura. "Sit on that and try to calm yourself," he said with a frown of concern. "You won't help the dog by being so tense. He can sense your distress."

Laura complied—at least with the directive to sit. If her life depended on it, she couldn't have forced her muscles to relax. The horrible growls and howls of pain kept echoing in her mind.

"How did Keever get loose?" she asked as Sandy crouched beside her and leaned back on his heels.

"I don't know," he said grimly. "But I'm sure Pete's out there now examining the chain. If he finds anything suspicious, he'll let me know."

"He'll let *us* know," Laura said harshly. "It's my dog lying here hurt."

"Keever had some pretty bad looking wounds himself, but since he was free while Blancheur was chained, he probably came out a little better. Keever outweighs Blancheur, too. I should go check on him, though."

Laura's anger dissipated. "I'm sorry. I forgot Keever was hurt, too. Go on. I'll stay here with Blancheur. And if we need to move Keever into the kennel also, we can put him in the office. That way we can keep the door closed and the two of them won't be able to get at each other."

"I'll put Keever up in our cabin if necessary. They'll both heal a lot faster if they can't even smell each other."

He rose again and left the kennel. Mentally pleading with Erik to hurry, Laura laid a hand on Blancheur's head. He would probably anesthetize Blancheur before he stitched the worst wound and cleaned some of the other areas with antiseptic. As much as Blancheur loved her, she feared he would bite her if she tried to put a stinging compound on his cuts, and her father had found only an empty tin when he searched for the salve they normally kept on hand. She recalled putting it on a list of items to restock the cupboards with, but she didn't remember buying any.

Rubbing her back, Laura vaguely recalled the wrenching stumble on the back steps, then dropped her hand and sighed in anxious relief as the tall, rangy vet came in.

"Buck was blubbering so bad I sent him up to the house for Katie to take care of," Erik said without preamble. "He loves that damned dog of yours."

Kneeling, Erik opened his supply case. His experienced hands quickly examined Blancheur while he asked Laura exactly what had happened. She appreciated his forthrightness as he interspersed their conversation with his opinion of each of the wounds, which he announced were mostly the type to leave a scar but not life-threatening. Even the deep wound on the dog's neck had missed any vital spots, he assured Laura.

"But I'll need to stitch that one," he admitted. "And I'll want you to help me put Blancheur under the anesthesia."

Heedless of the damage to her cloak and dress from Blancheur's still damp, blood-spotted fur, Laura scooted over and lifted the dog's head into her lap. Sandy came in as Erik uncorked a bottle of ether from his supply case. He knelt beside Erik and they nodded a greeting to each other.

"What can I do?" Sandy asked.

"Thread that needle and get it ready for me," Erik said. "How's your dog?"

Sandy picked up the needle, and Laura glanced away. She could handle the blood, but when Erik started sewing on Blancheur, she would have to leave.

"I'll want you to look Keever over," Sandy said, "but I don't think he's too bad off. He did get a bad bite in a leg muscle, though, and he won't be pulling any sleds until that heals."

"Bad news when a couple male dogs get into it," Erik mused. "How'd you let that happen?"

"Looks like it was an accident. A weak link we didn't notice in the chain. There's no indication it might have been tampered with."

Laura's gaze flew to his. "Who on earth would want Blancheur and Keever to get into a fight? What purpose would that serve?"

Erik and Sandy glanced at each other, and Laura's anger built as she waited for them to comment—or try to protect her from their suspicions because she was a woman.

Sandy spoke first. "Money," he said tensely. "Our two teams are already top odds-makers for the race. With them out of contention—or at least not at top speed—"

"The race isn't for six weeks!"

"You two worry about that later," Erik interrupted. "I've got this dog under, and I don't want to keep him that way any longer than necessary."

Laura chanced a look at the needle Sandy handed Erik and felt her face blanche. Sandy immediately scooted over and lifted Blancheur's head from her lap.

"You look like you could use some air," he murmured sympathetically. "Why don't you step outside?"

"Thank you," Laura breathed. Scrambling to her feet, she hurried from the kennel.

The fresh air quelled her nausea, and Laura blocked out what was happening in the kennel by concentrating on the scenery around her. Yesterday evening a small snowstorm had passed over, but the heavy, overcast skies appeared to predict a stronger storm later today. Instead of deep blue, the water in Lake Superior had a gray cast to it, and she could see rolling swells in the distance. Near noon, the temperature still seemed to be falling, rather than climbing toward the usual afternoon mildness.

Perhaps sensing the tension in the air, the dogs quietly paced or lay before their doghouses. Normally they would clamor for Laura's attention when she appeared. Here and there a younger pup whined and pricked its ears, and Trouble bounded on top of his doghouse, tail wagging. Yet even the worrisome yearling didn't show his usual exuberance.

Not disbelieving Sandy but needing to see the evidence for herself, Laura pushed away from the kennel wall and headed for Keever's doghouse. The empty chain lay in the snow, and she concluded Pete had taken Keever to the cabin to recuperate. When she picked up the chain, she had no doubt Sandy was right. The link had snapped at a spot noticeably thinner than the area surrounding it.

Why hadn't they examined these new chains before they used them, she wondered. But then, they'd never had any trouble like this before, so who would think to bother?

"Laura!"

Turning toward the call, Laura saw Cristy on the back porch.

"Katie's made some hot chocolate," Cristy called. "Would you like me to bring you out a cup?"

"I'll come get one." Dropping the chain into the snow, she walked toward the house. Cristy disappeared inside, and by the time Laura climbed the steps, the other woman had a cup of chocolate waiting for her.

"Thank you." Accepting the cup, Laura winced in pain.

"What's wrong?" Cristy asked. "Do you hurt somewhere?"

"My back," Laura admitted taking a sip of hot chocolate. After savoring the cinnamon-laden sweetness, she swallowed and moved over to a stool on the back porch. "I think I'll sit down a minute. I slipped on some ice on the step earlier. If you see Father before I do, Cristy, would you remind him to put some salt there before someone else gets injured?"

"Of course." Cristy's gaze swung toward the kennel. "How is your dog? And Keever? Tracie would be devastated if anything happened to either one of those animals."

"Please assure her they'll both recover."

"She'll believe it better if you tell her when we eat," Cristy said with a smile. "You're her heroine, you know. She's already decided she wants her own sled dog team by the time she's ten, like your father told her you had."

"I've been promising to take her for a run with me." Laura smiled. "But Sandy keeps me so busy training, I haven't had time. And—" She paused and shook her head. "I won't be able to reassure Tracie about the dogs' injuries at dinner, Cristy. I'll be sitting up with Blancheur tonight. The first night after a traumatic injury like he's suffered is touch and go. I'll want to be there with him to make sure he stays as peaceful as I can make him, so he won't tear out his stitches. I'll be going back out to the kennel as soon as Erik finishes caring for him."

Cristy placed a hand on her stomach and her mouth whitened. "Stitches?" she murmured.

"My sentiments exactly," Laura said with a grimace. "Look, there's Sandy, so I better go." She surged to her feet, hesitating just a second. "Tell Tracie everything will be fine and that Buck can bring her out to see Blancheur after a while, if she really wants."

"She'd probably feel better if she could see the dog for herself."

"She's a lovely little girl. Sandy and his wife raised her well."

"I didn't know Colleen very well," Cristy admitted, touching her cheek to brush back a strand of hair. "I only visited them a couple of times. But I remember her as a wonderful, giving person. Sandy loved her so much, we feared for his sanity when she died."

Becoming aware of the cup in her hand, Laura set it on the porch railing, having suddenly lost her desire for her favorite beverage. "He seems to be the type of man who loves deeply and truly," she said in one of those bursts of words she sometimes couldn't control.

"Very," Cristy agreed.

8

𝒜 LOG SHIFTED in the pot-bellied stove in the corner of the room, and Laura's eyes flew open. Her father insisted on setting up a cot for her beside Blancheur's bed, although she assured him she wouldn't sleep at all. Of course, she finally gave up the fight to hold her eyes open when Blancheur didn't stir for over an hour. The lantern on a beam overhead was out, and she could only see faint outlines in the room, except for the fire glow in the stove. Extending a hand, she touched Blancheur as the door opened.

"Laura?"

Sandy's voice. She sat up and said, "I'm awake. The lantern has gone out. Probably out of coal oil."

"Stay there, and I'll light another one."

She rubbed her eyes and waited until Sandy took another lantern from the supply shelf and lit it. It sent a glow through the room as he carried it over to the beam and replaced the empty lantern, then knelt to examine the dog. "How's he been?"

"Quiet. But I'm sure he wouldn't have stayed that way if I hadn't been here with him. How's Keever?"

"He woke me up scratching at the door, wanting back outside. I repaired the chain earlier, so I tied him up again. Then I got a huge hankering for a piece of Katie's pie and figured I'd check to see if you were awake and hungry, too. We didn't get much of a meal, sitting out here instead of at the table with everyone else."

"I told you to go on in," Laura reminded him. "There was no sense in both of us missing Katie's wonderful feast."

Sandy ignored her and rose to his feet. "You want a piece of that pie? Katie sent two pumpkin ones home with Tracie. I'm sure she won't mind us having a couple pieces."

Laura smiled up at him. "As a matter of fact, I'd love a piece of pumpkin pie. She didn't by any chance send some turkey home with you, too, did she?"

"White meat," Sandy said with a grin. "That turkey must have been huge, because she said that was only half of what was left. It's enough to feed the three of us for two days, if we never touch another thing."

"White meat's my favorite."

"I'll be right back."

While he was gone, Laura assured herself Blancheur would continue to rest comfortably by carefully coaxing one of the sedative pills Erik had told her to give him every six hours down the dog's throat. Then she added some logs to the stove.

She had no qualms about being alone with Sandy at this time of night. She trusted him, since they had rationalized the kiss as an aftereffect of their fear during the moose attack. They'd spent hours and hours together since then with no problem, and he continued to be the perfect gentleman, except when he came near to losing his temper with her. That, she knew, was concern for her safety, and . . . and . . . well, she decided with a firm set to her mouth while she cleared off a space on the office desk, conscientiousness on his part. He'd told her the first time they met that it wouldn't do his reputation any good if one of his students was injured or killed.

Besides, her life was planned out. She wanted her one chance at excitement—the Alaskan race—and then she'd settle down as a good little wife and mother. As *David's* good little wife and mother of *his* children.

By the time Sandy returned, she had another lantern lit and hanging on a peg in the office. A funny warmth stole through her when Sandy set his offering down and removed the linen dish towel wrapped around it with a flourish. His teal blue eyes picked up the lantern light and shone with satisfaction. He'd bundled up the turkey and pie for them by removing half of one pie and piling slices of turkey into the empty portion of the pie pan, then protecting it all with the dish towel.

They'd never shared a meal on the trail, although Sandy periodically checked Laura's emergency rations pack in case an emergency caught them out. They planned their runs to always arrive back at Ladyslipper Landing for meals.

Her stomach broke the stillness with a loud growl, and Laura burst into giggles. "Good thing you brought this food. Otherwise my stomach might disturb Blancheur. He might think there was another dog in here and tear his stitches lose trying to protect me."

Shaking his head at her nonsense, Sandy pulled the chair out for her. She sat, then remembered Pete had taken the only other chair to the back of the kennel to fix a weak leg. Sandy looked around the office, searching for a chair.

He picked up a stack of papers on the corner of the desk and piled them onto a nearby file cabinet. Then he nonchalantly propped a hip onto the desk, belatedly asking Laura, "You don't mind if I sit, too, do you?"

The stab of desire hit her with a wallop in the stomach—and lower. Maybe it was the late night aloneness allowing it to get out of control, when she'd managed to ignore it for so many weeks. Maybe it was the way his stance snugged his trouser leg so tight against his thigh.

"Of course not! Sit!"

He tilted his head questioningly in response to her sharp

tone of voice, but she reached for a piece of turkey. Sandy scooted back on the desk, his thigh so near her forearm she could feel the heat from it. Gritting her teeth, she stared at the piece of turkey in her fingers, wondering how the heck she could take a bite with her jaws clenched like this. But if she let go of her control enough to relax her jaws, she might surge to her feet and jump as far away from that desk as she could.

Or jump *onto* the desk and see if she fit as well in Sandy's arms as she remembered doing the day the moose charged them.

He seemed completely unaware of the tension straining her body. "Hey." He flicked a finger at the turkey in her hand. "As Tracie would say, we's grownups. If that doesn't appeal to you, you can have your dessert first."

Picking up a piece of pie, he held the pointed end to her lips. Her eyes flew to his, and the moment their gazes touched, Sandy's eyes darkened. His hand wobbled, and the end of the pie brushed her lips.

She shoved the chair back violently and stood, her hand immediately going to the opposite forearm, rubbing the tingles caused when it brushed his thigh. She backed away, but the filing cabinet behind her halted her escape.

"Laura, what's wrong?"

She heard more than a courteous concern in his voice—in only those three words. How could she tell he was forcing himself to ask that question? How did she know he was as aware as she was that the crackling in the air around them came from the waves of yearning flowing between them?

When she moved her hand from her arm to her lips, her finger encountered a tiny piece of pie. Instinctively, she stuck out her tongue and licked it from the end of her finger, the spicy sweetness making a dramatic impact on her too-heightened senses.

Sandy exploded off the desk. "Good God, woman!" he yelled. "How the hell much more do you think I can take?"

"I'm engaged," she halfway moaned, once again knowing exactly how he felt.

"I know that!" he yelled back. "Damn it, I know that!" He

ran both hands through his hair and glared at her. Voice softened with torment, he repeated, "I know that."

Laura heard a soft growl outside the office and realized Sandy's voice had disturbed Blancheur, even in the depths of his drugged sleep. "I . . . better go check on him."

"I'll go." Sandy took one step away from the desk, his boot landing on the pie he'd dropped on the floor. His leg skidded, and his arms flew up. Laura rushed forward, grabbing him to steady him. Her impetus pushed him against the desk and he sat, saving them both from a nasty fall.

She was between his legs. Her arms were around his waist—and his arms were around her. Their lips were only a scant breath from each other's. Then they weren't.

He kissed her with a fury she drank in joyfully, an unnecessary palm on the back of her head to hold her. He kissed her as though this would be the only other kiss he would ever have from her—as well it should be. Would be. She clung to him, savoring every tingle in her body and every moan rumbling in his throat—every whimper in hers. Storing every bit of it in her mind so she would have this memory to savor in her private thoughts down through the years.

He lifted his head. "Oh, Laura," he breathed.

She didn't pull away—couldn't. His fingers tensed, and she knew he was trying to do the proper thing for both of them—push her away from him. Yet an invisible velvet net held them together, and her lips desperately wanted just one more taste of his.

She had no idea how long they stared into each other's eyes, but finally Sandy released a sigh of surrender and bent his head. He barely touched his lips to hers, then brushed them back and forth. The next kiss clung a scant bit longer, and the one after that longer still.

When she tightened her arms around him, her breasts flattened on his chest. An unfamiliar hardness between his legs pressed against her stomach, and he hissed a tortured sound. Sealing their lips together, he swept his tongue into her mouth and filled her with spiraling sensations which made her lose all contact with the real world. Her entire universe right then consisted of her and Sandy and the glorious need burning between them.

A picture of the cot outside the office door flashed in her mind. Then a picture of her and Sandy entangled on it. It shocked her back to her senses, yet it took her an interminably long time to bring Sandy back to his. Did she purposely prolong the ecstasy, she wondered at one point? Because she knew this would never happen again?

When Sandy unbuttoned the front of her shirt and trailed his lips and tongue down to her breast, she knew this had to stop. Quickly. Soon. Very soon. Her nipple pebbled and a new jolt of pleasure stabbed down to her stomach, then centered a little lower—right below where that hardness pressed against her stomach, flinching and jerking.

David had never, ever made her feel like this.

His name in her mind did it. "David!" she said aloud, and Sandy froze.

Several long, intense seconds passed before Sandy raised his head from her breast. The dampness his mouth left behind cooled on her skin, a direct contradiction to the heat flaring inside her. He dropped his arms, and she stepped back.

As soon as she was no longer in his way, Sandy surged from the office. Her eyes widened, and the fire inside her shifted to anger. How dare he leave her without saying anything about what had just happened between them? And it had definitely been between them, not one of them alone causing this furor.

Buttoning her shirt, she raced from the office and saw him disappear out the kennel door. The door didn't even have time to shut before she shoved it open again and went through after him. Outside light from a brilliant silver moon highlighted the area, but the beauty barely registered on her—except for the fact that it gave her plenty of light to see Sandy heading toward his own cabin.

"You wait right there, Sandy Montdulac!" He whirled and she stomped toward him, feet sinking into several inches of new snow. "You can't just walk away from what just happened. We need to talk."

"Why? What the hell can we do about it?"

The truth of his words stunned Laura, and she halted abruptly. The crisp, cold air cooled the flush on her cheeks, and she blamed the air for the quick sheen of tears misting her eyes. Determinedly she blinked them away, because they interfered with her view of Sandy. He stood a few feet away from her, but the distance yawned as large as from one shore of the huge lake they lived upon to the other.

"Nothing, I guess," she forced out. "We can't do anything about it. Just see that it doesn't happen again."

"Is that what you came out here to tell me? To make sure I never let anything like this happen again between us?"

"No," she said, and her heart wrenched when Sandy took a hopeful step toward her. She backed away a step. "No," she said more firmly, knowing she had to make sure he understood her double meaning. "It *can't* ever happen again, but I'm not blaming you alone. We both have to make sure it doesn't happen again. I . . . I love David. I won't betray his trust."

"Maybe you ought to spend more time with David then, instead of so damned much time with me!"

"I'm not spending the time necessarily with you," she said as logically as she could manage. A corner of her mind called her a liar, but she ignored it. She had pleaded tiredness or being busy several times recently when David wanted her to do something with him. "I'm spending the time with my trainer and working toward the goal I've set for myself. After that, I'll finalize all my plans with David."

"Then what the hell did you follow me out here to talk about? You haven't said one thing I don't already know."

She'd forgotten her coat, and she shivered in the cold. "I just felt that what happened inside should be discussed." She tried to bite back the next words, but they escaped anyway, in a low voice. "Deserved to be discussed."

"No more than your discussing what stud should cover what bitch in your breeding program," Sandy snarled. "The two of us should never be paired—on paper or in reality."

Laura gasped with a pain so deep it nearly dropped her to her knees. "You . . . you bastard!" She tried to throw the words in his face, but they came out barely above a whisper.

"Remember what you think of me from now on," Sandy said. "As soon as both of our dogs are back on their feet, we need to do those overnight training sessions I told you about. Your feelings toward me will keep you on your own side of the campfire."

Pulling herself together, she glared at him. "Don't schedule anything from the middle of December through the first of January. I'm spending the Christmas season with friends in Duluth, doing some shopping for my trousseau!"

"Yes, boss."

The instant he stalked away from her, Laura ran back to the kennel. She wouldn't give him the satisfaction of dismissing her, instead of the other way around. She shoved the door open and plunged through, closed it and leaned back against it, fighting tears she told herself were from the acrid anger filling her senses.

She should fire him. But that would mean explaining to her father, and eventually to David, her reasons for doing so. It would mean forgetting about the Alaskan race, not only for this year, but for the rest of her life. It would mean forgetting about her plans for the kennel—the wonderful boost having won the Alaskan race would give the reputation of her dogs.

She could be content being David's wife and the mother of their children. If she had to, she would make herself be content with only that in her life. However, it would be much more satisfying to also have her kennel and the dogs it produced recognized as notable.

No more than your discussing what stud should cover what bitch in your breeding program. The two of us should never be paired—on paper or in reality.

Sandy's voice filled her mind again, and she swiped away the tears in her eyes. Damn him! He hadn't acted like she was just a convenient bitch in heat when he said her name in that voice filled with the wonder of the feelings between them.

She frowned in concentration, replaying the rest of their conversation in her mind. He'd snarled at her. Did everything he could to counteract what had happened between them. To make her despise him. To make her keep her distance?

He'd never said what he thought of her. What his true feelings were. He hadn't kissed her like a man who wanted her to keep her distance.

But he was right. They needed to keep the barriers up between them. She should feel totally ashamed of her actions. Why, if she ever stuck her tongue in David's mouth, he would probably spit it out as though he'd inadvertently found a bone in his piece of lake trout!

So why didn't she feel ashamed? Why did it hurt so bad to think of keeping those barriers up? To think of never being in Sandy's arms again?

To recall the snarling words he threw at her? To know—to know that his words were a defense against his own feelings.

She stumbled over to Blancheur. He slept peacefully, and Laura crept onto the cot. After pulling the goosedown comforter over her, she realized the lantern in the office was still burning. The remains of their interrupted meal were also still sitting there, a grim reminder of why neither one of them had eaten even one bite.

She had enjoyed that one tiny dab of pie, she thought with a wry smile as her eyes closed. But it was just a prelude to the delicious feast to her senses an instant later.

Crawling up to full consciousness through lingering threads of a disturbing dream, Laura woke the next morning as Pete came in the door. Damp tear tracks streaked her cheeks, left behind from the dream.

"Hey, sleepyhead," Pete called. "What are you doing lollygagging in bed? Erik's already pulling up outside to check the dogs."

A puff of her breath frosted in the cold air. "That's too bad." Laura snuggled beneath the comforter and surreptitiously wiped the hem on her cheeks. "You build up that fire over there and I'll get up. You spent the night in a nice warm bed with your wife, while I tried to catch what sleep I could on this lumpy cot."

Pete glanced in the office door as he grabbed some wood from the woodbox. "Looks like you had some company here, too."

Laura's face flushed. "Sandy came out to check on Blancheur. He thought I might be hungry."

"Doesn't look like you ate much."

"I thought you said Erik was coming," she said to change the subject. "Maybe he went to see Keever first. I think I'll go inside to bathe." She threw back the comforter and checked on Blancheur. "Blancheur's awake, so keep an eye on him, will you?"

"Sure." Pete closed the stove door, and Laura hurried over to grab her cloak and throw it around her before she went out in the cold. "Uh . . ." Pete said.

"What?" She paused with her hand on the doorknob.

"I don't have to clean up the squished pie on the floor in there, do I? Looks like Sandy's footprint in that mess."

"Whatever. Or whoever." She waved a negligent hand and hurried through the door, barreling straight into Sandy. She knew who it was even before she glanced up. She knew those hands reaching out to steady her—those muscles on the firm chest under her palms—the scent of male and woods and cedar soap she associated with him.

"Whoa," he said. "It's too early in the morning to be rushing about so fast."

She stepped back, barely keeping her mouth from dropping in astonishment. His voice was calm and in control, with nary a sign of the turmoil they'd gone through a few hours before. Over his shoulder she saw Erik, the taller of the two men, and focused her attention on him. Two could play this nothing-happened game!

"Have you already looked at Keever?"

"He's fine," Erik replied. "Just needs a couple more days out of harness to mend completely. But it's going to take Blancheur longer than that."

"I'm sure it will, and I want him completely healed before he hits the trail again."

"We'll have to talk about that," Sandy put in as Erik pushed on past her and went into the kennels.

She tossed Sandy a surprised look. "What do you mean? He doesn't need to be on the trail again until there's no chance he'll reopen those wounds. I can use one of the other dogs for lead for a while."

Sandy shook his head. "That dog has a lead dog's heart, like Keever does. He needs to be back on the trail as soon as possible, even if it's only for easy runs. If he sees you heading out of here with another dog in his place, it could do two things to him—break his spirit for good or make him harder than hell to handle once we do put him back in harness."

He paused, then continued, "Males are funny that way. They want there to be only room for one of them in their owner's hearts."

Laura's own heart plunged to her toes, and her stomach twisted. She caught his double meaning—caught it well. When she flicked her eyes at his face, his gaze skittered away. "Then we'll have a break for a few days," she said. "I can spend some time with my father. And David."

His indrawn breath let her know her jab hit him somewhere in retaliation for the hurt he unloaded on her during their moonlit quarrel. Why then, didn't she feel a sense of sweet revenge as she hastened toward the house?

Sandy went on inside the kennel, straight to Blancheur in order to determine for himself how serious the dog's injuries looked this morning. Erik was still examining the dog, and Sandy sat on the cot, instantly aware of his mistake when Laura's scent rose around him. Even some of her warmth lingered in the comforter, stealing into the back of his thighs with fingers of sensation as light as her dainty hands. Yet he'd seen the deceptive strength of those hands, and these sensations cut through him with the same force.

Jumping to his feet would call too much attention to his discomfort, so he gritted his teeth, trying to concentrate on what Erik was saying.

"I would think about two weeks before you can use him

at full muscle again, Sandy. He'll definitely be in shape by the middle of January for the Northshore Race, though."

"Laura told me she's going to be in Duluth for two weeks over Christmas, but I can ask Pete or Buck to drive her team while we train. I want both of these teams in tip top shape for the Northshore."

"It's true then? You're planning on running in that race too, huh? There's been a lot of speculation about whether you'd just concentrate on Laura's team or give her some competition yourself."

"Laura's team isn't the only one around here that has a good chance of winning the race. I've been making inquiries, and a couple of Thunder Bay teams I've heard about sound excellent. For that matter, as scroungy as that Buck is, his team's a fine looking bunch of animals."

Erik laughed and shook his head. "Yeah, I will say one thing for Buck. He likes his booze, but if it came to a choice between needing to pay me to look at one of his dogs or buy a bottle, he'd wait on the bottle. That day he didn't take care of Laura's dogs properly was a mistake, and I think Buck would've rather died of thirst himself than let that happen to the dogs he was responsible for. I've seen him drinking since then, but never falling down drunk like before."

"Long as it taught him a lesson. People make mistakes. The main thing is to learn from them and go on."

"I agree with you there." Erik rose to his feet. "Well, you've got everything you need here to take care of both of these dogs. And plenty of help, with both Pete here and Buck coming in part time. I've got to go look at my sister's cat."

"Her cat?"

"Yeah, and let me tell you, that animal despises the ground I walk on. It hisses and arches its back every time I walk through the door!"

"Probably because it smells dogs all over you most of the time," Sandy said with a chuckle.

"Yeah, that's what my sister says. But I don't have time to go home and take a bath every time before I see that cat. Sis gets hold of me if the animal leaves one tiny bite of food in its bowl. Figures there's something wrong with it."

"People are like that with their animals."

"Yeah, and Sis is an old maid. Her fiancé went down on one of the ships in the lake, and she's never looked at another man, not that a lot haven't come courting. She has Hermie, and says that's all she needs."

"Hermie?" Sandy asked with an arched eyebrow.

"Her fiancé's name was Herman." He grabbed his fur-flap hat from the end of the cot and picked up his supply bag. "I better go look at Hermie before she gets hold of the police and has them out looking for me—tells them it's a family emergency. She did that once, when I didn't come check on Hermie as quick as she thought I should."

Erik paused at the door. "You know, I haven't had the nerve to tell her Hermie is a female. I hope Hermie doesn't get out some day and come back in the family way."

Shaking his head, Erik went through the door. At last Sandy could get off that damned cot and move away from it. Still Laura's presence lingered in every inch of the building. An old jacket she sometimes wore hung on a peg inside the door. A shelf in the supply cabinet, where someone had left a door open, held the trousers and shirts she preferred when she worked around the dogs. He recalled Katie saying once with a sniff of disgust that she would iron those clothes for Laura, but not put them away in Laura's room. They compromised on leaving them out in the kennel.

He hadn't slept another wink after he left here last night. He'd relived each and every second of the time he held her in his arms—each and every touch of her and his every sensation in response.

Each and every word of their quarrel afterwards, and each and every lie he'd forced out of his mouth. Even the lewd insinuations he barked out in an attempt to anger her so she would back away from him. Hate him. Keep her distance so he couldn't touch her—kiss her—drown in her essence. The essence of Laura, the beautiful, caring, bubbling, womanly person he would give almost anything to have for his own.

Almost anything, except his self-respect.

He wondered what it would be like to know that a woman loved him like Erik's sister loved her dead fiancé. Loved him so much it was impossible for her to even think of allowing another man into her life. That she would rather spend her life alone after his death.

He and Colleen had shared a deep love, a comfortable love. But had he become lost in one of the killer blizzards in Alaska during a race, or died some other way, Colleen would no doubt have married again. After a proper mourning period, he hoped, but he couldn't imagine her pining away for him for the rest of her life. She'd been raised to be a wife. Instead, she had died and left Sandy and Tracie to go on with their lives.

On the other hand, Laura's indulgent father had obviously given his daughter a huge measure of independence. She chose other interests in life than flirting and attracting a man for a potential husband. A father to a brood of children.

The potential husband and father had come into her life anyway and remained firmly planted. She loved David Hudson. Had told Sandy so. She'd come running after him last night with one purpose in mind—to tell him their shared passion had been a huge mistake. To get his agreement it would never happen again.

It wouldn't. He might be considered a criminal on the run by the Alaskan authorities, but he wasn't a criminal in his own mind. He'd done what he had to in order to keep the daughter he loved with all his heart by his side.

And he wasn't a thief. He wouldn't attempt to steal another man's woman. Fate, assisted by his father- and mother-in-law, had stolen a hell of lot from him, but he still had his honor.

9

A WEEK LATER Laura paused at the door to Sandy's cabin and watched Sandy and Pete mush up the trail leading away from Ladyslipper Landing. Blancheur had been replaced with Snowstorm, one of his own pups, now two years old. Snowstorm looked so much like his sire, Laura's heart ached with yearning. But she glanced over her shoulder at the doghouses on the far side of the yard, where Erik had told her to start tying Blancheur out for a few hours each day. Her true lead dog stood there, his head swiveling from her to the disappearing team. As usual, she had to admit Sandy was right. Had it been her instead of Pete on the sled runners, Blancheur would probably tug frantically on his chain, risking opening his wounds again.

She turned back and knocked on the door. Tracie opened it immediately.

"Hi, Miss Laura. I'm ready. All's I gotta do is put on my coat."

Cristy carried Tracie's coat over. As she knelt to help the

little girl put it on, she said to Laura, "Are you sure you don't mind taking her with you? It's no imposition?"

"Good heavens, no," Laura denied. "I have to keep my legs in shape, so I won't lose all Sandy's training. When Blancheur's ready to hit the trail again, I need to be able to keep up with him. The best way I can make sure of that is to walk every day. Blancheur won't get upset if he sees me walking out of the yard—just if he sees me with other dogs, leaving him behind. I'm delighted Tracie wants to come along and keep me company."

"Where are you headed today?"

"Into town. I know it's a long way, but if Tracie gets tired, we'll stop and rest. The temperatures are rather mild, and I don't think we'll have any trouble. We'll eat lunch there and ride back with Father this evening, so don't look for us until then."

"Aunt Cristy?" Tracie asked.

"What, darling?"

"You think I could take my money with me? Miss Laura could help me do my Christmas shopping."

"I'd love to do that," Laura said before Cristy could protest it might be another imposition. "I love shopping, and I'm glad you reminded me Christmas is coming up so soon, Tracie. I can start my own shopping."

Christy smiled tolerantly in agreement, then left them for a moment. When she returned, she handed Tracie a small child's purse. "Your money's in here, darling. You won't lose it, will you?"

"I won't, Aunt Cristy." Tracie hung the strap around her neck and patted the purse. "See? It fits right there."

Laura held out her hand. "If you're ready, so am I."

Tracie took her hand and nodded emphatically, and Cristy gave Laura a knit cap and tiny shawl. "It's nice out right now, but she might need this on the way back. Her mittens are in her pockets."

A few moments later, Laura and Tracie headed down the trail toward Grand Marais. Her father, Buck, Pete and other people visiting Ladyslipper Landing traveled the trail daily, either on horseback or sleighs, leaving it firm and easy to walk upon. She and Tracie made good time, but she kept their pace just below brisk, not wanting to tire the little girl.

She quickly realized she didn't have to worry about that. Tracie's ebullient energy bubbled over in both her skipping gait and cheerful chatter.

"This is really nice, Miss Laura," she said at one point. "I like being outside more than anything, but sometimes I have to play inside while Aunt Cristy cleans the house or paints. Look!" She pointed up a tree. "There's a squirrel!"

Unafraid and drawn by the little girl's voice, the fat gray squirrel crouched on a limb, fluffy tail twitching in time to its chittering barks. Tiny brown eyes sparkled, and Tracie's delighted laughter rang out. The squirrel leapt to its feet, racing up the tree trunk and turning around on a higher limb. Then it scurried to the other side of the tree and peered back around at them.

"Look, Miss Laura!" Tracie clapped her hands in delight. "It's a'playin' peek-a-boo with us!"

"It sure is," Laura agreed.

They watched the squirrel until it raced away through the treetops, leaping from limb to limb and showering snow to the ground in its path. Instead of being disappointed at the squirrel's desertion, Tracie eagerly continued their walk, searching for the next surprise.

Spying a huge pine tree with cones scattered on the ground beneath it, Tracie raced over. Squatting, she picked up two of the cones, then glanced at Laura. Her eyes, so identical to Sandy's, caused Laura to catch her breath.

"Can we gets a bag in town and pick up some of these on the way home?" Tracie asked. "Mama used them to decorate at Christmas time. I can show Aunt Cristy what Mama used to do. We hadda leave our decorations in Alaska. And Aunt Cristy hadda leave all Gramma and Grampa Montdulac's stuff in Wa—Washington, 'cause we couldn't bring it on the train."

"Of course we can stop and gather some pine cones," Laura agreed. "And you know what?"

"What?" Tracie asked eagerly, getting to her feet and stuffing the two pine cones into her pockets.

"There's way too many Christmas decorations in the attic at my house for me to use. Every year Katie has to stop me from bringing all of them down. If it's all right with your daddy, you and Cristy can use some of them at your house."

"Yippee! I was a 'wonderin' what we'd do for decorations. Christmas is special, you know."

"I know," Laura agreed, wishing she would be around to watch Tracie open presents on Christmas Day. Always before she'd looked forward to her Duluth trip for Christmas with relatives and friends who had moved away. This year David had already said he couldn't accompany her, since he had two important cases he needed to prepare for trial in January. Her father, also, had hinted at some business dealings, which might make it impossible for him to be gone the entire two weeks she planned to be in Duluth. He did promise to come down for at least a couple days, and they'd compromised by agreeing to have their own Christmas celebration, which would include David, the day she arrived home—January second.

Finally, after an hour's walk, which would have taken them only fifteen minutes by sled or sleigh, Grand Marais came into view. If she'd really wanted to maintain her leg strength, she would have ridden into town and then made the uphill climb to return to Ladyslipper Landing, Laura mused. But then she wouldn't have had Tracie's delightful company, for she couldn't imagine the child holding up to the steep ascent.

They stopped by Tom's office first, to let him know they had indeed walked into town and remind him not to leave them behind that evening. He invited them to lunch, and they decided to meet at Mrs. Sterling's at noon. As they headed for the general store a few minutes later, they encountered David on the walkway.

"Hello," he said, glancing beyond Laura's shoulder. "Uh . . . did just the two of you come into town?"

"Uh-huh," Tracie answered as Laura wondered what had distracted David's attention. "Aunt Cristy is paintin'." She gave Laura a mysterious look, then David a childish wink. He winked back before he reached down and picked her up.

"Well, then, Tracie-Racie," he said, tossing her into the air and easily catching her, "I guess Laura sprung you from a day locked up in jail, huh?" Settling her on his forearm, he wiggled his fingers on her stomach, and Tracie giggled wildly.

"My name's just Tracie," she insisted when she caught her breath. "Not Tracie-Racie!" She patted David's cheek. "But you can call me Tracie-Racie."

"Tracie-Racie, it is." He rather belatedly leaned over and kissed Laura's cheek. "Sorry, honey," he said. "I got diverted by this other beautiful lady here. Could I buy both of you beauties lunch later today?"

"Father's already spoken for us." Laura tried for a saucy tone, but to her ears it fell flat. David didn't appear to notice. "But why don't you join us. Twelve o'clock, at Mrs. Sterling's?"

Setting Tracie down, David nodded. "I'll be there. See you then."

"He's a real nice man," Tracie said as David strode off and they headed the opposite way, toward the general store. "Aunt Cristy said you and him's gonna get married next summer."

"That's the plan," Laura agreed. "We still have lots of things to decide upon, but we'll take care of them after I get back from Alaska."

Tracie fell abnormally silent for the duration of the walk to the general store. Once inside she perked up again. She stared over the displays of goods—everything from perfumed soaps for ladies to pipe tobacco for men. The smells intermingled with the warmth from not one, but two potbelly stoves used to heat the vastness. As usual, several elderly men sat at a table beside one of the stoves, playing gin rummy and gossiping about everything from which young woman had her sights set on which young man, to who would run for election next for the Board of Commissioner terms. Laura knew exactly what types of discussions they held, since she had crept up on them to eavesdrop when she was younger.

Every eye around the table swiveled to see who the new

arrival was and they all said their greetings. She responded with a "hello" to the "howdy's," "hey Miss Laura's," and "g'morning's."

Tracie evidently knew at least a couple of the men well, because she looked up at Laura and said, "Can I go over and say hello to Pops and Clinker?"

"Of course."

She skipped away, and Laura continued to the counter, where Cathy Berglind stood. Cathy gave Laura an even snider look than normal, and Laura wished Mrs. Berglind were attending the store. She'd never been able to figure out whether Cathy's sarcastic attitude came from some quirk in her personality, which left her unable to maintain friendships, or something else. The fact was, because of her derisive, gloomy attitude, Cathy had no friends in town, and the only reason anyone bothered with her was because there was no other store in town. If they needed supplies, they had to deal with Cathy when her parents left her in charge of the counter.

"Hello, Cathy," Laura said politely, unsurprised at not receiving a greeting in return. "Katie asked me to see if you'd received a new shipment of cinnamon yet."

Cathy glanced over her shoulder. "I don't see any cinnamon lying on the shelf above your name. After all these years, you should know that's where we put the special orders for people, so they can check themselves when they come into the store and not bother us if we're busy."

Laura bit her lip to keep from telling Cathy she didn't consider her standing there behind the counter with her arms crossed, glaring at the customers, being busy. At one time she had thought Cathy interested in David, but when she'd teasingly mentioned that to her fiancé, David had shivered at the horrible thought.

"I don't know that Katie special ordered the cinnamon," she said with a sigh of resignation.

"Well, then, you can check the spice rack to see if there's any there. That's where it would be if we got a new order in."

Pursing her lips, Laura turned away before she could tell Cathy exactly what she could do with the cinnamon. Tracie skipped up to her, holding out a lollipop.

"Look, Laura! Pops gived it to me. But he said I gots to wait 'til after lunch to eat it, less you say I can have it now."

"Huh," Cathy muttered, but Laura kept her attention on Tracie.

"Well, it's still a good hour before lunch, sweetheart. I don't see any reason why you can't go ahead and have the lollipop now."

"Thanks, Miss Laura!" Tracie tore the wrapper off and stuck the lollipop into her mouth, then casually tossed the paper at a trash can by the counter. She whirled away before she could see the paper miss and fall to the floor. Laura chuckled tolerantly and bent to pick up the paper herself.

"No wonder the child has no manners," Cathy said. Laura straightened and gave her a warning glare, but Cathy didn't back down. "Well, it isn't. She runs wild all the time, just like you're letting her run through my store right now. And heaven forbid her aunt pay any attention to the child when your fiancé is around. Cristy's too busy making eyes at David! I'll tell you, Laura Goodman, for your own good you better put a stop to them spending so much time together."

She narrowed her eyes, an even more malicious glint entering them. "Or, from what I hear, maybe you don't care if someone else steals David from you. Just what *do* you and Sandy Montdulac do out in the woods?"

Laura leaned on the counter, pushing her face as close to Cathy's as she could. Cathy stood her ground, but a tentative glimmer of fear replaced the maliciousness.

"You are an absolute bitch, Cathy Berglind," Laura said through clenched teeth, not caring that her voice carried.

Cathy huffed in outrage, but Laura didn't give her a chance to speak. "No, my female dogs are bitches, and they're very likeable animals. You're a jealous, troublemaking, gossiping witch. I've put up with you for years and years, but I will *not* have you insulting that precious child or her aunt. And while we're on the subject of your witchiness and gossiping ways, let me tell you that if you don't start controlling that vicious tongue of yours, I'll find some way to make you control it."

She pounded a fist on the counter, and Cathy lurched back against the wall. "My father has several enterprises in this town," Laura said. "I'm sure he could be talked into starting another store to give this one some competition and perhaps bring the prices down."

"Oh, no! Now what have you done, Cathy?"

Mrs. Berglind stood at the curtain separating the storage room from the rest of the building, her worried gaze going from her daughter to Laura. "What happened, Laura?"

Letting out a wail, Cathy pushed away from the wall, then raced past her mother. Her footsteps clumped up the stairwell, which led to the family's living quarters over the store.

"Laura?" Mrs. Berglind repeated.

"It's nothing for you to be concerned with," Laura relented. "Cathy just stuck her nose into business that didn't concern her, and I guess I overreacted a little."

Mrs. Berglind shook her head sadly, wringing her hands together. "All of our children are married and settled, with fine families and wonderful, satisfying lives. Connie's husband would love to give up his woodcutting business and help us out in the store, but he won't put up with Cathy. I just don't know what to do. Cathy's my daughter, too, but Dick's ready to retire if we could just get Connie's husband in here to take over."

She pulled her hands apart and walked to the counter. "I'm sorry, Laura. I didn't mean to tell you my troubles. What can I do for you today?"

"Tracie and I are going to do some Christmas shopping, Mrs. Berglind. I was checking with Cathy to see if you'd received a new order of cinnamon first, before I looked around."

"It just came in today." Mrs. Berglind started back to the storage room. "I'll unpack it and have some waiting here at the counter for you."

"Thank you."

10

*I*T SURPRISED LAURA what a difference having Cristy and Tracie around made, now that she wasn't out on the trail every day. It became habit for her to go over to the cabin each morning after Sandy and Pete left with the teams and Buck arrived to take care of the feeding and cleaning. Some mornings Cristy wafted around with a distracted look in her eyes, which Laura came to recognize as a deep desire to get to her painting. Tracie and Laura would head out for their walk, then have lunch with Katie. Afterwards, they read or played either a game of make-believe or a board game. Other times they decorated Laura's house or Sandy's cabin for Christmas.

A couple mornings Cristy asked if she could join their walks, saying she'd stayed inside way too many days in a row and needed to refill her creative well. Her friendship with Laura deepened, and whenever Laura recalled Cathy's gossiping comments, she mentally waved them away as just that—gossip.

Two days before Laura had to leave for Duluth, Tracie, Cristy and she made another day of shopping. Lunch with Tom and David was a gay affair, and afterwards Laura made plans to have dinner with David the following evening. Tom closed his office early and shopped with the women, and they headed back to Ladyslipper Landing in mid-afternoon.

Tracie nodded with sleepiness by the time they arrived, and Tom offered to carry her to the cabin for Cristy.

"I'm going over to the kennels, Father," Laura said. "Buck brought some supplies we needed today, and I should enter them in the books. Pete hasn't had a lot of time for that lately."

Tom murmured a quiet agreement as Tracie snuggled into his arms and Laura walked away. She detoured by Blancheur's doghouse and released him. To keep him somewhat in shape, Blancheur had accompanied her and Tracie on their walks after that first day, and according to Erik the dog would be ready for a brief run in the harness tomorrow.

She'd debated delaying her trip for a week in order to spend some time on the sled again. However, whether it was spending time with Sandy once more or the looming threat of the overnight campouts, she decided to only do this one run and wait until she returned after Christmas to resume full training. Blancheur would be fully ready by then. She'd tell Sandy her decision when he came back from the training run today.

She settled at the desk in the kennel office, and Blancheur curled up on the floor. When she reached for the ledgers, Sandy's face swam in front of her. In an uncharacteristic fit of annoyance, she slammed her palms on the desk surface and closed her eyes.

She'd hinted in her correspondence with her friends and relatives in Duluth that she might not make her holiday trip down there this year. She needed this training time as much as Blancheur did, and she knew without doubt missing the fun and gaiety wouldn't bother her that much. More and more she was realizing that she could have just as much fun celebrating Christmas at Ladyslipper Landing as she could in the big city.

Yet she had given in to her relatives' pleas to reconsider and still make her trip. She'd given in not because she wanted to experience the gaiety, but because she needed to distance herself from the temptation of a pair of teal blue eyes, broad shoulders and a voice that whispered her name with a longing that fired an even deeper yearning in her.

Hopefully a couple weeks away from Sandy would give her time to gain some perspective on her feelings. She could never break her engagement to David. She couldn't do that to him. He'd done nothing to deserve her giving his ring back.

Besides, it wasn't as if her being free would assure her of a chance to pursue her feelings for Sandy, she thought, chastising herself as soon as she realized how selfish that sounded. She would make David a good wife. They had everything in common and their friendship to build on. So what if David's kisses didn't fill her with a whimpering need to make love to him. They would have a quiet, placid life together.

Wasn't that why she had insisted on participating in the Alaskan Race to begin with? Because she knew her life with David would be lacking in the excitement she craved? She'd thought herself so mature when she decided to have this one huge adventure and make the memories last the rest of her life—her placid, unexciting life with David.

She'd spent many a restless night listing in her mind the reasons a future with Sandy was out of the question. On the other side of the balance sheet, she'd mentally listed the reasons to continue her engagement. David was a good man. David would make a fine husband and a wonderful father. David would treat her with respect, in bed and out, although David wouldn't make her tremble with desire. David had every quality a woman wanted in the man she married and lived with the rest of her life.

David wasn't Sandy Montdulac.

Opening her eyes, Laura reached for the ledgers again. Buck was already gone, and she'd noticed full food bowls and fresh water waiting for the sled teams when they returned. The water might be frozen over when the teams got back, but it would be Sandy and Pete's responsibility to replace it. Buck had done his job.

In a tray beside the ledgers, she found more than just that morning's entries needing input. With Pete busy training the team, it was up to her to do this job, and she mentally rolled up her sleeves and went to work.

When the kennel door opened and closed a long while later, Laura glanced up. The clock showed two hours had passed, and it was getting close to supper time. At least the bookwork was caught up. It would do until she got back from Duluth.

Instead of Pete, whom she expected, Sandy strode into the office, halting abruptly when he saw her. For a brief instant a look of hunger entered his eyes, but his gaze quickly blanked.

"I didn't know anyone was in here," he said without greeting her.

"Hello to you, too," she said irritably.

"Hello, Laura," he said reluctantly.

Sighing, she pushed the chair back and rose. "I'm leaving for Duluth the day after tomorrow, Sandy. But Erik was by early this morning and gave Blancheur the go ahead to get back into the harness for short runs. I'd really like to know how the teams are doing before I go, so I planned on making the run with my team myself tomorrow. If you prefer, I can ask Pete to go with me."

"I'm the one training you. If your dog's ready, I'll make the run with you."

He glanced around the small confines of the office, and Laura could feel the tensions sizzling in the air. Why was it that at times she could almost read his mind and other times he was an enigma? Now she knew he was recalling what had happened the last time the two of them found themselves alone in the kennel office—the last time they'd been alone at all.

Two steps on her part would take her into his arms. With his longer legs, he would only need one step to bring them together. All her rationalizations and assurances that Sandy Montdulac meant nothing to her fled. The knowledge that David was the man for her future melted away into a figurative puddle of snow at her feet.

Sandy turned and strode out of the office. "I need to make sure Buck got all the supplies I ordered," he tossed over his shoulder. "We can talk out here."

She hesitated for a moment before following him, relieved when her mind searched for and found the stern admonishments she had spent so many days formulating. No matter how drawn she was to him, Sandy had made it clear during their moonlight quarrel that he wanted to be nothing more to her than her trainer. She ran through the facts once again—facts she had listed over and over in her mind on sleepless nights.

They were woman and man, but the pull between them had to be ignored. It was only a physical thing, with no other basis to build on.

They were complete opposites, with her enjoying life and Sandy carrying with him a moroseness it would take a saint to tolerate. Yes, she sensed some shadowy need behind the moroseness, some deep pain he tried to hide. But it wasn't her place to delve into his life. He'd told her a little about his marriage, but the barriers between them had frozen tight again afterward.

She loved David! She had her life planned with David. David tolerated her enthusiasm and nonconformity—actually admired that in her. Well, at least until they were married. But she had agreed to settle down then and be a good example for their children.

Sandy was so different from David. He expected to be the caretaker and provider, the rulemaker. He only bore her nonconformity because she paid his salary. He would never accept a woman like her for a wife. For Tracie's mother.

She gasped at the last thought, which came out of the blue, perhaps because of the wonderful times she'd had with Tracie in the last two weeks. Any lingering thought of postponing her Duluth trip flew from her mind. She wasn't afraid of impossible situations—look at her determination to win the Alaskan race, something no woman had never attempted. Yet anything beyond an employer-employee relationship with Sandy Montdulac, or a friendly aunt-type relationship with Tracie, was more than impossible. It was utterly unattainable. She had enough sense to realize that, given all her ponderings during those restless nights.

Rather than going over to the supply cabinets, where Sandy stood with the doors open and a list in his hand, she waited outside the office door. She became aware of the deepening chill in the room and noticed the potbelly stove barely glowing. Building up the fire would be wasteful with evening coming, so she took her cloak from the peg. Its protection afforded her an extra measure of comfort as Sandy came toward her.

"The supplies are fine," he said. "I'll have to admit, I had doubts about Buck when you rehired him, but he's a good hand. I've never smelled liquor on him here, but I've seen him drinking in one of the saloons in town at night."

"I didn't know you went into town at night."

"Why wouldn't I?" he snapped. "My evenings are my own."

"Of course they are!" she said in frustration. "I was just carrying on polite conversation."

His shoulders heaved and he jammed his hands into his coat pockets. "Sorry," he said tersely, turning his gaze away from her. "You need a report on the teams. They're doing extremely well. It is time to get Blancheur back in charge of your team, though, before they get too used to Snowstorm. In fact, after you get back from Alaska, put Snowstorm up for sale so he can lead his own team. He's too good to play second fiddle to Blancheur, and he'll never be happy in harness behind him now."

"Thank you, Mr. Montdulac, for your *advice*. I'll take it into consideration for my plans with my dogs." Laura was sorry the moment the words were out of her mouth, but her emotions were too much on edge around him right then. He flicked his eyes at her face, then shrugged and remained silent.

"I assume you'll have Pete working with Blancheur again while I'm gone," she said in a less antagonistic tone.

"That's the plan."

"The day after I get back, I'll be ready to take over my own team fully. The Northshore Race will only be two weeks after that."

"Of course."

He held himself so rigid, avoided her gaze so studiously, she fought the urge to hit his chest—or do something to make him look at her. That would be flirting with disaster, though. The last time the explosion between them had been nearly catastrophic.

She opened the door. "If you need anything else before I leave, please let me know tomorrow. Your wages are on the desk in the office. The extra is from Father. He gives all his employees bonuses at holiday time, so you don't have to be stubborn about accepting it—thinking it's from me. Pete and Buck have extra in their pay envelopes, too."

She started through the door.

"Laura?"

Hopefully she turned back and caught the deep sadness in Sandy's eyes before he could blank it out.

"If I forget to mention it tomorrow, have a good time in Duluth—and a Merry Christmas."

"And you," she whispered. After a searching look at him, she whirled and headed for the house. A film of tears misted her eyes, but she hurriedly blinked them away. On the back porch, she suddenly remembered she'd left Blancheur in the kennel, but when she looked back, she saw Sandy lead the dog toward his doghouse.

Night fell early in December, yet Katie kept the supper time at six o'clock, as always. The landscape was already black and white, as well as variegated shades of gray, the moon waning in its final quarter from the fullness of two weeks ago. A dim light crept through the tops of the tall pines, but starlight winking overhead sparkled in glittering pinpoints.

When Sandy got to Blancheur's doghouse, he unsnapped the lead rope. Blancheur bounded away before Sandy could secure him to the chain, and Sandy's chuckle of laughter carried on the still air. The sound crawled through her on sensations of yearning, and she couldn't tear her eyes away from him.

His blond hair needed trimming again, and it gleamed in the darkness. He tossed a lock off his forehead, then pushed his coat aside and placed his hands on his trim hips. Blancheur circled around him, barking joyfully and scattering new-fallen snow in his path. It was a far cry from the distrust the dog had shown Sandy when they first met.

"Hey, you. Dog!" Sandy called. "Laura took you for a walk today already. It's time to settle in for the night."

Blancheur's antics had a few of the other dogs sitting up, and here and there Laura could hear a whine. In a moment, the entire pack would be howling and barking. Sandy snapped his fingers and whistled, and Blancheur trotted over to him. When Sandy lunged for him, Blancheur teasingly danced away.

Losing his balance, Sandy tumbled to the ground. Blancheur pounced on him, and the two of them tussled, rolling over and over in the snow. Jealous, a few of the other dogs jerked against their chains, barking for attention. From the other side of the yard, Sandy's dogs sat on their haunches and howled into the night air.

Sandy sat up and grabbed Blancheur around the neck, rubbing his head with his other hand. Voice rumbling with laughter that made Laura crave being closer, he said, "Dog, look what we've done. We've got the rest of the pack all stirred up. Come on now. Let's put you on your chain."

He stood, and Blancheur obediently allowed him to snap the chain on his collar. When Sandy straightened, the dog rose on his hind legs, propping his forelegs on Sandy's chest. He slurped Sandy in the face, and Sandy jerked his head back with a laugh. Then Sandy wrapped his arms around Blancheur and they stood silent for a moment. Dropping his head, Sandy buried his face on the dog's neck briefly before stepping away.

"See you in the morning, boy," he said. "I want some time with Tracie before she goes to bed."

He strode across the yard, still not noticing Laura in the darkness of the porch overhang. He stopped and patted Keever for a minute, and the dogs in the yard settled down. Laura waited until he disappeared into his own cabin before she went into the house.

What a different man he was when he didn't know he was being watched, she thought as she walked through the kitchen. For a while after they started working together, she'd hoped he would let down his reserve, and he'd started to the day the moose attacked them. Yet after their night in the kennel, he'd refrozen the blocks of ice between them into glacial thickness.

Tomorrow would be a good test for her. She would keep their relationship on a business basis and then have time away from here to firm that resolve. She'd show him they could be trail partners and nothing else.

11

Motioning for Laura to halt, Sandy "whoa'ed" his team on top of a hill the next morning. "This is an easy downhill grade," he told her, "and Blancheur's aching for a run. Why don't you go ahead? I'll watch from here and examine your driving style. See if I notice anything you've gotten lax on in the past two weeks."

She bristled, and Sandy held up a hand. "Sorry. I didn't mean that like it sounded. You may have gotten lax, but the only reason I'm concerned is because it's my job to keep you in top shape. Anything I point out will be helpful criticism, so you can have a better chance at winning a race."

"I was hoping I could forget training just for today," Laura said, her voice almost pleading. "Like you point out, this is my first run in two weeks, and it's also the last one I'll have for another two weeks. Couldn't we just enjoy today and get serious after I return?"

He studied her for a moment, already knowing he would

agree to anything she wanted today. Already knowing he was going to miss the hell out of her the next two weeks. Even on the days she wasn't on the trail with him—the days he had to put up with Pete—he'd known he would see her in the evenings.

Not that he had any right to look forward to seeing her. But his damned heart overrode his head. It took every bit of willpower he could dredge up last night to let her walk away without telling her how desolate he would be while she was in Duluth. As usual, he'd fought his feelings by acting like a bastard with her.

"Go ahead," he said, failing utterly to put a growl of annoyance in his voice. He would allow himself just these few hours of pleasure with her. "Just enjoy yourself and forget about training."

She flashed a brilliant smile and turned back to her dogs. "Mush!" she shouted joyously. "Mush, Blancheur! Let's run!"

With a yap of pleasure, Blancheur leapt forward, the other dogs willingly following his lead. It was a great team, Sandy admitted. He'd never seen a better one, except for his own. He'd been beaten in Alaska because of circumstances beyond his control, when Keever stepped on a jagged stone in the trail near the finish line. Sandy had pulled the team in the moment he noticed Keever limping, which gave the second place team time to pass. There were always other races, but lead dogs with hearts like Keever and Blancheur were few and far between.

Thankfully, second place money had been enough to get him and Tracie, as well as part of his team, out of Alaska.

He watched Laura fling her head back and breathe in the crystal pure, cold air, hanging onto the sled handles and riding the runners, her dogs carrying her along at full speed. Her slight weight kept a drag on the sled on the gradual downhill grade, but he had in mind a steeper grade to train her on in January. Sometimes the sled would get going so fast it threatened to overtake the dogs, and tossing out a drag line was necessary. It took practice to know when to do that and not lose the momentum of the race.

Laura had enough sense not to let Blancheur run too long at full speed, but in the meantime he could tell she fully enjoyed herself. He was so tuned in to her after all their time together he could sense her emotions—see her jubilant face in his mind.

Excited, her green eyes sparkled like rain-washed leaves after a spring shower. Cold air blushed her cheeks with a red tint, and her full mouth would be open in exhilaration. Unless it was a bitter cold day, she refused to tie her hood into place, and today's temperature hovered above zero, mild to a born-and-bred northerner like Laura. More often than not her hair came loose from the tight coils she started out with every morning, streaming down her back in waves—silk fire a man could warm his hands in. It flowed behind her now.

Damn, he would miss her while she was gone. And damn, he needed to win that Northshore Race, so he could get the hell out of Grand Marais before he broke down and admitted to someone how deep his feelings had become. The person most likely to be on the receiving end of his admission was the object of those feelings—the woman who rode on the sled runners as light as a fairy and as excited as a child.

The woman who had the potential to fill a day with laughter and whose voice threatened to melt the ice around his heart. The woman who fired his senses with the way she came alive in his arms one dark night. The woman who belonged to another man. The woman he didn't dare become involved with because he was on the run.

As he had known she would, Laura swung her team into a circle and headed them back toward the hill, bringing them to a halt at the bottom.

"Come on," she called, waving a beckoning hand. "It's a wonderful day for a run!"

Shaking his head, he ordered his dogs on. Laura was right, he agreed as soon as he got started. It was a lot more fun once in a while to let yourself go and enjoy the run instead of worrying about whether you were taking advantage of every opportunity to cut off a winning foot or two from your path. His dogs sensed the difference, and Keever raced down the hill, barking now and then in pleasure. His team passed Laura's without a glance, tearing full speed along the path broken by the other dogs. Though his own dogs, led by a lead dog back in top physical condition, could have gone on, Sandy ordered them along the same curve Laura's team had taken, heading them back to where she waited.

Laura stood tense, gazing out over the lake on their left. As he halted his team near her, she let out a cry.

"No! Oh, Sandy, look!" She pointed at the lake. "Our dogs frightened a doe out of the woods. She started across the lake and fell through the thin ice out near the middle. Now she can't get out."

She turned an anxious gaze on him. "She'll drown, Sandy. What can we do?"

"Nothing," Sandy denied. "It's too dangerous for us to try to help her."

"We can't just stand here and watch her die! Oh, Sandy!"

"It's the way of the wilderness . . ." he began, but Laura grabbed a rope from her sled and raced toward the lake.

His surprise and fear for what she had in mind gave her a head start as he stared at her in disbelief. Then he shouted and tore out after her.

Lighter than he, Laura raced across the snow without floundering, while he broke through the firm crust time and again. She reached the frozen edge of the lake before him, but he quickly made up the distance across the ice, swept somewhat clear of snow but with enough powder to give him some traction. He caught her still a safe distance away from where the doe struggled in the water, front legs scrabbling on the ice but failing to make purchase. Already Sandy could see the doe tiring, both from her useless struggle and her fear.

"Listen!" he said. Laura tried to jerk away from him, and he shook her slightly. "There's nothing we can do, Laura."

"We have to try!" Tears misted her beseeching eyes, tearing at Sandy's heart. "What if it were a person out there?"

"It's not. It's an animal."

A splash drew his attention to the deer, and his hold loosened on Laura, allowing her to turn. The deer had fallen completely back into the water, but her head reappeared. She somehow managed to get her front legs back onto the ice again, and she looked over at them, bleating in fear.

"Sandy. Oh, Sandy, please," Laura pleaded.

She placed her small hand on his chest. In an instinctive reaction, he cupped her cheek, his fingers folding into the auburn silk of her hair. His gut wrenched, and his mind told him to pull away, but his heart won, even overriding the danger his mind threw in to caution him. He couldn't deny her when she was within kissing distance. If he couldn't have her kisses, at least he would have her gratitude and respect.

He dropped his hand lingeringly—which she didn't protest—and took the rope from her. Stepping back, so he could think about the rescue instead of her, he quickly fashioned a loop in the rope.

"I'm not a cowboy," he told her, "so I'm going to have to hope I can get this over that doe's head. In the meantime, you stay back. Your weight added to mine is liable to send us both through the ice."

"You'll need my help when you're ready to pull her out," she insisted.

He held the rope out of her reach. "I've got this now, Laura. And I will *not* take a chance on your drowning to save a damned deer. You do what I say, or I'll forget this whole thing."

She stuck her bottom lip out, but nodded in agreement, backing away a few paces.

"Stay there unless I call you to help me. Then get down on your belly and crawl as soon as I order you to. That way, your weight will distribute on the ice and be less likely to break through."

After another warning look, Sandy turned and walked closer to the doe, testing the ice at each step before he put his full weight on it. Finally he neared the thinner ice.

The doe still had her legs on the edge of the hole,

enlarged around her now by her flailing. Her head lolled weakly. He shook out the rope, gauged the distance, and gave it a toss. It settled over her head on that first try.

Sandy dropped to the ice himself. He belly-crawled a few feet forward, since he barely had hold of the end of the rope and needed more to get a firm grip. Suddenly the ice creaked near him and he froze in fear. The fissure he expected didn't materialize, and he carefully turned his head.

His stomach knotted and his heart hammered. Laura lay on her stomach not too far from him.

"I won't come any closer unless you need me," she hurriedly assured him. "I just wanted to be close in case you did."

"If you crawl even one inch farther," he snarled, "I'll push that damned deer back into the water and drown her myself!"

"No, you won't," she said with a smile. "But I'll stay here."

He dropped his head and shook it, but a jerk on the rope got his attention. The doe was struggling again, her strength renewed. It would be a close call as to whether he could give her enough help to get out of the water before the rope strangled her or not. She was large—not yet winter starved as she would be near the spring—probably well outweighing his own one hundred and seventy pounds. He braced himself and slid a few inches forward. The doe's head disappeared again beneath the water.

He twisted around, butting his boots against a patch of jagged ice frozen in a wave formation. It gave him enough leverage to lean back against the rope again, and when it tightened, the doe once again tried to climb out of the hole. She lunged and almost made it, but the pull on the rope jerked his upper body forward.

Suddenly he felt Laura's arms around his waist, and he started to turn and shout at her. Just then the doe made a new lunge, and with the added strength of Laura's hold, they held the animal firmly. The doe scrambled onto the ice and stood, head down. The slipknot Sandy had tied loosened of its own accord, and the rope fell to the ground.

"What's going on?" Laura shifted to peer around him, and Sandy twisted onto his stomach. Shoving on her shoulders, he sent her scooting across the ice before he scrambled to his feet and went after her. He scooped her into his arms and hurried back across the ice. When they got to the shoreline, he turned and looked back at the doe, already bounding toward the far side of the lake.

"Oh, I hope she doesn't freeze to death," Laura said.

"We've done all we can. She'll probably keep moving until her coat dries. Or try to, anyway."

He turned his gaze on Laura and saw the trepidation fill her green eyes. "Uh-oh," she murmured.

He firmed his jaw, but she placed a tentative finger on his lips and the rigidity died a fast death. "I know," she said. "I broke another rule. I didn't obey you right to the letter, and it could have been dangerous. Dangerous for both of us. I'm sorry. I'll . . . I'll accept any punishment you pronounce, but please don't quit. Please."

He heaved a defeated sigh. "You could have denied you remembered the rule."

"I'm not a liar, Sandy. I remember everything you've ever said to me."

That was a totally dangerous conversation. And still holding her in his arms was even more dangerous. Why the hell didn't she struggle—insist he put her down? Why the hell didn't he put her down anyway?

She was light in his arms, yet every inch a woman. A definite contradiction, he mused. How could such a little bit of nothing still have all the right curves—all the right feminine elements to tantalize and tease him?

There didn't seem to be room in that slender body to grow a child, but. . . .

He dropped her legs, yet had sense enough to hold onto her with his other arm. Her eyes widened in surprise, and she tightened her arms around his neck in reaction. It was a damned good thing they both wore all those layers of clothes, or he would have felt every delicious inch of her slide down his body. But he quickly realized not even the clothing protected him, because his mind remembered every part of her from that night in the kennel office.

His gut kicked in response, as did his groin. Laura gasped, and he realized she'd ended up with her jacket wedged between them, pulled up far enough for her stomach to press against his beginning arousal.

Instead of pushing away from him in fright, Laura whimpered and her fingers tightened around his neck, pulling on a lock of his hair in a pleasure-pain way. His pleasure came from knowing she felt the same heady desire he did. The pain barreled right over the pleasure, carrying with it all his promises to never let this happen again. Carrying a reminder of the small amount of honor and respect remaining to him after he was forced to leave Alaska with his life in shambles, his future ruined—a reminder of his stupidity in allowing that to happen.

Not wanting to humiliate her by letting her think her effect on him was easily controlled, knowing he owed her this honesty, he reluctantly eased Laura away from him. Carefully watching her eyes, he could tell the moment her desire changed to the beginning of embarrassment. He had to get his hands off her, but when she started to push past him and head for the sleds, he growled her name in a voice that halted her.

Keeping distance between them, he jammed his hands into his pockets as she turned back to him.

"I'm sorry," she said. "I . . ."

"Shut up, Laura," he growled in a low voice. "The other night we only yelled at each other, and I should have explained myself then."

He paused, trying to figure out the best way to say what needed to be said. Being Laura, she ignored his order to be quiet and filled the void with her own words—an attempt at her own excuses and apologies.

"I should be totally ashamed of myself, I know. My God, if David had any idea . . . and what must you think of me—belonging to him and being so ready to stay in your arms?"

"Shut up, damn it. I . . ."

"Maybe once I could be forgiven for. Maybe even twice. But a third—"

He grabbed her and kissed her. Just to shut her up, he lied to himself. And somehow the great god of willpower gave him enough strength to let her go, step back and jam his hands into his pockets again. Somehow that same god kept his hands in his pockets when her eyes got dreamy and she touched her fingers to her mouth.

"Listen to me, Laura. Please," he pleaded, and she ever so slowly nodded her head.

"If there was any possibility at all of there being a future for you and me, I might fight for you. There's all sorts of rationalizations we could make. Believe me, I've made them to myself many sleepless nights. That you would be doing David a disservice by marrying him when you felt so strongly about another man. That you'd be doing yourself that same disservice."

She nodded very slightly once more in agreement, but she must have sensed the fatalistic sentence to come because he saw none of the earlier sparkle in her eyes. They changed to a flat green, dark with dusty shadows. He had to keep them that way—deaden any slight hope she might have. Hell, any slight hope he might have himself.

"I have no plans to ever take another wife," he said in an even voice. She flinched slightly, but her shoulders remained unbowed and her gaze on his face. "And I care too much about you to only have an affair and leave you behind when I go."

When pain filled her eyes, he curled his hands into fists. "Yes, go," he repeated. "I haven't said anything to your father yet, but I imagine after—" He steeled himself for another lie. "—after I get back from Alaska, I'll probably leave Grand Marais." He never even planned on going to Alaska, but he couldn't tell her that. Cristy and Tracie's comfort depended on that lie being fostered for a while yet.

"What will you do?" she whispered in a broken voice.

"Something to do with my dogs." He shrugged. "The plans your father has for me include going into one of his businesses—the shipping business. I have absolutely no desire to become involved in that again." Another lie. He would give his eyeteeth to use his mind once more, and a position like that would enable him to provide a secure life for his daughter and sister.

"I understand." Laura wrapped her arms around herself. "I won't . . . tempt you any more. . . ."

"Damn it, you aren't to blame for this!" Pulling his hands free, he ran his palms down his face. When he looked at her woebegone face, he swiveled and stared out across the frozen lake to avoid her gaze—to keep his willpower strong. She was so tiny—so fragile. Yet so strong and impetuous, so much a woman capable of being a companion to a man rather than a woman a man had to feel responsible for and protect.

"It's both of us," he said sternly. "I sure as hell didn't beat you off. In fact, I'm the one who let this get out of hand. I'm older and I've been married. I know how strong the feelings can get between a man and woman, especially on a man's part."

A snowflake feathered down, and he quickly examined the sky. Black clouds were blowing in. He should have kept the weather in mind, as he usually did when out on the trail. Almost at once the snowflakes thickened, and he quickly turned back to Laura.

"It's starting to snow. We've got to get back, because this looks like it's setting in for a while." Suddenly he noticed her ungloved hands. "Laura, when did you take your mittens off?"

She shivered. "When I decided to help you with the rope and the deer. If I'd have had to help you pull, the mittens wouldn't have let me get a good hold."

"You know how easily your hands get cold. Get your mittens back on."

She complied, and he motioned for her to follow him back to the sleds. The lazy flakes continued, beautiful, but deceptively dangerous. He pulled her snow anchor free for her as she climbed onto the runners.

"You might need to push Blancheur a little to get back

before this gets too bad to travel in," he said. "If you do, I'll make sure he rests tomorrow to make up for it."

"All right." She reached for the handles, and her hands fumbled, her right one refusing to grip. She grimaced and tried to wrap her fingers again.

"Laura, let me see your hands."

"They're all right. I'll be fine."

"Damn it. . . ."

"Will you quit cursing at me?" she cried. "You've said 'damn' or 'hell' a dozen times in the last few minutes!"

"Don't change the subject! If we were in the Alaskan race and ignored possible frostbite on your hands, you could end up having both of them amputated. Get those blasted mittens off and let me look at them!"

"Get your mittens on, Laura," she mimicked. "Get your mittens off, Laura." She pulled them off and held her hands out.

"Oh, God," he breathed as he took her hands in his and examined the patches of white skin, which could easily turn into frostbite. "All this over some damned deer, which will probably die anyway. I should've just shot her and put her out of her misery."

"You wouldn't do that," she said logically. "Just give me a few minutes here. I'll warm my hands inside my coat sleeves. . . ."

He clasped both of her small wrists in one of his hands, then quickly unbuttoned his jacket, followed by a couple buttons on his shirt. Carefully he placed her hands against his chest, cringing at their coldness. Inadvertently he'd laid her hands very close to his own nipples, and they contracted, sending a message downward.

Hell, cold was supposed to suppress desire, wasn't it? Yet the fragility of her small hands and his worry combined in an emotion as powerful as his sexual drive. He wrapped his jacket around the both of them, satisfying that protective need the only way he could. How the hell could he have thought she was so strong a few minutes ago? Right then he wanted to wrap her in a cocoon and do nothing with the rest of his life except make sure she never got cold again—never wanted for anything.

He could never provide Laura Goodman everything a woman of her station would want—not now. Not after his life had fallen apart. He suppressed a sigh.

Suddenly he realized she hadn't spoken a word since he took her hands. She hadn't moved her hands, either, and she stood docilely in his embrace. He pulled her a little closer, hoping she would lay her head on his chest and knowing that was the very last thing he should be wishing for. Damn, he'd just listed all sorts of reasons why they had to keep away from each other, and here he was wanting a closer embrace!

The snow thickened even more, and he cursed himself for not paying attention to the sky and weather. They needed to get going, but he wouldn't risk one tiny finger on her fragile hands.

"Sandy?"

"What? Are your hands completely warmed?"

"Almost," she whispered raggedly. "But you've got a hell of a way of making me keep my hands to myself."

"Don't curse, Laura." He pulled her tight against him and buried his face in her hair.

12

On the way to Ladyslipper Landing, Sandy stopped Laura every mile to check her hands. If he could have gotten away with it, he'd have left her dogs out on the trail and taken her back on his sled, wrapped in the furs he carried and lying there like a helpless female. Helpless female she was not!

He tried, though. Only when she reminded him that his stubborn arguing was allowing the storm to heighten—and that he would also have to tie her hand and foot to the sled—did he give in. She led, since she knew the trail home blindfolded and being ahead gave her a little satisfaction. So infrequently did she get a one-up on Sandy, and his admission of her knowing the landscape better than he made up in a little for her stupidity in not putting her mittens back on immediately. She'd spent twenty-one winters in the Northland. She knew darned well even days the sun made look deceptively warm could be deadly to exposed skin.

Sandy's cabin finally came into view, lights shining from

every window, then the welcoming sight of her own house and the kennels. She "whoa'ed" her dogs, and Sandy was beside her before she could step off the runners.

"You go inside and get warm," he ordered. "I'll take care of your dogs today."

"You said one of the rules—"

"—is caring for your own dogs," he overrode her. "But I'm breaking my rule this time. Get inside."

Suddenly something glimmered in her mind, but Laura refused to acknowledge it. Instead, it sent her pushing past him toward the back porch. But when she reached for the doorknob, the thought hit her that she'd be leaving early in the morning, pending the storm not turning into a blizzard. She wouldn't see him again for two weeks.

She turned. She could barely make him out through the heavy snow, but make him out she did. He hadn't started unharnessing the dogs yet. He stood there unmoving, and though she couldn't really see well enough to determine which direction he was looking, her senses told her that he was watching her. Snow mounded on the shoulders of his coat and hood. She should get inside, because something told her that he would stand there until he saw the door open and her pass through.

Something else told her that he was filling his own mind with his last glimpse of her for two weeks. Then that thought she'd tried to ignore blasted into her consciousness.

He cared for her, more than just a casual liaison type of affection. He'd indicated that a couple hours ago out on the trail, but she'd been much too involved in fighting her own feelings to comprehend the magnitude of it. Yet there were definite reasons Sandy would never pursue his attraction to her, not the least of which was her betrothal to David. Something else held him back.

She waved a hand, waiting a full five seconds before Sandy returned the gesture. After she went through the door, she moved over to the window on the mud porch to look out as she took off her wraps. He stood there for another long time, then began to unharness the dogs.

Removing her boots last, she set them on the mat inside

the door and went into the kitchen. Katie waited at the table, two cups of steaming chocolate in front of her.

"We were worried," she said. "Tracie and Cristy just left. We thought you'd be back before this—right after the snow started falling so heavily."

"We were on our way," Laura said evasively. Katie's discerning look told her the misleading statement didn't go overlooked, but the elderly woman didn't comment as Laura sat down and gratefully reached for the hot chocolate. "Ummmmm." She licked her upper lip. "Delicious, as usual."

"Thank you," Katie murmured. "I made some cookies, too, unless Tracie ate all of them."

She heaved herself to her feet, and Laura let her go, since Katie would frown that deadly glare if Laura offered to get the cookies herself. While she waited, her mind wandered back to the trail.

Perhaps Sandy hadn't realized exactly what he was saying, she mused. Or perhaps he hadn't thought her perceptive enough to realize he'd left out much more than he actually said. She was certain something unfortunate shadowed his life. He didn't appear to be the type of person who would drag his child and sister away from a good life such as they had in Grand Marais to the rigors of harsh, wilderness living. Not unless he had no choice.

Katie set a plate of cookies on the table, and Laura reached for one. "Is Father home?" she asked.

"In his study," Katie told her. "He's slowing down to half days for the holidays, like every year."

Laura stood and picked up her cup. After a smile of thanks to Katie, she wandered out of the kitchen, down the hall to the study. The room was empty; instead she found her father in front of the huge stone fireplace in their living room, ensconced in the overstuffed chair he preferred. He sat there, relaxing, his feet on the footstool as he watched the snow fall outside the huge bay window. A cup of chocolate sat on the little table by his side.

"Laura," he said when he glanced up. "Please join me, darling." When she sat in the lady's chair across from him, he continued, "I'm sorry, my dear, but it looks like David won't make it out here tonight to take you to dinner before you leave. He stopped by the office right before I left, and he was worried about the storm clouds. I told him he could come on out with me and spend the night if necessary, but he said he had a case he needed to work on."

"It's all right, Father. I'll see him in the morning before I leave, if the storm stops in time for me to be able to go. If this keeps up, the supply ship may not arrive tomorrow so I can go back on it."

"I checked with the weather forecasters before I left," he said with a wink. "You know, those old men around the stove at the general store?"

Laura laughed and nodded. Amazingly, those old men were extremely accurate. "What did they say?"

"That it will quit by midnight. Then we'll have a couple days of clear weather before a larger storm hits."

"It's the time of year for it," Laura said with a sigh. "I'm surprised Sandy and I have had as much clear weather as we have for our training runs. Some winters it starts snowing in November and doesn't stop until May."

"How is that going, darling? And how's Blancheur?"

"Blancheur's almost perfect again. And I guess it's going all right. Sandy's not one to give a lot of praise, but if you mess up, you definitely hear about it."

Tom reached for his chocolate and took a swallow. "Cold," he muttered. "Ah, well, it's just as good that way." He finished off the cup and set it down, then studied Laura. "Do I detect that Sandy thinks there might be a flaw somewhere in my perfect daughter? I might have to have a chat with him about that."

His teasing tone belied his stern words, and Laura chuckled. "He only wants to make sure I stay safe. Today, I was foolish and left my mittens off too long." She explained about the deer, knowing he would chastise her more if she kept that from him than if she confessed. Taking a cigar from the box beside him, he lit it while she talked.

When the cigar glowed strongly, Tom puffed out a

mouthful of smoke and said, "I assume, though, you didn't suffer any permanent damage to your hands."

As she recalled exactly how the damage was avoided and once again imagined those hard chest muscles beneath her fingers, a blush heated her cheeks. Yet she forced herself to meet her father's gaze. "No, no damage. And I'll be more careful in the future."

Tom nodded and inhaled on his cigar. "The house looks lovely," he said after he blew out the smoke. "Too bad you won't be here to enjoy it."

"I enjoyed the time spent decorating. Cristy and Tracie are a lot of fun and good company."

Tom nodded an acknowledgment, but didn't say anything else. Finally Laura recognized a familiar ploy on her father's part. Ever since she had been little, Tom would fathom when she had something on her mind and silently make himself available for her confidences. This confidence, however, had to be handled delicately, because she also felt she had a secret with Sandy. He hadn't told her father of his decision not to accept the shipping position, and that knowledge divided her loyalty. Maybe she could evade the issue and still get some information.

"I really appreciate your finding Sandy for me, Father. I don't believe you could have found any better man on earth—more knowledgeable about dogs and racing."

Tom nodded agreement, but instead of commenting, he continued to enjoy his cigar.

"And, as I said, I truly enjoy Tracie and Cristy. I guess they surprised me somewhat. I don't mean to sound . . . well, judgmental, but when I think of people from Alaska, I think of prospectors and trappers. I keep forgetting there are cities and towns there, too."

"Cristy came with Sandy from Washington State," Tom corrected. "It was a shame, but her and Sandy's mother and father both died, leaving her to depend on Sandy."

"Oh, I knew that," Laura said. "Sandy told me. You know, I wonder why he came all the way to Minnesota, instead of staying out there? Do you think he wanted to get far away from the memories of his wife? He talked about her a little one day, and you could tell he really loved her."

Tom flipped some ashes into a glass ashtray at his elbow, then studied Laura for a few seconds. "Real love is a beautiful thing," he said, not directly answering her question. "I had that with your mother, and not finding it again is what's kept me a widower all these years. If I could choose only one wish for you, it would be for you to live your life with a true love, Laura, darling."

She smiled at him, then glanced out the window. "Thank you, Daddy," she said, using the name she'd dropped a few years back. He held out his arms, and she rose. Crossing to his chair, she settled on his lap, as she had hundreds of times before. They sat that way for a long time, alternately watching the fire and the snow through the window. Finally Katie came to announce dinner, and Laura realized she hadn't really gotten any more information about Sandy from her father.

Yet maybe she'd gotten something even more important from him.

Something about the couple striding resolutely up the walkway toward the general store two days before Christmas caught Cristy's attention. When Tracie's hand tightened on hers, she glanced down to see a look of fear on her niece's face. Tracie pulled her hand free and turned back the way they'd come.

"I decided I don't wants to go to the store, Aunt Cristy," she said. "I'm gonna wait for you back at Davie's."

Cristy hurried after her, catching her within a few steps and pulling her to a halt. Tracie's eyes flew past her, and Cristy saw the couple enter the store. Tracie relaxed slightly, but Cristy sensed her determination not to continue on down the walkway.

"What's wrong, Tracie? What made you afraid all of a sudden?"

"Can we's just go into Mr. Tom's office?" she asked. "I gots cold." A shiver punctuated her words, but Cristy had a feeling the chill had more to do with who Tracie had seen than the actual temperature.

Taking her hand, Cristy led Tracie inside the nearest building, which was indeed Tom Goodman's office. She didn't see his secretary at her desk, and the door to Tom's office was closed. Leading Tracie over to the potbelly stove, she sat her in one of the chairs.

"What's wrong?" she repeated. "You need to tell me, Tracie."

Tears pooled in Tracie's eyes, and she bit her lips. Cristy knelt before her, cupping her chin in her palm. "Please, darling. I can't help you if you don't tell me what's wrong."

All of a sudden Cristy was afraid some danger from Alaska had arrived in Grand Marais. She hated to upset Tracie further, but she needed to know, since she was responsible for Tracie when the child was in her care.

"Does your being afraid have anything to do with what happened in Alaska, before you came to Grand Marais?" she asked.

Reluctantly, Tracie nodded her head, and wiped the back of her hand under her nose. "Uh-huh."

Cristy pulled a handkerchief from her reticule and handed it to Tracie. "Does it have something to do with the people we just saw on the walkway?"

Dropping the handkerchief, Tracie flung herself into Cristy's arms. "It's Grandma and Grandpa," she wailed. "Please don't let them take me away from Daddy, Aunt Cristy! Please!"

Fighting her own burgeoning fear, Cristy gathered Tracie close. Thank God her niece had seen the Dyers and recognized them. Cristy had never met them herself. Since she'd become aware of why Sandy couldn't return to Alaska, she'd imagined all sorts of terrible things about them, though.

Tom's office door opened, and Cristy rose, Tracie in her arms. David stood in the doorway.

"I thought I heard her cry," he said. "Would the two of you like to come in here?"

"Yes." Cristy carried Tracie toward him. "Where's Tom?"

"He went home just a second ago. He left out the back door."

His eyes traveled over her hungrily, as they had been doing lately. She had to tell him they needed to stay away from each other. Soon.

"I was just leaving myself," he said. "Gonna lock up for Tom."

"I'm glad you're here. I thought we'd have to go to your office to find you."

Motioning for her to sit, he pulled the other visitor's chair close to her. "What's wrong?"

Tracie straightened in her arms. "We can'ts tell him, Aunt Cristy. It's a secret."

David laid a hand on Tracie's head. "Darling, you remember me telling you that I was a lawyer?"

"Uh-huh."

"Well, before men are allowed to be lawyers, they have to promise that they will never, ever, tell anyone's secret. It's called an oath, and if we break that oath, we can't be lawyers anymore. And since I really, truly like being a lawyer, I can promise you that your secret will be safe with me. The only times a lawyer tells a secret is with permission, and to protect other people."

Tracie stubbornly stuck out her lower lip, and David gave Cristy a beseeching look. "It's tearing me up to know the two of you are worried about something and won't let me help."

It took all the willpower she had not to answer him—tell him she wanted nothing more than to fling herself into his arms and let him take over her problems. Worse, she almost did just that, even knowing how she would be betraying Laura and the morals she'd been taught all her life. Only knowing her mother would be disappointed in her, even in death, kept her in place.

"I can'ts tell you," Tracie insisted. "But maybe Aunt Cristy didn't promise Daddy she wouldn't tell anyone."

The rationalization from the young mind told Cristy how terribly afraid Tracie must be. George and Elvina Dyer evidently posed a threat more horrible than Cristy had imagined—so horrible that Tracie was willing to break a promise to her father. Squeezing Tracie comfortingly, she began to tell David what she knew.

"I found the court order among Sandy's things when I was cleaning his room one day," she said at the end of the story. "A box fell off the closet shelf when I was hanging up some of his shirts, and an official looking document caught my eye as I put it back. I'm not exactly sure how the Dyers managed it, but they stole custody of Tracie from my brother, and now they're here in town. Somehow they followed Sandy all the way across the country."

Cristy's voice broke. "O—oh, God, David, what can we do? Sandy will die if he loses Tracie."

"I'm not goin' back to Alaska with Grandma and Grandpa!" Tracie cried. "I won't go! I won't!"

David knelt on the floor and wrapped an arm around Tracie's small shoulders, placing his other arm around Cristy. He offered too much comfort and she needed it too badly to refuse the gesture.

"Tracie, you and Cristy have done the right thing in talking to me about this," he said softly. Tracie looked at him hopefully, her sobs quieting. "There are things I can do to protect you from the Dyers. At least, I'm pretty sure there are."

"Pretty sure?" Cristy asked, immediately picking up on his hesitation.

"It's the holidays," he said with a worried look. "I have a feeling the Dyers deliberately came here now, thinking the legal officials would be unavailable at this time of year. What I can do to help will depend on whether I can get hold of Judge Barstow in Duluth. Otherwise, we'll have to hope Police Chief Ingstrum can be reasoned with."

"P—police?"

"Don't worry, Aunt Cristy," Tracie said, patting her on the cheek. "Chief In'sun likes me. He gives me peppermints all the time."

Cristy exchanged a look with David, neither of them having the heart to tell Tracie the police chief liking her had nothing to do with enforcing the law. David stood, indicating for the two of them to join him.

"Where did you see the Dyers?"

Cristy explained the couple had gone into the general store, and David frowned. "Cathy's at the counter today. I was in there a half hour ago."

Having heard over and over what a gossip Cathy Berglind was, Cristy avoided her whenever possible. If the Dyers asked Cathy for information about Sandy and Tracie, without a doubt she'd be more than willing to fill them in on even more than they asked.

"We can go out the back way, and get my horse and sleigh." David locked the front door of the office, then turned back. "I want to take both of you out to Ladyslipper Landing and I want you to stay there. Even Chief Ingstrum won't bother you there, if I can assure him Judge Barstow is coming here to conduct an emergency hearing. He won't want to antagonize Tom."

"Maybe Mr. Goodman will be so upset at being involved in this situation, he'll tell us to leave," Cristy said.

"Not the Tom Goodman I know," David assured. "Just be glad he's still here, instead of in Duluth with Laura." He placed a finger on his chin. "Wait a minute."

Sitting at Tom's desk, he searched in a drawer until he found some paper. He picked up Tom's fountain pen and dipped it in the inkwell, saying as he wrote, "We'll detour by John Beargrease's cabin on the way to Ladyslipper Landing and see if one of his sons will go to Duluth for us by dogsled. I'm writing a short letter to Judge Barstow, explaining the situation. He's a friend of mine and Tom's both, and if there's any way he can get up here, he'll come, despite it being the holidays."

A half hour later, they arrived at Ladyslipper Landing. Sandy was gone, and David refused to leave them alone in their own cabin. He took them down to the main house and ordered them to stay in the kitchen with Katie while he explained things to Tom. Tracie didn't seem to pick up on the fact her secret was spreading, which told Cristy exactly how scared her tiny niece was.

David came back to the kitchen after a few minutes and motioned for them to follow. He led them into Tom's study, which she and Tracie had helped Laura decorate. Given the crisis they were there to discuss, the merry decorations looked incongruous.

"I'm going to send Buck out to find Sandy and get him back here," David said as Cristy sat down with Tracie on her lap. "I'll return in a minute, I promise."

"Thank you," Cristy breathed.

Tom stood and walked around the desk as David left. "I don't want you to worry about anything," he said. "You've both become very dear to Laura and me, and I'll do everything in my power to protect you, Tracie."

A stab of guilt pierced Cristy at his words. Yes, Laura had become almost like a sister to her—the sister she'd never had. At the very least, Laura was her best friend. And Cristy had fallen in love with her best friend's fiancé.

13

*P*URE LUCK, LAURA thought to herself as Judge Barstow helped her down the supply ship's gangplank. To cover up her indignant reflections, she directed a brilliant smile at the judge. Pure luck had let her overhear Mrs. Barstow at the party, bemoaning the fact her husband had to make a trip to Grand Marais between Christmas and the New Year for some sort of emergency hearing. When Laura sought out the judge, he hadn't known much more than his wife—only that David Hudson had requested he come, and David had written that Tom Goodman would also deeply appreciate the judge handling this very important matter.

She hadn't minded cutting her trip short at all, since she'd spent the entire week constantly wondering what was going on back home. Well, wondering a little more about what one certain person was doing, but overall she missed her father, Cristy and Tracie, also. Oh, and David, too.

Not surprisingly, given the request for the judge's appearance in Grand Marais, her father hadn't shown up for

Christmas Day at her friend's house. After that Laura had no qualms about sending Judge Barstow a note, telling him she would join him the next morning on the supply packet.

The judge checked his pocket watch. "It's almost one o'clock, Miss Goodman. I better get on over to the courthouse. Will you accompany me?"

"I believe I'll stop by my father's office and let him know I'm back early," Laura said. "I'll come over after that."

"Your father may already be at the courthouse," Judge Barstow said.

"It'll only take me a minute to check. Thank you for the company on the trip."

"My pleasure, my dear."

The judge hurried away, and Laura followed at a slower pace. Judge Barstow was a very nice man, but he thought it good manners to keep her amused. She hadn't had a moment to herself during the trip. Not that it would have mattered, because she still had no earthly idea what would merit summoning a judge from Duluth. When the judge got a fair distance ahead of her, she quickened her own pace and arrived at her father's office a couple minutes later.

His secretary wasn't at her desk, and Laura could see her father's empty desk through his open office door. Just to be sure, she peeked into the other office. Then she hurried back to the walkway and a few doors down to David's office.

Papers strewn all around and law books open on every surface indicated David had been there recently. But his clerk's desk was empty, as was David's. A quiver of apprehension stole through her. The mess in David's office was unlike him. He usually stayed so calm and in control, even when working on an important case. Concern heightening, she left for the courthouse further down the street.

Suddenly Laura halted in the middle of the walkway. She'd been so distracted she hadn't noticed the area around the courthouse. Dogsleds, horses and sleighs surrounded it, with snowshoes and wooden skis setting against the front wall of the building. Every person for miles around must have interrupted their holiday celebrations to be at this hearing. She stifled a stab of anger at her father and David for not notifying her about whatever was going on.

Since she didn't see any people outside the building, she assumed the hearing must be in progress. She raced down the walkway and up the courthouse steps. Inside, she hurried over to the courtroom, then paused at the door to catch her breath. When she finally eased the door open, she saw every seat taken and people standing against the back wall. Despite the crowd, however, the room was almost silent.

Scooting inside the door, she closed it softly. Buck stood to one side, his battered hat in his hand. She sidled up to him and tapped his arm.

"What's going on?" she whispered when he looked at her in surprise. "I just got back from Duluth."

Buck nodded toward the front of the room. "See them there scalawags over there by themselves at t'other table?"

"That man and woman? They're strangers here, aren't they?"

"Yep." Buck scowled fiercely. "An' iffen everybody gets their way, they ain't gonna be 'round long enough to ever be anythin' else. They's here to try to take little Miss Tracie 'way from her Daddy, and we ain't a gonna let 'em!"

Laura gasped. "What do you mean? My God, where's Sandy?"

"He's over there at t'other table." Buck tilted his head toward the opposite side of the room, where David and Sandy sat at a table with her father.

Thanking Buck with a smile, Laura strode down the aisle. She couldn't find a seat on the bench behind David's table, but one of the Beargrease men on the second bench back offered her his seat, and she took it gratefully. No one paid any attention to the stir their exchange of places caused, because just then Judge Barstow came into the courtroom, dressed in his black robes. As Laura settled on the bench, she recognized the back of Cristy's head in front of her, but saw no sign of Katie or Tracie.

"Please stay seated," Judge Barstow said when some of the people started to rise. He took his seat behind the dais. "I've only just arrived in town and have had a limited time to examine what this is all about. I did, however, glance at the paperwork left for me in the judge's chambers by Chief Ingstrum, as well as the brief left by Attorney Hudson. Now, who is Mr. Dyer?"

The strange man stood, and the woman beside him crossed her arms and nodded her head. Her entire attitude—her stiff back and haughty sniff—indicated she felt herself about to be supported by the high and mighty auspices of the law. Without even knowing her, dislike welled up in Laura.

"I'm George Dyer," the man said. "And I'm here to get you to enforce the court order I brought with me. I assume it's among the papers you have in your hands."

"That it is," Judge Barstow agreed. "But it's also an order from an Alaskan court."

"That order gives me custody of my granddaughter, Tracie Montdulac," George Dyer said in a supercilious voice, ignoring the judge's comment. "I expect you to make her father turn her over to me, so we can take her back to Alaska with us."

"What you expect—" Judge Barstow leaned forward a bit. "—and what the law is, are quite possibly two different things, Mr. Dyer. Since I've made the trip all the way here from Duluth, I'm willing to listen to any arguments you may have. However, unless there's something missing from the paperwork I have, there's only one ruling I can make."

The woman beside George Dyer jumped to her feet, slapping George's hand away when he tried to push her back into her chair. "Now, you listen to me! I've got a few things to say here."

Judge Barstow rolled his eyes. "As I said, I'm willing to listen. And you are?"

"Elvina Dyer, the child's grandmother. She's my only granddaughter, and I insist you give her to me, as it says in that order. We were granted custody of the child after my daughter died, and I want to see she has a proper upbringing instead of being raised in the wild among a bunch of backwoods trappers and Indians!"

A mutter of dissent moved through the courtroom, but Judge

Barstow tapped his gavel, silencing it. "Mrs. Dyer," he responded with a long-suffering sigh. "Did you and your husband consult with an attorney before you came here today?"

"We tried, Your Honor," George replied. "But the other attorney in town wouldn't take our case when he found out why we were here."

"Did he perhaps mention you might be wasting your money hiring him for this?" Judge Barstow mused. "That perhaps the other attorney in town had the stronger case? That happens in towns where they don't have permanent judges for their court. The attorneys consult and try to work things out beforehand, so the courts aren't clogged with clear-cut cases being argued just for the sake of argument."

"He was on the side of this town," Mrs. Dyer spat. "He tried to trick us into leaving without my granddaughter."

Judge Barstow shook his head. "You are entitled to your day in court, if that's what you want, Mrs. Dyer." He looked at David. "Do you have anything to say, Mr. Hudson?"

David rose to his feet. "If I'm reading you right, Your Honor, I believe you're getting ready to say it for me. At the risk of having my clients think I'm not earning my fee, although I did spend an inordinate amount of time on my brief—" He smiled at Sandy, then looked back at the judge. "—I believe I'll just let you make your ruling. No sense forcing the people in the courtroom to sit through the same information twice."

Judge Barstow inclined his head, then picked up one of the pieces of paper in front of him. "This is your court order, Mr. and Mrs. Dyer. As you have both admitted, and as I've seen, this is from an Alaska District Court. If you'd consulted legal counsel—or, I guess, if you'd paid attention to the advice the legal counsel you *did* consult gave you—you'd have known the Alaska courts have no jurisdiction down here. At least, the law books I've read indicate that, and if my memory is fuzzy, the brief Mr. Hudson prepared gives exact case law on it. Now, you may find another judge who might let you tie up his courts with arguments on this matter, but I'm not willing to do that. I have more important things to do than listen to obscure interpretations of the law some lawyer out to make a name for himself might want to use for an argument."

He laid down the paper and picked up his gavel, tapping it on the dais. "My ruling is that, according to the laws of our nation, Tracie Montdulac is already in the proper custody—the custody of her father. Court dismissed."

Cheers erupted in the courtroom as Judge Barstow left the dais and headed for his chambers. Realizing she'd gone undetected by her father, David and Sandy, Laura slipped down the aisle amid the confusion. Back on the walkway she hesitated, trying to determine who it would be best to confront and ask for information about what was behind the hearing. Deciding upon David, she hurried to his office and went inside, taking a chair in the corner of the room to wait.

A short while later, men's footsteps clumped down the walkway. They paused outside the door, and Laura could hear their conversation as they stood outside one of the large windows.

"I'm taking Sandy on home," her father said. "Katie and Tracie will wonder what happened, and I'm really glad we've got such good news for them."

"I thought I had the law figured out," David replied, "but you never can tell. As much as we research, at times the Judge knows something we've overlooked and we lose. I'm happy that wasn't the case this time, Sandy."

"I don't know quite how to thank you, David," Sandy said. "Your fees. . . ."

"I told you, brother," Cristy said. "*I* took care of that. David asked for my help redecorating his office, and the advice and paintings I'm doing for him are my contribution to our family. If you argue with me one more time, I'll . . . I'll dump cold water in one of your boots and let it freeze like I did when we were growing up."

"No, no," Sandy said in a voice laced with mock-horror. "Anything but that. But we'll talk about this later. Right now, I'm going home to Tracie."

"Give her my love, too," Cristy said. "I'll be there in a while. I need to talk to David about something. Since he's coming out for the celebration, he's offered to let me ride with him."

There was a minute of silence, and Laura imagined the men shaking hands. Then two sets of bootsteps left, and the office door opened. David and Cristy walked in and Laura started to rise, but her cloak snagged on a splinter in the chair. Silently grimacing, she fingered the snag, but the dimness in the corner of the room made it hard to figure out just how to remove her cloak without damage.

While she worked on it, she listened to the conversation, immediately aware of a strain she'd never noticed before between David and Sandy's sister.

"You did a fine job, David," Cristy said.

"Thank you," he replied in a formal tone. "Now, what was it you wished to speak to me about?"

"I think I need to sit down."

"Of course. Please forgive my lack of manners."

David walked past his clerk's desk and pulled back a chair from in front of his own desk, then stood waiting for Cristy to cross the room. Laura managed to free her cloak from the splinter, but her puzzlement over this change in David and Cristy's usual camaraderie held her in place.

"Uh . . ." Cristy said, staring around the room and avoiding David's gaze. "Maybe I can just stand. I just need an accounting of what I still owe you."

"Dammit, Cristy," David said, his voice going from formal to tortured. "Sit down and we'll talk. I already told you that there's no way I'm going to charge you for handling this. I love Tracie as much as you do."

"I can't let you do that—"

"Cristy, I don't know how much more I can take of this! Of us! Of the way we've been acting around each other the last couple weeks!" He pushed the chair away and it slammed into the front of the desk. He took a step, but Cristy backed away from him. "We need to talk, Cristy. And not about the legal work!"

"No!" Cristy shook her head and retreated another step. "I know what you want to talk about, and there's absolutely nothing to discuss."

"Nothing, Cristy?" David's voice lowered to a murmur. "What about the reason you won't or can't be near me? What about the way we've gone from being friends to having to keep distance between us. What about the temptation to give in to the feelings that have grown between us? You can't tell me that you don't feel them, too. You've changed toward me just as I've changed toward you. I've forced myself to keep my hands off you and be true to Laura. Admit it, Cristy. At the very least we should talk about this and get it behind us."

"I won't admit anything! I don't know what you mean."

Cristy shook her head violently. Turning as though to flee, she ran into the clerk's desk, hitting her hip and tumbling onto the surface. She pushed herself upright, but David had already closed the distance between them. He wrapped his arms around her and pulled her close.

"Are you hurt?" he asked anxiously. "Oh, Cristy, I'd die before I'd do anything to hurt you."

"I'm fine," she said. Then she gave a sigh and looked up into his face. "My hip's fine, but my heart's going to hurt for the rest of my life. Please, just . . . please let me go."

David bent his head until their lips were so close they almost touched.

"David, please don't," Cristy whispered

He complied, releasing her as though she were about to burst into flames in his arms. Turning from her, he buried his face in his hands. Looking at his back Cristy finally saw Laura in the corner and gasped in dismay.

Laura stood, confused for only a moment. She'd just heard her fiancé imply he was in love with another woman—seen him on the verge of kissing that woman. By all rights, she should be fighting mad and ready to tear Cristy's hair out. Shouldn't she? Instead, she only felt relief. After she quickly examined her emotions, she made a decision.

"Please," she murmured, and David's head flew up.

He stared at her, then back at Cristy. "Listen, Laura," he said. "This is all my fault."

"Hush, David." Laura walked over and took his arm. Then she reached for Cristy's hand and placed it in David's.

"I hate to disillusion you about your attractiveness, David," she said around a chuckle, "but I spent part of my time in Duluth wondering if our getting married was the right thing to do. And now, I know it isn't. What we have is habit, David. You and Cristy are in love, and you shouldn't throw that away. I hope you'll ask me to the wedding?"

"Oh, Laura," Cristy cried. "We didn't mean for it to happen. We fought very hard to ignore our feelings. I feel horrible, and even more so because you're being so nice about this."

Laura shook her head and laughed. "Cristy, I'm not only being nice, I'm being honest. I care for David. I care for him a lot. But I've never had the type of feelings for him that I sense you have. I care enough about David to want him to be happy, and I'd never want him to marry me just to save face—or whatever crazy idea society will have about us ending our engagement. I truly want you and David to be happy, and if the townspeople think they'll see any tears and miserable prostrations out of me over this, they'll be sadly disappointed."

"You really mean it, don't you?"

"Haven't I been saying that? Now, the only thing I need is a ride to Ladyslipper Landing, since I'm sure Father has already left."

"What are you doing back?" David belatedly put in, although Laura noticed he slipped his arm around Cristy.

She gave him a stern look. "It seems no one notified me there was a crisis here pertaining to people I care about. I'll take you and my father to task for that later on. Right now . . ." She winked at Cristy. "Right now, I'm going over to Mrs. Sterling's Restaurant and have a piece of pie and some coffee. Perhaps you'll make sure David doesn't forget me on the way home, Cristy."

"I will," Cristy said, her attention transferring to David.

"I hope so," Laura whispered to herself as she moved to the door. She turned slightly, enough to see David cup his hand around Cristy's face, his gaze worshipping her, before she slipped through the door. Once on the walkway, she realized she'd forgotten to return David's engagement ring and pulled off her right mitten to remove it. Taking it from her finger, she placed it in her pocket. She could give it back to David on the way home.

She laughed out loud, then shook her head as she headed toward Mrs. Sterling's. She'd just been the victim of a broken engagement and jilted by the man she'd thought would be her husband for a large part of her life. By all rights she should be wailing to high heaven, tears coursing down her cheeks and freezing in the cold.

Instead she wanted to jump for joy. Or at least skip down the walkway. She hadn't skipped in years. She took a tentative hop, delighting in the bouncy freedom and skipping another few steps. When she came to the general store, the door opened and Cathy Berglind came out. Laura tossed her a smile and stopped.

"Hello, Cathy. Tell you what. Since it's the holiday season and a time for forgiving and gift giving, I have something to make you very happy. You can be the first one to start spreading the gossip. David Hudson and I are no longer engaged."

Cathy's eyes widened, then she pursed her lips. "Oh, Laura," she said in a falsely sympathetic voice. "I'm so sorry."

"I'm not," Laura said with a laugh. She skipped on past Cathy, her mouth watering for a piece of Mrs. Sterling's blueberry pie. Hopefully the restaurant owner would have ice cream to go with it.

As she walked up the restaurant steps a minute later, Laura realized what the cadence of her steps had been saying in her mind. *No excuse. No excuse.* She knew what it meant. There was no excuse for her not to explore the feelings between her and Sandy now.

Pausing with her hand on the restaurant door, she tilted her head as a dreamy thought came to her. Wouldn't it be wonderful to have a man—Sandy—gaze at her the way David looked at Cristy? It was such a nice thing for Fate to take a hand and allow both her and David out of their engagement. Allow them each a chance to find true love, rather than the friendship they mistook for love before Cristy and Sandy came into their lives.

14

*A*NYONE WHO COULDN'T see the change in the relationship between David and Cristy that evening had to be blind, Laura mused to herself. Yet Sandy truly appeared ignorant of it. She couldn't blame him, she guessed. His total attention focused on Tracie, and he never let her out of his sight. Recalling her own fear and anger when David finally explained the situation to her, Laura kept a close eye on the child herself.

She still hadn't totally forgiven her father or David for not notifying her along with Judge Barstow in Duluth. She might as well get over her pique with David, however, because her cold shoulder didn't matter one iota to him. His attention stayed on Cristy, and he could care less if Laura wasn't speaking to him.

Her father was a different matter. As soon as their dinner was over, he murmured quietly for her to meet him in his study while the others had coffee and hot chocolate in the living room. She slipped away unnoticed and joined him.

"What's going on, Laura?" he asked. "You're acting like you're peeved at me over something."

"I'd think it would be obvious, Father. I *am* rather perturbed at you—and David, too—for not letting me know about the Dyers being in town. I could have come back even earlier and been here for Sandy. As it was, I had to find out about the hearing by eavesdropping on a private conversation. I worried all the way back on the supply ship about what could be going on."

Tom shook his head. "I expected you'd be upset over that, darling. The Beargrease boy had already left for Duluth by the time I found out what was going on myself, since David stopped at their place on the way here from town. He thought it prudent to get help as quickly as possible to keep Tracie out of the Dyers' clutches."

"Oh. Then I forgive you." She hadn't been that upset at him anyway. The other path her thoughts had traveled off and on the rest of the afternoon and evening kept her spirits high.

"Thank you." Tom chuckled tolerantly. "But that's not what I was alluding to. I notice you're not wearing your engagement ring, and David hasn't said two words to you all evening. In fact, it looks suspiciously like he's falling in love with Cristy."

"He's already in love with Cristy," Laura said with a gay laugh. "Has it been that long since you were in love yourself that you can't recognize it?"

Tom raised his eyebrows, and Laura pursed her lips at him. "I should make you wait for an explanation, like you conveniently ignored me in Duluth," she threatened.

"Laura," he warned. "I thought I was forgiven. Not that *I* actually did anything wrong."

"You are." She raised her head in feigned superiority. "I'll be a much bigger person than you and explain things."

"For a woman who's engagement seems to be off, you don't seem very brokenhearted."

"I'm not, Father. In fact, I'm very happy for Cristy and David; I really believe that what they have is true love. Remember what you told me the night before I left for

Duluth? That real love is a beautiful thing? We're seeing that beauty now, and it's made me realize what I feel for David is only friendship. I'm very, very glad we both found out before we got married and ruined our lives."

Tom walked over and hugged her. "I don't believe marriage to David would have actually ruined either of your lives, Laura. However, given what we know now, it could have shortchanged you both somewhat. And I'm very proud of you, Laura, darling. I was sure you were grown up before, but this tells me you've indisputably become an adult."

"You don't seem surprised, Father. That David and I won't be getting married, I mean."

"No, I'm not," he admitted. "Until recently, I would have been, but not this last month."

"Why? What did you see that I didn't?"

"Oh, I think you see it, too, Laura. But one thing I've always promised myself is to not make your decisions for you. I'll always be there for you, darling, but I want you to live your own life, not the life I pick out for you."

"I love you, Daddy," she said.

"Me, too, darling. Me, too." He kissed her forehead, then said, "We better return to the living room. Since you're back, I promised Tracie we could open gifts tonight instead of waiting until next week."

"Oh, I've got the gifts I bought in Duluth upstairs in my room. I'll be right down with them."

Picking up her skirts, she hurried to the stairs. In her room she opened the satchel where she'd packed the gifts for her trip home. Unerringly she picked out one small gift and slipped it in her skirt pocket. She'd give that one to someone in a private ceremony.

At first she tried to pile all the gifts into her arms, but the heap tumbled to the bed before she could take one step. Laughing, she started packing them back in the satchel.

"Tom said you might need some help."

She whirled. Sandy stood in the doorway, and Laura smiled at him. When he didn't return her smile, a frown creased her forehead. Downstairs around Tracie he had been about as cheerful as she had ever seen him. Now he carried that darned moroseness on his shoulders again. She stamped her foot.

"What on earth has turned you so dour again? And on Christmas?"

"Christmas was day before yesterday," he said with a shrug. Avoiding her eyes, he walked over to the bed and picked up packages until his arms were full, then headed for the door. Laura grabbed his arm, and he paused without looking at her.

"I've got my arms full," he said.

"Sandy, tell me what's making you unhappy." Since he wouldn't look at her, she dropped his arm and moved around in front of him. "You didn't by any chance think David was paying way too much attention to your sister tonight, did you?"

"They both explained what happened to me the minute they got back today. I'm very sorry about your broken engagement, Laura, but I can't say I'm displeased for Cristy. Hudson is a fine man. I'll forever be in his debt."

"Didn't they tell you it was a mutual decision for David and me to end our engagement?" she asked in exasperation.

"Yes. And I hope you find someone you truly love when you do decide to marry again. Excuse me, but Tracie's waiting to open presents."

Before she could stop him, he stepped around her and went out the door. For a moment she stood there, trying to understand what he had said—or more to the point, what he *didn't* say. Her hand inched into her skirt pocket and fingered the present. Looking over at the bed, she saw a couple of boxes Sandy had missed and retrieved them. She could wait, she guessed, to continue this conversation with him. They'd be alone on the trail tomorrow or the next day, when they began training again.

She carried the presents downstairs, where excited voices told her everyone was getting impatient to unwrap the gifts. In the living room, she placed her last two gifts—except for the one in her pocket—under the tree.

Tom and Katie had lit the candles on the tree branches,

and as soon as she moved back, Tom asked David to help him turn out the lanterns in the room. Everyone gasped in awe at the surreal beauty of the glow from the fireplace and the candles on the tree. Silence lingered for a few seconds until Katie's elderly but still melodious voice rose in an old carol.

Other voices joined in, and David pulled Cristy into his embrace while Tom reached for Laura. She glanced past Tom to Sandy, who sat on the floor with Tracie on his lap. He wasn't singing, but he listened to every note from his daughter's mouth. When the carol ended, Tracie leaped to her feet.

"Can we open presents now?"

"Tracie," Sandy admonished.

"Oh. Please? Please can we open presents now?" she beseeched.

Amid tolerant laughter, Tom and Katie relit the lanterns.

The next morning, Laura opened her eyes to exactly what she hoped. She'd taped the charcoal sketch of Sandy, Tracie and Cristy to her lamp base until she could get a frame, and it was right in line with her vision.

The gift had been labeled from Tracie, and Cristy assured everyone who received one that Tracie had come up with the idea herself. In fact, Cristy said, Tracie helped with the housework to pay for Cristy doing the sketches. The child had already picked up on the fact a person made or earned gifts to give to others, and insisted she was quite old enough to pay for her gifts, too, thank you very much.

Laura's lips curved in a smile, and she cradled her cheek on her palm for a few seconds, studying the sketch. Then she bounded out of bed. Sandy had at least spoken to her long enough last night to confirm they would start training again today. A glance at the clock indicated she was up even earlier than normal, but she dressed anyway and hastily made her bed.

On her way downstairs, she smelled coffee. Katie was already ahead of her, despite their late evening.

"Morning, Katie," she said, waltzing across the kitchen

and kissing the elderly cheek. "Did you have a nice time last night?"

"As always," Katie agreed. "Breakfast will be in half an hour, but the coffee's ready now if you want some."

"Thank you. I'll get it." She poured a cup and headed for the back porch to get her coat and boots. "I'll be back in a little while."

"Your father's already up and about, too. He's out at the kennel."

"Oh. That's unusual. I hope nothing's wrong."

"Don't believe so," Katie said with a shrug. "It's just an early morning for everyone. I saw the lights on in Sandy's cabin, also, when I stepped out to see what sort of day it was going to be."

"And what sort of day will it be?"

"A beautiful one. Now go on and enjoy it, so I can get my work done."

Grinning at her, Laura carried her coffee onto the porch. By the time she pulled on her boots and coat, her coffee had cooled in the frigid air, and she drank it down, leaving the cup on a windowsill to pick up when she returned.

Outside she realized Katie was right. The sun was just rising, beautifully variegated hues of pink shading the cloud-free eastern sky. Her breath frosted ahead of her, and her footsteps crunched on the snow as she headed for the kennel.

She found her father and Sandy in the office, faces serious when they looked up in response to her entrance. Her father motioned her into the office.

"Good morning," he said. "I'm glad you're here, because we all need to have a discussion. Pete should be here as well, but since he's not, I'll let you and Sandy tell him when he arrives."

Her high spirits dimmed as she studied him, then glanced at Sandy, who immediately flickered his gaze away. "Well, I started to mention what a beautiful day it is," she said in attempted flippancy, "but the atmosphere in here doesn't bear that out."

"There's nothing really wrong, darling," Tom said. "It's

just that I don't believe either you or I want to lose the best trainer in the business, and I believe I've come up with a solution. You'll have to make the decision, however."

"Lose Sandy?" she gasped. "But why?"

"Please sit down, Laura."

Tom pushed a chair toward her, but Laura shook her head. "I'm fine. What's going on?" She gazed steadily at Sandy, silently demanding an explanation, but he continued to ignore her.

Tom finally spoke. "If you'll think for a moment, Laura, you'll understand. There's no way Sandy can return to Alaska—at least, not in so visible a capacity as one of the drivers in a highly publicized dogsled race. Back in that jurisdiction, he'd be arrested for defying the Alaska court order. It's probable he wouldn't be released until he turned Tracie over to her grandparents."

"No!" Laura's hand flew to her throat. "Then I'll go without him."

At last Sandy looked at her. "Thank you for not pointing out I was aware all along I couldn't accompany you. Even when I first accepted this job."

"I could never be sorry that you came into my . . . our lives," she insisted. "And Tracie and Cristy, too, of course. I'm sure you had your reasons. I imagine the most important one was your intention to protect Tracie from those vile creatures I saw at the courthouse."

Sandy shoved his hands into his trouser pockets. "The Dyers aren't truly evil," he admitted. "After all, they're my wife's mother and father. If they'd been sensible, I would have let them see Tracie as often as they liked, but Elvina wanted to take complete control and cut me out of their life. They were too powerful for me to fight in Alaska, but thanks to David, they didn't get away with that here."

A green stab cut through Laura's heart at the mention of his wife, but she mentally chastised herself. "So all you have to do is stay out of Alaska. That's no problem. I'll take Pete with me for the race."

"That's exactly what we decided," Tom said. "I'm glad you agree. So as soon as he gets here today, Pete will start training along with the two of you. He'll use Sandy's dogs, so he can get used to them and them to him. We'll want Pete driving a team that can keep up with yours in the race, so he can stay with you. Sandy will work on training a team of the greener pups. However, in the Northshore Race, Sandy will want his own team, so Pete will drive the newer team for the experience."

Laura's heart clenched at the loss of her privacy with Sandy on the trail, but short of having him quit, she had no choice. She wondered if . . .

"I've also told your father I'll be training Pete along with the dogs, so he'll know all I do about racing and breeding. And that I won't be available for the shipping position next spring, either," Sandy told her in answer to the unformed thought in her mind. "My being honest with Tom now will give him plenty of time to look for someone else. I felt I owed him that, given his tolerance of my lying to him about being able to accomplish what he'd hired me into this position for."

"Given the choice you had," Tom said, "I would've done the same thing, Sandy. I've already told you I won't hold that against you. And Laura and I have until spring to change your mind."

"You'll both be wasting your time, Tom. But it's nice to know I can count on you for a reference."

Laura clenched and unclenched her hands in time with her heartbeat and remained silent. What could she say? All her hopes and dreams were crashing around her feet, and it was a wonder her father and Sandy didn't hear the noise.

It was her own fault. She'd picked and chosen what she wanted to believe from the things Sandy told her. He hadn't led her on even one tiny bit. All along he'd let her know there was no future for the two of them. That he had no intention of ever trying to build one. That he would take his lovely little daughter with him when he left.

Somehow she controlled her emotions and excused herself. "I'm going to check on breakfast." Thankfully, her father didn't remind her in front of Sandy that breakfast would probably be the same time it had been for twenty years—about fifteen minutes from now. She hurried toward the house and maintained that careful control while she removed her boots and coat before entering the kitchen.

"Katie," she said, "all of a sudden I feel terrible. Would you mind if I just had tea and toast in my room? I don't believe I'll even go on the run today, unless I feel better after I eat. If I don't come back down, would you tell Sandy for me?"

The old eyes apprised her astutely for a second, and Katie slowly nodded her head. "It's time for your woman thing, isn't it, dear?"

"Ummm, yes. I guess it is." Not for another day or so, she thought as she escaped up the stairs. And she knew Katie wouldn't use that excuse to Sandy. It would be much too embarrassing to even allude to. Katie was only giving her an out if she wanted to use it.

Stripping, she put her nightgown back on. She wasn't lying. She did feel as though dozens of horses' hooves had pounded over her. Tomorrow she would crawl out of bed again, a new day available to start her new life. A life without David and with the knowledge she would lose both Tracie and Sandy by spring. She needed today to come to terms with all of it. To banish any inkling of self pity.

Laura Goodman did not wallow in self pity!

And Laura didn't. At least not wallow. Well, at least not on the surface. The next morning she rose and dressed, assuring everyone who asked she'd only had a minor illness. She waited until Pete arrived before going out to the kennel, but that was the only concession she made to her self-consciousness around Sandy.

For a brief instant when she first saw him, she wanted to ask Pete to leave. Ask Sandy why he didn't care for her—what was wrong with her. Ask him if it would make a difference if she cut her hair or changed the color. If her resemblance to his wife drove him away. Ask him all the questions tumbling through her mind the previous day, as far away from answers now as they were then.

Ask him where he found the willpower to act like they

had never shared those passionate kisses or felt the need between them. If the one tentative conclusion she had reached was true or another uncertainty: Had she mistaken the feelings between them for love, the same way she mistook her friendship with David?

But Laura Goodman had her pride. Laura Goodman would survive this and the next time she would be older and wiser. She would be more careful and more capable. She could examine her feelings for the next man to come into her life with a more critical eye and with the lofty experience of two failed relationships behind her.

She would love a man who would give her children of her own, children who would never be taken away from her.

Shoving everything into a corner of her mind for now, she ordered herself to attend to business. The dark, lonely night would be soon enough to ponder it all again—to search for resolutions to unresolvable questions.

Sitting in the desk chair, she indicated for the men to join her. For the next half hour they went over the new plans and strategies as though this were the better plan all along. Normally she bantered with Pete, but today she kept her tone businesslike. Pete looked at her strangely a couple times, and she assumed he was trying to understand her change in attitude.

She could read Pete's confusion at least. Sandy spoke in the same businesslike manner as she did.

"Then you agree with me, Pete?" she said in conclusion, keeping her gaze on him and not asking Sandy for his opinion in something she didn't now consider him having any input into. "Buck is able to handle things full time here at the kennel, like he was doing before?"

"He seems to have learned his lesson," Pete replied. "And he's a damned good man with the dogs, as well as passable with the books. But you know he's planning on running in the Northshore Race, too, so we'll need someone here during those few days."

"Sandy can . . ."

"I'm entered in that race, too," Sandy broke in. "And I won't be running as trainer, either. I'll be competition for both of you, and we'll see how well you both handle that."

"One of my brothers needs work," Pete said. "I can vouch for him. He's dependable."

"Ask him if he's interested, will you?" Laura rose to her feet. "I'm going to take my ration pack into the house and freshen some of the stuff in it. I'll be ready to go out on the trail in about an hour."

"There's one more thing, Laura," Sandy said, halting her at the doorway.

She turned. "Yes?"

"The three of us will be camping overnight three days from now. I want to get the dogs back in shape first, but they should be ready by then. Pete and I mapped out a more rugged route than our usual runs, and we'll be out two nights. We'll spend these nights on the trail whether they're clear or stormy, so plan your clothing and supplies accordingly. I'll check both your packs before we leave, and I don't want to find either one of you missing something important."

"If I am, I'm sure you'll remind me of it." Laura deliberately walked over to the desk again and leafed through the calendar. "No, those nights won't work," she told him as though he'd asked her opinion rather than stated an already-decided conclusion to her. "The day you want to leave is New Year's Day, and I'll have been at the celebration in town with Dav—with Father most of the night. It's an annual thing and we've already made plans to go."

She glanced at him briefly. "I'm sure Cristy will go with David, and I assume you know that you and Tracie are invited, too."

"I'd forgotten," he admitted curtly.

"We'll all be much too tired to make an extended run that day, even Pete, since he and his family always attend the party and dance. That is what I assume you have planned, isn't it? Something as close to a race as possible—with the two overnight stays on the trail?"

He nodded.

"I don't have anything else scheduled after the party, so

let's wait and start out the next day. I'll inform Father and Katie as to what days we'll be gone."

She continued as she walked away, "I assume you and Pete will inventory the supplies and make sure we have the proper food to take along. If you need anything from town, please put it on our bill at the general store, as usual."

Proud of herself for holding together, she didn't realize she'd forgotten to get her ration pack from the supply shelf until she reached the house. She knew the contents, though, and could carry replacements for the staler rations when she returned to the kennel.

She could also replenish her store of emotional fortitude—or guts, as Buck called it. All she needed was a few minutes of privacy again, away from those teal blue eyes, which were filled with unreadable shadows.

15

SANDY THOUGHT ONLY children anxious for Christmas to arrive X'ed off days on the calendar, but he stared at the one hanging in his kitchen the morning they were to begin their overnight trail run. So far, only three X's were marked, and he added a fourth one. He restrained himself from re-counting the days until the Northshore Race—thirteen—and the days after that until Laura would depart for Alaska and he could leave Grand Marais—thirty-four.

Hell, he didn't need to count the days. The numbers were ingrained in his mind like descending numbers on an upside down yardstick.

He'd pushed it a little when he told Laura and Tom he'd leave in the spring. Laura would head for Alaska the fifth of February, still the dead of winter in northern Minnesota. But she would need a week and a half of travel time—by rail across the States and then ship up the western coast. He'd warned them they should also plan for at least a week of training time in Alaska to familiarize themselves with the climate and terrain. The week-long race would be run the end of February, and Laura would be back in Grand Marais sometime the second or third week in March.

Once she was gone, though, he would have some leeway to make his own plans and be gone before she returned. A lot depended on whether or not he won the Northshore Race, or at least placed in it. He'd managed to save some money from his wages, but with the daily needs of his family, not to mention Christmas, it wasn't nearly enough to make a move—unless he already had another job waiting for him.

He had, however, subscribed to a couple newspapers and even a dog breeder's magazine, which had employment ads in them, on their layover in Duluth. Already, he'd sent out several letters.

"Good morning, Sandy. You're up even earlier than usual." Cristy poured herself a cup of coffee at the stove before sitting at the table and yawning hugely. "For some reason I woke up early, too. Maybe because I knew you were leaving for three days today."

"I hope you manage to feed Tracie something that isn't burned during that time," he teased lightly. "Does David know you can't cook?"

"I told him, so there!" Childishly, she stuck out her tongue at him, reminding him of his daughter. Their features did resemble each other, although both he and Cristy had blond hair.

"And he told me that Laura can't cook, either," Cristy continued saucily. "He'd already known if he married Laura, he'd have to hire a cook unless he wanted to eat out every night."

Sandy refilled his own coffee cup and joined her at the table. "You handle talking about David's former fiancée very easily."

She shrugged. "It happened. He was engaged to her, and Laura is a very good friend of mine. David's, too. Living in Grand Marais, we'll be seeing a lot of her, and I don't want any uneasiness between us."

When he didn't respond, she said, "We've set our

wedding date for February fourth, the day before Laura leaves for Alaska. I want her to be in my wedding. And I want to be married to David before you leave. I'll spend a lot of time getting David's house in town ready for us to live in, but I'll keep Tracie with me during the day, so don't worry a bit about her when you're on the trail with Pete and Laura."

"I don't worry when she's with you, Cristy. I tease you, but you know I trust you."

"I know. And Sandy, I don't want you to take this the wrong way." He gave her a cautious look, and she went on, "If you need to leave Tracie with me for a few days or weeks, until you find another job, I want you to know she's welcome."

"Thank you," he said in a growl. "But Tracie goes with me."

Taking a deep breath, Cristy gazed at him sternly. "I promised myself I'd stay out of your business, Sandy, but if a sister can't tell a brother when he's being an asshole, who can?"

"Cristy, watch your damned language," was all he could think of to say. He stood, preparing to go over to the kennel.

"Sit down, Sandy," Cristy ordered

Instead he leaned on the table. "Look, little sister. Just because you're getting married doesn't make you a full-grown adult with the experience behind you to give out advice to other people. I—"

"*You*," Cristy said, standing up to face him, "are throwing away the best thing that ever happened to you since Colleen died. But that's something you'll have to find out for yourself. And your decision to move is affecting more than just your own life—your own feelings. I can't just stand by and watch you uproot Tracie again and take her off somewhere in the wilderness to grow up with a pack of dogs and mushers! She's much too loving a child and enjoys being with people too much for you to force her into that sort of life."

Sandy sat down with a hard jar. "I'm not . . . I mean . . . Cristy, you don't know what you're saying."

"I think I do. And so do you, if you'll quit being so darned self-involved and look around you. You're hurting people, Sandy, by keeping yourself so closed off and now planning to drag Tracie off to heaven-knows-where and lock her up with you in your loneliness. I can't stop you, but I can't let it happen without trying to make you listen to me and see what you're doing."

"What the hell am I supposed to do then?" Sandy shouted, and Cristy flinched. "Lose my daughter, like I've lost everything else in my life—my wife, my home, my money? Leave Tracie here with you to raise, or give her to her grandparents?" Shoving his chair back violently, he stood and flung his coffee cup across the kitchen. It shattered on the wall.

Before Cristy could gather her wits and overcome the fear he saw in her eyes, Sandy stomped from the kitchen to the mud porch. Jamming his feet into his boots, he wrenched the door open and went out, pulling on his coat and cap as he walked.

"No, Sandy," Cristy said into the silence left behind. She could feel the smile on her face. "You're supposed to start having emotions again, like you just did. You're supposed to start feeling again instead of being the ice man you've been since you picked me up in Washington."

She went out on the mud porch for the broom and dustpan, glancing through the window. Sandy strode angrily across the snow-covered yard toward the kennel. "You're supposed to turn back into the fun-loving, wonderful brother I knew growing up. Laura got you started on that, but you froze over again. I hope Laura can find the fortitude somewhere to keep trying—and see that the fissures she initiated aren't completely closed up again."

Shivering, she carried the broom and dustpan back into the kitchen and shut the door. She cleaned up the mess from the cup without anger at her brother, then poured herself a fresh cup of coffee and took it to the writing desk in the living room to examine the list of things to do before her wedding.

Tears filled her eyes, blurring the list, when she recalled

Sandy's face the previous evening when he came in and found her working on the list. She'd known immediately he would begin worrying about the cost of the wedding and hastily assured him that she had enough money from her paintings to pay for the small ceremony she and David planned.

Still she could see the hurt in his eyes—the damage to his pride over not being able to give her a huge wedding.

"Pride is a good thing at times, brother," she whispered. "But not when you make it as important as it seems to be in your life. When you let it affect other people's lives in a negative way. And as much as I like Laura, she has a touch of willfulness, which I suppose comes from being a little bit spoiled. I wonder if your two lives can ever merge? If Laura can understand all the heartache you've gone through, which makes you cling so desperately to the pride you have left? She's had it so easy in her life."

Pulling her handkerchief from her robe pocket, Cristy wiped her eyes. Sandy could shout at her all he wanted and demand she keep her nose out of his business a million times. Perhaps it was being so happy herself that made her want the people she loved to be happy, also. Whatever it was, she had no intentions of letting her brother wallow in his loneliness if she could help it.

"Pride's a lonely bedfellow," she quoted to herself.

She could at least pretend to be miserable, Sandy thought to himself the second night on the trail.

The blizzard had hit an hour earlier, although they'd had plenty of warning when the sky started clouding over that afternoon. The storm's fierceness made it very probable they'd have to spend an additional night on the trail, but he'd told Tom that he was packing plenty of supplies for just such a contingency. Only if they failed to return the day after the blizzard stopped would a search be launched.

Laura and Pete didn't seem to care one way or the other whether their trip ended tomorrow or the day after. He thought he'd have to preach about the need for them to form a bond and be able to trust each other fully on the trail, forgetting Laura and Pete had a firm friendship already. Had he a right, he might even find himself jealous of their camaraderie and easiness with each other.

They unloaded their sleds and pitched the tent together, leaving Sandy to his own devices, as he had insisted. He wanted them to form the habit of being partners and trailmates immediately and hadn't realized they intended to have a rollicking good time doing the necessary chores. Yet he should have. They enjoyed themselves together at the kennel, and Laura always loved being on the trail. Pete shared her high spirits, as he did at the kennel when they bantered back and forth over the bookwork or whose turn it was to order supplies.

When it had been only Laura and him, she tried to bring him out of his moroseness at times. Now, with Pete to banter with, she had no reason to tolerate his moodiness or grumpiness. In fact, she barely acknowledged his presence unless he spoke to her directly.

The hell with it. He had what he wanted, didn't he? Pete was a suitable partner to watch over Laura if she continued with this asinine insistence of running in a dangerous Alaskan race. Laura was extremely proficient on the trail, doing her share of the chores as though she'd been doing that all her life. In no time at all, and despite high winds and blowing snow, all three of them were inside the tent warmed by a kerosene heater, which also served as a stove. The two of them dug into the food packs, arguing over what to fix for supper.

"You know, Pete," Laura said. "Before we start out for Alaska, I think we should sit down and decide what our meals will be on the trail."

"Well, if you'd eat decent, stick-to-you food instead of stuff your stomach will forget you even fed it a half hour after you eat, we'd get along better. I'm not about to go hungry when I'm pushing myself and my dogs to make a hundred miles a day."

"He's right, Laura," Sandy put in. "I know women are told from the time they're born they need to watch their figures, but on the trail, you use up ten times as much energy as you do off the trail. You need a meat and potatoes diet, as well as lots of sweets for energy."

"Sweets I can handle," Laura said with a laugh, the first time she had said anything even halfway pleasant to him in days. "I only wish Pete's idea of what to fix on his day to cook wasn't dumping a bunch of odds and ends in the pot and seeing what it tastes like when it's done. I prefer eating my peaches separate from my potatoes."

"Hey," Pete said. "They looked like carrots. I thought I was making stew. I can't help it if frozen peaches look the same as frozen carrots."

"That's what we have a lantern in here for, dummy." Laura flipped a hand towel at Pete, and he caught the end of it, jerking it from her with an unexpected twist.

"It all gets mixed up in your stomach anyway," he said with a chuckle.

"I'd prefer to actually wait until it gets to my stomach to mix it up. Now, it's my turn tonight, so you don't have anything to say about what I choose."

Bending her head, she dug in the pack again, the long braid she'd taken to wearing falling over her shoulder and gleaming in the lantern light. Sandy knew the weather had turned too frigid for her to leave her hood back, but he missed seeing the brilliant fire of her tresses streaming behind her. Even the braid gleamed, however, and he'd touched her hair enough times to remember how it caressed a man's hand.

"Oh, no," Pete grumbled. "Laura, if you pack any turkey when we go to Alaska, I'm going to feed it to the dogs! I guess Katie must have over-estimated what size turkey to cook for Christmas this year, because we've had some sort of turkey almost every day for lunch at Ladyslipper Landing. And my wife made turkey soup, turkey sandwiches—and darn it! She even cut up turkey and put it in my eggs one morning! I'm gonna start gobbling the next time I even smell turkey!"

Laura sniffed at him. "Well, gobble, gobble, because I happen to like turkey."

"It's not filling enough for a trail run," Pete told her.

"Goose might be, since it's got a lot of good fat on it, but turkey's too lean."

"Yuk. I hate goose. But all right, no turkey for the Alaska run," Laura conceded. "I'd already made up my mind that's what we'd have tonight, though, and since you cooked last night—"

"From what I've heard," Pete broke in, "what you do might not be called cooking." He glanced over at Sandy. "I believe you've overlooked one portion of her training, Sandy. I'm going to step in here and say Laura needs to find enough time to take a few cooking lessons from Katie before we leave—if nothing more than at least how much salt to put in something."

Sandy nodded, recalling what Cristy had told him about David planning to hire a cook so Laura wouldn't have to bother with that chore. One more thing to add to his list of reasons the distance between them was unbreachable. He could never afford a cook, although when he left Ladyslipper Landing with Tracie, he would have to find some way to hire a woman to take care of her while he worked.

Since Pete had his attention on him, it was Sandy who noticed Laura reach toward the pot of now boiling water. His eyes must have flickered, because Pete jerked his head around and grabbed for Laura's hand, shouting a playful "no!" at her. She dropped the frozen piece of turkey breast into the water before he could stop her, then pulled the salt shaker from behind her back. Pete had more success with that. He grabbed it from her and carefully measured in a small palmful of salt.

"Did you see how much I put in there?" he asked. "That'll be enough for the potatoes and anything else, too, so don't add any more."

"Yes, boss," Laura said with a chuckle.

Sandy stood up from his camp stool. "I'm going out to check on the dogs."

Neither Pete nor Laura admonished him to stay out of the blowing cold, he thought as he ducked out the tent flap. Of course, he probably would have snapped either one of their heads off, telling them he didn't need their concern. Or maybe they wondered why he even bothered going out, given the violent weather and the knowledge the dogs were no doubt already curled into warm balls, waiting out the storm while snow piled over them and insulated them.

Laura accepted spending the night together in the confines of the tent without any problem the previous evening. *He* had slept barely two hours. Her scent filled the tent, and her even breathing invaded his senses.

Hell, he couldn't see two feet in front of him, and he had better judgment than to try to find the dogs in this whiteout. Still it was better than sitting in there feeling lonely even with two other people within touching distance. Out here, the loneliness had substance.

Above the wind Laura's gay laughter sounded, followed by Pete's rumbled response. Walking over to one of the sleds, Sandy sat on it, facing away from the wind and letting its roar drown out the sounds inside the tent. How could he stand being inside that tent for another entire day and night with Laura so near yet so absolutely untouchable? How could he handle the thirty-three days left until she left for Alaska?

He could go ahead and leave now, he supposed, or at least right after the Northshore Race. But if he heard later that Laura and Pete had made some stupid mistake in the Alaska race that caused either one of them to be injured—or killed—he wouldn't be able to live with himself. Though they appeared to be ready for the race now, they might get lax if he weren't around to keep them in training. He alone knew a person was never totally prepared for the rigors of an Alaska race—that only the actual event would give you the experience to build on the next time you undertook one of those races.

The wind heightened further, but Sandy gritted his teeth, fighting the cold. As he had to do every time Laura's close proximity threatened to make him throw caution to hell and forget the consequences, he reiterated why he could never have her.

He could never give her a comfortable life, as she had now. Maybe he could build up financial security again.

Maybe in another fifteen years, the same length of time it had taken him to make not a fortune, but the secure financial base George Dyer had cheated him out of. He'd barely salvaged his pride from the mess in Alaska, and despite what Cristy appeared to feel, Sandy couldn't swallow it and become what a lot of people might consider a fortune hunter. He couldn't court Laura and be forced to depend on her father's good will in order to give her a prosperous lifestyle if they married.

He couldn't bring himself to accept the shipping position Tom Goodman offered, either. He couldn't stand to remain in Grand Marais and try to rebuild his finances, because it would take way too long to get the security he'd had before. His pride wouldn't allow him to offer Laura less, and she'd surely find someone else in the meantime. His heart wouldn't allow him to live where he could constantly see her after she became another man's wife.

Finally knowing he would risk frostbite if he stayed out any longer, Sandy re-entered the tent. The meal still wasn't ready, and he sat on his camp stool and pulled out a book he'd had the foresight to bring with him. He read the same page ten times before he felt he understood it well enough to turn to the next.

16

At LEAST THEY had a pretty day for the start of the Northshore Race. Laura gazed at the ice-blue sky with powder puff clouds, which overlay the gay crowd and busy streets of town. Another wicked storm had hit in the middle of the week, leaving high drifts behind, but the weather forecasters around the potbelly stove in the general store seemed in agreement the clear, frigid weather would hold for the race. According to the rumors Buck duly reported to Laura, the good weather had some of the mushers grumbling. They'd hoped bad weather would make Laura shake her pretty little female head and sit the race out. Those hopes came from out-of-towners, Buck had said loyally— not locals who knew Laura's grit and determination.

Plenty of out-of-towners were here. She'd perused the entry list the day before, finding teams from Grand Portage, Thunder Bay, and other parts of Canada. The thousand dollar prize money was more than a lot of these old trappers would earn in their entire lives, and for a while Laura felt guilty about the certainty she would be the one walking—no, mushing—away from the race with the money. Then she decided she would be foolish to pass up this opportunity for race experience, not that Sandy would allow her to do so anyway. She would donate the prize money to one of the charities in town.

She'd done everything except carry around a ten-foot pole to measure how far to keep away from Sandy the past two or three weeks. Her heart hadn't healed at all, but perhaps she could keep it from shattering anymore. Mostly she just gritted her teeth and looked on Sandy as any other man of her acquaintance.

Huh! Tried to, anyway. On the trail she avoided his teal blue eyes and focused everywhere except on his bundled-up figure. She noticed a lot of things she never had before, like how bright the black-capped chickadee's feathers looked against the snow. Pete didn't seem interested in discussing her new observations. The only times he paid attention were when they found game trails, which he could tell his brothers about in order for them to check out new trapping grounds.

With practice she maintained a façade around Sandy, which she thought feigned appropriate lack of interest in anything other than his knowledge of sled dog racing. They talked without bristling or snapping at each other—as long as she remembered the ten-foot-pole distance she set for herself. Any closer, and those silken strands of yearning were almost inescapable.

It was useless to try to distance herself from Tracie. She'd just have to endure that horrible wrench when Sandy took her away. It would probably devastate Katie, too. Although the elderly woman had more experience than Laura in letting go of loved ones, Laura doubted the pain was less severe because you had experienced it before.

Amid clusters of people and bright, multi-colored flags the Commissioners had used to decorate the streets, the tiny object of her thoughts raced up to Laura now. Laura held out her arms, and Tracie leapt into her embrace.

"I told's Daddy I hads to come and wish you luck, too,

Miss Laura. And Aunt Cristy and David are comin' over here." She shook her head. "We's all had an awful time."

"What sort of awful time?" Laura said with a growl and a mock-fierce face. "Who's giving you an awful time? I'll go awful them right back!"

Tracie giggled wildly. "You'd have to awful you and Daddy, 'cause it's you two givin' us the awful. We wants both of you to win the race. Oh, and Mr. Buck, too. And Pete. But it just can'ts be, can it?"

Laura gently pinched Tracie's pert nose between her thumb and forefinger. "No, it can'ts, darling. Unless there's a four-way tie, and I've never heard of one of those in a race. There *might* be a two-way tie, though."

"That don't help none." Tracie shook her head. "I can count, you know—all the way up to a hundred. A two-way tie'd still leave out two persons." She sighed dramatically. "I guess we's will just have to be happy with whoever wins."

"Guess so, darling. Oh, I see David and Cristy coming. Where's your daddy? He needs to line up for the start of the race."

"He's comin', too. He don'ts like to put his dogs on the trail cold." She nodded in satisfaction at this exclusive knowledge of her father's race plans. "He gives them a little run first, then brings them to the startin' place right a'fore time for the gun to go off."

"I'd think that would tire them right from the first," Laura mused.

"No, it don'ts. He just takes them 'round the block, so they gets the k . . . kinks outta their legs."

"I see." She smiled at David and Cristy as they approached. "Hello. Here to congratulate the winner before she even starts the race?"

"Not unless you're referring to this cute little button," David said, chucking Tracie under the chin. "If she got on a sled and started driving a team to Duluth, I'll bet every one of these old mushers would pull over to the side and let her go. Then their eyes would be frozen with tears and they'd never get them open in time to catch her."

"Why, David, how profound," Cristy said with a laugh. "Maybe you're not such a stodgy old lawyer after all."

Laura tilted her head as she watched them, waiting for a stab of jealousy. None came, only a warm feeling of happiness for the two of them. She truly wished them well, and looked forward to having Cristy around for a friend.

"It's almost starting time," David said, reaching for Tracie. "Come here, Button. Let's let Laura get ready."

Tracie hugger her neck and whispered "good luck" before she went into David's arms, and Laura gave her a wink. As the other teams headed to the starting line, she checked her harness. Buck and Pete halted their teams on either side of her, and her father pushed through the crowd to her.

"I've turned the starting procedure over to Dick Berglind," he told her. "Didn't want to be accused of bias." Slipping an arm around her waist, he hugged her. "Good luck, darling. And please, be careful."

"You've got Buck, Pete and Sandy watching out for me, Father," she said with a laugh. "How could I be anything else?"

"Things can happen," he warned. "Just promise me."

"I promise, Daddy," she whispered, standing on tiptoe to kiss him on the cheek.

"Listen up, everyone!" Dick Berglind shouted through a bull horn, and the crowd quieted at his command. "We're drawing the numbers for the order of the race starts now. The teams will leave thirty seconds apart, and that time will be noted on Erik's high dollar stopwatch. So anyone with a gripe, see Erik after the race. The same staggered departure times will be used tomorrow morning, after the layover at the way station, but they'll depend on the time lags between the arrivals of the teams off the trail tonight. All of you get there as soon as you can!"

Only a few chuckles sounded in the strained and expectant atmosphere. Laura had counted twenty entrants in the race, and it took Dick fifteen minutes to draw the numbers and line the teams up. She hadn't even realized she'd been searching for Sandy until he emerged from the crowd and pulled his team into the seventh position. Her own name came up for eighth, and she pulled in behind him, a good dozen feet separating them as John Beargrease indicated. The proud Ojibwa had been awarded the important position as starter's helper in honor of his work in planning the race route, and despite her nervousness she remembered to thank him. She received a secretive wink in return.

"My friend Pete Tallwolf tells me the Ladyslipper Landing team is the one to beat," he said in a low voice. When she smiled back at him, he continued, "But there are three teams from there running in the race, counting Buck's team, which might be part of your kennel. Pete didn't say which one he meant."

Laura laughed with him, and after he walked away she watched Sandy check his dogs' harness for a few minutes, vaguely aware of hearing Buck draw number ten and Pete, eleven. Evidently satisfied with his team's readiness, Sandy walked back to her sled.

"Nervous?" he asked without a greeting.

"Very," she admitted. "It's going to be extremely different competing against these strangers instead of in a friendly run against you and Pete or Buck."

He nodded agreement. "The first thing is your safety," he reminded her, as he had at least a dozen times the past week. "Don't take any chances."

"I understand," she said saucily. "If I die in this race, I won't have another race to prove myself in."

A brief haggard look crossed Sandy's face, leaving his eyes dark and shadowy even when he smoothed his face into stoniness. "You could end up injured to the point where it would take you too long to heal in time to make the Alaska race."

She shrugged. "Since I'm not getting married this summer, there's no reason I couldn't still shoot for the following year's race. I heard you telling Father just a day or so ago that Pete's turning into a very capable trainer."

"You be careful, damn it!" he snarled. Dropping his chin on his chest, he closed his eyes. When he looked back at her, he said "Please" in a softer voice. Then he stomped back over to his team and rechecked the harness, which she had no doubt was in the exact same shape as five minutes previously.

Dick Berglind called number twenty and the name of the musher, and Laura walked up to Blancheur. Squatting beside him, she stroked his head. "I told everyone I wanted them to stay back during the start, Blancheur. I didn't want them distracting you and me."

He licked her face, body quivering as though he caught her tenseness and realized this was no regular run. Sandy reminded her it was Blancheur's first race, too, and to keep an eye on him so he wouldn't get distracted by the strange teams. His guidance would decide the actions of the rest of the team.

"We've got a good start position," she told him. "The first two or three teams out will have problems breaking through the loose snow. I imagine the lead teams will change several times, and we'll probably have plenty of chances ourselves to break trail. But one thing I like about you Siberian huskies is that you're lighter than the malamutes. If we find some windswept crusts of snow, we can probably cut off some distance by heading out over them. The malamutes will break through easier than you dogs will."

She'd proven that time and time again on her training runs, and Sandy had been forced to admit her choice of huskies was valid. She also had the lightest sled possible, made from cured birch and cedar, and with her slight weight, compared to the muscular trappers on the other sleds, her team could fly across the snow.

There were few rules in this free-for-all race, as Sandy had indicated there were in the one in Alaska. It was every man—or woman, as the case might be—for himself. But anyone proven to have deliberately sabotaged or injured another driver or team would be dealt with under the same conditions as though a crime had been committed.

Suddenly Laura realized the team ahead of Sandy had just pulled out. Concerned, excited and tense, she hadn't even heard the starter's pistol. She only had sixty seconds before she would be on the trail herself, pitted against nineteen men of varying physiques and dispositions. Hurrying back to her snow anchor, she stood ready for her own name to be called. First John Beargrease moved into position by Sandy's sled, with Erik holding his stopwatch beside him.

She fiercely admonished herself when she realized she was hoping Sandy would turn around and give her one last look. Shoot, they'd be passing each other closely on the trail, hopefully with her passing him and not relinquishing the lead—at least once they got near the end of the race.

John Beargrease raised the pistol in the air, and Sandy turned. He gave her a thumb's up and a tentative smile. She responded with an excited wave, calling "good luck" over the pounding in her heart. He nodded and the pistol cracked. Sandy's dogs were off in a beautiful start, and John and Erik moved to her sled.

Glancing briefly to the side, Laura saw her father, Cristy, and David and Tracie all trying to be very quiet and not distract her. The hell with it. She waved wildly at them, then jerked her snow anchor free and laid it on the sled. When the pistol cracked for her, she called a gay "Mush! Mush!" to Blancheur and they were off.

The first couple miles were fairly easy going, since the lead teams had broken trail. But, as she suspected, those teams soon tired and other teams were forced to take over while the initial teams rested. The first leaders would be back in contention soon, however, after restoring their strength by travelling at an easier pace.

The word from Duluth was a clear trail for the last forty miles of the race, since the blizzard hadn't reached that far and they'd only had a few flurries the past couple weeks. Today would be rough going, but tomorrow, on the easier path, would weed out the qualified teams and skilled drivers from the lesser ones. The competition would become fiercer, she reminded herself.

All too soon, she passed Sandy, who waved her on with a laugh.

"Your turn," he called. "Give us a path to travel on!"

She saluted him and went on by. Having to bound through the loose snow to break a trail for his teammates, Blancheur immediately slowed. A good foot and a half of loose snow covered the trail, the depth a distinct drawback to the huskies. Their smaller stature made it harder going than for the larger malamutes, and Laura quickly re-thought her race plan. She would take her turn breaking trail, of course. If not, she would risk antagonizing the rest of the mushers for not pulling her share of the load.

Yet she could drop back among the laggers, if she wished, feigning lack of endurance to stay in front. That would give her fewer times to find herself in the lead and make less demands on her dogs. Tomorrow, on the easier trail and with her lighter dogs, she could take the lead and maintain it.

She only had a slight qualm about the deceptiveness of that ploy, because there wasn't a doubt in her mind it was something every *man* in the race would employ if given the opportunity or the aptitude. She'd planned on winning by cutting off distances whenever possible, but this new scheme would give her both that opportunity and another advantage. Her dogs would be fresher and faster tomorrow if they endured less trail-breaking labor today.

An unfamiliar team took over the lead when Laura pulled to the side, and she let several more teams pass before mushing back onto the trail. Pete waved at her, and she gave him a cocky smile. Buck, though, avoided her gaze, just barely nodding at her. She put his strange action down to concentration on the race and forgot about it.

There were no requirements as to when anyone should stop and eat or feed their dogs. Any musher with any sense knew the dogs were of primary importance, and those who didn't wouldn't last the race. Laura fed her dogs lightly that morning, very early, so they wouldn't be running with full stomachs. The slow pace was good in another way, since she could pull over for at least a few minutes and give them another snack at some point, while she grabbed a bite herself.

Katie's contribution had been a huge lunch. Not having the heart to tell the elderly lady she couldn't weigh her sled down with enough food to feed her for a week, Laura left most of it in the kennel before she headed into town. She'd stuffed a couple sandwiches inside her coat so they wouldn't freeze and put her supper in her pack to eat over a fire at the waystation this evening.

After a while, the slow pace also gave Laura an unanticipated problem—boredom. To her left stretched the huge lake, which she never tired of watching, but the underbrush and trees cut off her view. The dogteams, many of them strangers to one another, meant there would be no wildlife, since they barked at each other and stretched their drivers' attempts at control time and time again. On the training runs her own dogs ran almost silently, as did the teams they ran with. Such was not the case in a race, she learned.

She also learned very quickly that boredom led to complacency. Lucky for her and her dogs, she learned her lesson as a bystander, not the musher involved.

Hearing shouts up ahead, Laura's heart pounded in fear. A moment ago she'd noticed David pull up near the lead when they crossed a wide, flat expanse. Now they were in thick trees, and she couldn't see what was happening.

Cobwebs fleeing from her mind, she shouted at her dogs to run faster.

When she recognized Sandy's jacket and hat where he and the dogs were pulled off the trail, she sighed in relief. The teams ahead of her kept right on going, but she joined Sandy. The teams behind her, except for Pete, ignored them and kept moving.

Sandy turned and saw her. "Go on, Laura," he called. "There's nothing you can do here."

Disregarding his order, she hurried over to where he stood, halting abruptly when she realized they were on the edge of a cliff. Tracks from a team led over the bank.

"Oh, no," she breathed. "Is he . . . who is it?"

"One of the Canadian drivers," Pete told her as he stared downward. "He's not hurt, but I think a couple of his dogs are—"

A gun shot sounded, and Laura clapped a hand to her mouth. A second shot rang out. She flinched and blinked away tears as the sounds reverberated through the huge trees. Suddenly a tender hand touched her shoulder and she turned to bury her face in Pete's chest.

But it wasn't Pete. She knew the moment the arms went around her and tightened to hold her close. As much as she wanted to linger in Sandy's embrace, she knew she had to keep her grit. Straightening, she stepped back.

"I'm all right. Can I do anything to help here?"

"No," Sandy said. "And neither can we, since he's not hurt. He'll get up here himself, and we need to get back on the trail. The order we arrive at the waystation determines the order we'll leave in the morning."

"I know," Laura said. "But I think I'll take this opportunity to give my dogs a little food. It's almost noon."

"No, you won't," Sandy said flatly. "I'm not ready to stop yet, and you're not staying behind here."

She glared at him defiantly. "I thought you told me that I'd be making my own decisions in this race. That you'd tell me what I did wrong afterwards. *If* I do anything wrong."

"Yeah, well that only goes if I see you making decisions not reflecting on my obligation to Tom to keep you safe. If you're foolish enough to do things that might cost you the race but still leave you uninjured, I'll keep quiet."

She pulled in a breath, preparatory to telling him off again, but he continued, "Surely you're not too wrapped up in winning this race to realize we don't know that man down there. And to have forgotten the fact you're a woman, which will have its own disadvantages, like we discussed and you promised to take into consideration. It's not a good idea for him to find you alone on the trail when he gets back up here. He might decide there's something he wants worse than winning the race."

Her anger made her lash out at him in retaliation without considering her words. "Oh, you mean he might decide to rape me as a consolation for losing his dogs and having no chance now of winning with a short team?"

Sandy dragged a hand across his face, then shook his head. The instant he started to speak again, Pete stepped over to them.

"I'm getting a little sick of this," he said. "At first it was interesting to listen to the two of you go at each other. Now we're in the middle of a race, and we ought to be helping each other out and keeping an eye on one another. So how 'bout we get the hell back on the trail and on our way to Duluth? You two can snap at each other after the race."

Chagrin replaced her dissipating anger, and Laura ducked her head. "I'm sorry, Pete, you're right." She looked up at Sandy. "I apologize. And I'll wait until you decide it's safe for us to stop and eat."

She headed back to her sled without waiting for his response.

Sandy stood there alone after both Pete and Laura disappeared down the trail. Below, he could hear the Canadian cursing as he unharnessed his dogs and started to lead the ones he had left back up the cliff. From his study of the cliff earlier, Sandy knew it was climbable. It would take the Canadian some time, however, since he'd have to crisscross back and forth rather than climb straight up. Once successful, he could haul his sled up with the rope he'd probably already fastened to it. Most mushers went over at least one cliff in their lives, and those who survived knew the drill in order to get back on the trail.

He needed to do that himself—get back on the trail. Yet the scent and feel of Laura lingered in his senses. When those shots had been fired he'd felt her pain as his own. Even knowing the dogs had to be destroyed to end their suffering didn't help alleviate the agony he knew Laura experienced. Her pain had stabbed straight into his heart.

Yet, like his usual jackass self, he'd protected himself from his feeling by demeaning her—scolding her. Even snarling at her. It didn't help at all to know he couldn't think of any other way to handle his feelings. The X's on his calendar weren't adding up fast enough.

He fisted his hands, then let fly at a tree trunk. Damn it! What was really bothering him was those goddamned X's were adding up too damned fast! Each one of them meant one day less he had left to be around Laura. Hear her voice. Get close enough for one more touch. Soon all that he had left would be a memory. A memory he could take out and brush off some day in the far distant, lonely future.

The far distant, lonely future when Tracie would have found someone to share her life with, and he might still be worrying from one day to the next whether he would have enough money to feed his dogs. And when Laura would have found a man who could give her the luxuries she expected and the love she deserved.

Hell, if love were the only thing necessary for happiness, he could give her plenty of that. He didn't remember which desolate night he'd come to terms with his love for her, but it had been after their overnights on the trail. Try as he might, he couldn't deny his jealousy over her easiness with Pete, even though the other man was married. Hell, he could admit Laura and Pete's relationship was no more than a deep friendship, but he was jealous of that, too. He couldn't even have a friendship with Laura, since he needed to hold back his admission of love for her.

The best thing he could do for her would be to get the hell out of her life. Sure, there was something between them, which could possibly grow stronger. But it would also quickly disintegrate if he were forced to accept her father's charity in order to give Laura the comfortable life she deserved. He would resent her, and she in turn would come to hate him.

Love wasn't everything. After all two of the insurmountable barriers between them had already fallen. She'd walked away from her engagement to David, and the judge at the court hearing assured him that he wouldn't be considered a criminal as long as he stayed out of Alaska. He didn't have to consider himself on the run any longer to keep Tracie from being taken from him.

His shattered career and loss of everything he'd ever worked for remained the biggest obstacle, and one he could never overcome in the foreseeable future. George Dyer had used forged documents to strip him of his financial security, and Sandy had no recourse against the man's heavy influence in Juneau. It had taken Sandy fifteen years to build that security.

If he still had the money George Dyer stole from him to offer Laura, he would gladly pursue her heart. However, he would never offer her less than she had now—less than he had been able to offer Colleen.

Keever growled, and Sandy glanced up to see the Canadian a few dozen yards away, leading his team over the edge of the cliff. Shaking off his thoughts, Sandy pulled his snow anchor free. The other teams would be far ahead by now, but none of them could get a huge lead in the deep snow.

"Kra!" he called, stepping onto the runners. He gave the dogs their head for the first time today, taking advantage of the newly packed trail. The wind whistled by him, and the trees closer to the trail blurred on the edges of his vision. Yet her name stayed safe inside his mind, the wind unable to blow it away.

17

As THE SUN was setting, Laura pulled into the waystation, and secured her dogs before checking in with the race officials to find out her position. She'd lost count of how many times the lead had changed and which teams were ahead of her—which behind. Except for Sandy. He was ahead of her.

"Your time puts you in tenth place right now, Miss Goodman," the official informed her. "That'll be your starting position in the morning."

"Then ten teams are still out?"

"Yeah, but here come several now."

A scattered group of six more teams arrived within seconds of each other, including Pete and Buck, and the officials carefully noted the times. Concerned for the missing teams, Laura cared for her dogs on instinct alone, staying aware of the conversation around her. Soon she realized the remaining teams were well overdue and the officials began commenting about heading out to check on them before total darkness fell.

The Canadian with the short team came in before a search could be organized, and when questioned, he said the last team he had passed was well over half an hour earlier. But he hadn't checked behind him to see how close the other team was travelling to his.

Another team appeared down the trail, but when it came in, a couple of the dogs left bloody paw prints in the snow. The officials pointed this out, and the musher shook his head.

"I took a shortcut back there across a lake. They must've cut their feet on some sharp ice."

"You can't run those dogs tomorrow," the official told him.

"I won't. I think too much of my dogs for that. Consider me withdrawn from the race. I'll head back to Grand Marais tomorrow instead, and carry them on the sled. Get Doc Sawbill to fix them up for me so I can get back home."

The official made a mark on the list in his hand.

The search team left a short while later, carrying lanterns on the sled. The next to the last missing team came in as Laura worked with Pete to set up the tent they would share. The official who stayed behind checked off the man's name, noted his time, then asked where he'd been.

"Just enjoyin' the run," the musher said, squirting a stream of tobacco into a nearby snow bank. "Shoot fire, I been almost last this here whole race, and I know I ain't a'gonna be anywheres near winnin'. Decided not to kill my dogs tryin', and rest up for the celebration party tomorrow night. I can get drunk just as well a loser as a winner."

"There's still one team out," the official said chuckling.

"Ole Sourdough's the only one I passed after my dogs got all wore out breaking trail," the musher said with a shrug. "But he shouldn't of been that far behind me."

Laura ate her supper—a healthy helping of Katie's stew—before the search team came back in, a second team following them. She could hear the man on the sled moaning in pain. Curses intermingled with the moans when the men who had brought him in carried him into the large tent occupied by the officials. As soon as she repacked her supplies, she walked over to see if she could help.

A scream split the air as she approached the officials' tent, and Sandy reached there the same moment she did.

"You don't need to go in there, Laura," he said quietly. "They've got plenty of help."

"Probably, but I'd feel better if I saw whether or not there was anything I could do."

He shrugged and held back the flap for her to enter first. She brushed by him, feeling the contact through the layers of clothing. He could have asked her how her day had gone, she thought with a mental pout. Then the musher screamed again, and she glanced over at him, paling. In the lantern light she could see the end of a bone sticking through the skin on the man's arm.

One of the officials looked up and saw her standing there. "There's no need for you to be here, Miss Goodman. Red's got a little medical knowledge and he'll patch him up until we can get him into Duluth tomorrow."

"What happened?" she murmured, aware with every inch of her body that Sandy had slipped a steadying arm around her waist when she gasped in horror at the sight of the bone.

"He tripped and fell on the trail," the official said. "Broke his arm, and strapped it to his chest himself. His dogs were bringing him in when we found him. We'll dose him with painkiller and keep him here on a cot tonight."

"Can't you set the arm?"

"Red's afraid to try. The break's too bad."

"Come on," Sandy said in her ear. "Let's get out of here."

Willingly she allowed him to guide her from the tent. She breathed in the icy air, and the roiling in her stomach calmed. Sandy led her over to a fallen tree trunk nearby and gently pushed her down on it.

"Sorry," she murmured, hunching her shoulders and curling her arms around herself. "Another failing of my being female, I guess."

"I've seen many men get shaky at a sight like that," he said, telling her that he understood her without further explanation. "Fact is, I doubt I'd have been any help in there without a half a bottle of whiskey in my belly first. And any whiskey tonight needs to be in that fellow's belly."

"Thanks, Sandy. I don't know if I could take your rubbing my nose in my being female and lacking a man's attributes to make it in a race right now."

"Oh, God, Laura. I don't mean to do that."

He sat beside her, throwing his head back and staring up at the black sky. She followed his gaze, scanning the clear, inky blackness studded with dagger-bright stars. Someone began playing a harmonica in one of the camps, and the slow, lazy tune kept time with a breeze playing through the towering tops of the pines. Far away a wolf howled several melancholy notes, which she recognized as a call to its lost mate.

"I only point out what you do wrong for your own safety, Laura," Sandy said insistently, keeping his gaze on the sky. "You know I still feel the same way. You've got no business going to Alaska. I doubt we finish up this race tomorrow without losing a couple more drivers and teams to something or the other, and this race is tame compared to the ten-day-long ones in Alaska."

"If I ever have children, I hope I train them differently than the way you're trying to train me." He stiffened, and she hastened to explain, "I don't mean that you haven't done a wonderful job with Tracie. But then—" She sighed. "—that's exactly what I do mean, I guess. In a way. I've listened to how you handle her, and you praise her when she does commendable things, discipline her when she does wrong. You've never said one nice thing about me or how well I've been learning from you. I have no idea—despite your insistence on how good a trainer you are—whether I've learned enough to hold my own in that race."

"You're very good, Laura," he said in a grudging voice. "Excellent, in fact." After a second's hesitation, he gave her praise that filled her with warmth. "I wouldn't hesitate to have you as a trail partner if I were running another Alaska race."

"Thank you. You don't know how much that means to me."

He glanced sideways. "Why do you want to do it? You don't need the money."

Shifting around on the log, she said, "How come you've never asked me that before? You've told me ten thousand reasons why I shouldn't go, but you've never asked me why I wanted to."

He waited a minute, then said, "Why do you want to do it, Laura? Is it because. . . ."

"Oh, poop!" she said. "There you go ruining it. You've already made up your own reasons, and you're ready to list them rather than being truly interested in my feelings."

"Poop?" he said with a chuckle. "Poop, Laura?"

The log quivered, and she realized he was shaking with silent laughter. The yearning to hear his full-fledged laughter once more filled her, and she stuck her face up close to his.

"Yes, poop, Sandy Montdulac! You told me once not to curse, and poop isn't cursing."

The log shook harder, and he snickered. "That sounds like something Tracie would try to get away with."

"Oh, she's got more imagination than that." Laura waved a hand, trying not to be too elated over his not drawing back from her. Instead, he kept his eyes trained on her face. She wished for a lantern, but she could imagine the blueness caressing her with warmth, rather than chill, for once.

"Tracie would say something like 'poop-de-doodle-do.'"

His guffaw rang like a clarion on the night air. She grinned, satisfied with herself, then joined him. The log shook a little harder, then an ominous crack sounded. The log broke, and she lurched into Sandy, tumbling them both to the ground before either of them could stop themselves.

She landed full length on him, amazed when he didn't immediately fling her away and scramble up. Instead, he laughed for another few seconds, wrapped his arms around her and asked, "Are you all right?"

She wasn't at all, but she had no idea how to explain the problem. The weeks of depriving herself of his touch all piled in on her senses and she couldn't move. Layers of heavy coats and shirts separated their upper bodies, and she knew he had to be wearing long underwear underneath his trousers, the same as her. Yet the barriers between them melted away so fast she listened to see if the snow around her was sizzling as it thawed. She recalled his body from the night in the kennel as clearly as though she hadn't ever stifled the memory.

"Laura?" he asked softly.

"No. No," she said. "I'm not all right."

He tightened his arms around her. "What's wrong? Where are you hurt?"

"It wasn't the fall, Sandy. I think you know that."

She pushed against his chest, embarrassed at what she'd said and determined not to make a further fool of herself. He'd made it as clear as a man could that he didn't want anything more to do with her than a trainer-trainee relationship, and her pride couldn't stand another shattering. But her body slid between his legs, and maybe Sandy didn't want her with his heart, but she'd bet his body sure would enjoy the chance to soothe the aching wetness flooding between her thighs.

She gasped in mortification mixed with need, the sound intermingled with a guttural groan from Sandy, which spread her ache upward, pebbling her breasts and trapping her breath in her chest. She dredged up the willpower to try to move away from him, only making it an inch or so before he grabbed her hips and held her in an iron grip.

"Don't! Ah, God, Laura, don't move. If you do. . . ."

She blinked in confusion. Of course she knew the problem. As soon as she'd begun her breeding program—long before she was ever involved with David—Katie had sat her down for a talk. The elderly woman had been frank, telling her if she planned on raising puppies, she needed to know the why and wherefores of how they would come about. And be aware of the lure to mate between animals—between a man and woman.

It's the strongest passion that God has given His cre-

ations, Laura, dear, she remembered Katie saying. *And it's the most beautiful one, because it creates life.*

A cloud drifted away from the moon, and a filter of light caressed Sandy's face. She almost laughed again; he didn't look as though what he was feeling was beautiful. Instead his lips were compressed, and his eyes tightly closed as though in pain. Just as quickly, the hint of laughter died, and a spiral of sensation curled from her core.

Scared of the spiking sensation, she broke his hold and surged to her feet. The muffled howl of agony from Sandy sounded as though he'd stepped on a hidden bear trap on a wilderness trail. Puzzled, she bent to rub her knee, which had come into contact with that hardness she was trying to escape, while Sandy curled on his side into a tight ball.

Suddenly another one of Katie's pieces of advice rang in her thoughts, and it dawned on her what had happened. *If a randy boy tries to touch you when you don't want him to, Laura, child, you ram that knee right here on him.* She'd used Laura's body for the demonstration, but her knee had hit the place Katie had meant on Sandy.

"Uh-oh." She didn't think it a good idea to stick around and try to explain it was an accident. Katie had also said something about how cold chilled a man's ardor. Maybe Sandy could roll over into the snow and get some relief.

18

PETE SNORED! OF all nights to enlighten her about that, he picked this one. Either that, or this was a new habit because Laura didn't remember him snoring on any of the training runs. Yet she'd been exhausted those nights, although she probably would have heard every tiny rasp if Sandy had snored. Today's journey hadn't been nearly as tiring as the training runs with Sandy, yet Pete didn't seem to have any trouble sleeping.

If she were a man, she could go over and crawl in with Sandy and Buck. She needed to get some sleep, but she couldn't get the picture of herself in between Sandy's legs out of her mind. If only the sensations she'd experienced would fade. The sensations might if the picture would pale, but each kept circling in her mind. Picture fired sensations. Sensations fired picture.

Sighing, she jerkily rolled to her other side, punching her small camping pillow with a fist. Somewhere near dawn she fell asleep, estimating the time because the tent lightened enough for her to make out the side walls.

And she overslept. She wrenched awake, feeling the cold in the tent from the missing camp stove Pete must have already packed. One of the rules, one of Sandy's, was that everyone was on their own as much as possible in a race. No one took care of anyone else's dogs. No one woke anyone else if they overslept. Scrambling from her sleeping bag, she jammed her feet into her boots and started out of the tent. She halted abruptly at the tent flap, hearing Sandy's voice clearly in her head, reminding her to protect herself from the cold as her first priority.

Trying to ignore the jittery tenseness of her muscles and the mental voice telling her to hurry, she clumped back to her sleeping bag and sat down. As she fastened her boots snugly, she could hear the sounds of the other mushers getting ready to start the race—the excited yips of the dogs, rattles of chains and gruff voices of the men.

The smell of coffee drifted to her, and her stomach growled. She would have no time to eat, but she'd packed some trail mix. The blend of honey, dried meat, nuts and raisins would have to do until they reached Duluth. The balance of the race today was less than half the distance from Grand Marais, and most of the mushers anticipated arriving early in the afternoon.

She raced out the tent flap this time, almost colliding with Pete. "What time is it?" she demanded.

"Ten minutes until race time," he said. "I did everything else, so you can take the tent down. The teams are already lining up."

"There's no rule about me having to take the tent with me," she said defiantly. "I'm running late, so it and the rest of the gear can stay here until I get back to pick it up! And if it's gone by then, whoever takes it is welcome to it."

Pete gave her an admiring wink. "Sounds like a decision a man would make. I'm going over to take my place in line."

"I'll be there as soon as I harness my team. I've got fifteen minutes yet, since I'm starting tenth."

She hurried to the area where she'd pegged her dogs, checking the sky as much as she could through the tall trees. That concentration, and her worry over how soon she could get to the starting line, kept her mind off what would happen the first time she ran into Sandy today. Almost. She kept wondering how long it took a man to recover from a kick like that.

Horrors. Would a kick like that do permanent damage? No, it couldn't. Since that protective move was common knowledge to be passed down among women, she imagined more than one man had suffered like that, then gone on to procreate. Besides, she'd watched some of the mating dances between her dogs get rather violent, and the stud still was anxious to cover the next bitch she put him to.

Her dogs whined and jerked against their chains, but she patted only Blancheur as she got to the sled. Fumbling with the rope on the feed sack, she finally got it open and hurriedly grabbed a few pieces of frozen fish. She'd give them a small portion of frozen fish this morning, then feed them a big meal when they hit Duluth. Within a minute all eleven of the dogs had their breakfast.

Laura threw back the fur covering on the rest of her sled, then cried out in anguish.

Her harness lay there cut into pieces. She picked up one portion of leather and stared at the clean slice. No doubt about it. Someone had deliberately slashed it apart with a knife. She gripped the leather in her mittened fist and slowly sank to the sled.

Who could have done this to her? She would report it to the race officials, but what good would that do? Extra harnesses were not among the emergency supplies the officials carried.

She tossed the harness down and bent her head, fighting tears. It shouldn't matter so much. She could race another time, and she didn't need the money. What hurt the most, though, was all the wasted time she had spent training both herself and her dogs. She'd had no idea what a big hole not finishing this race would leave in her life. How badly having her goal jerked out of her reach would devastate her.

"Laura, what's wrong?" Sandy came up to her and grabbed a piece of the harness beside her. "Who the hell did this?"

"Someone who obviously doesn't want me to win the race," she said sarcastically. "I'd think that would be clear."

"Go over to the officials' tent and come into Duluth with them," he ordered. "I'll stop by there on my way back to the starting point and tell them to expect you."

"Yes!" She stood, placing her hands on her hips. "You go on! You get back on the trail!"

He spread his hands out to his side. "Laura, there's nothing I can do. There's no sense in both of us being out of the race. It won't do your kennel's name any good if that happens, since our teams are supposed to be the top contenders."

She glared at him suspiciously. Sandy wouldn't sabotage her, would he? Why? In retaliation for what she did to him last night? She couldn't rationalize that. He might roar his anger and threaten her with dire possibilities he would never follow through on, but he wouldn't do something sneaky like this. Would he?

Biting her inside cheek, she told herself her suspicions were groundless. What did she expect him to do? Drop out of the race just because she couldn't finish? It wasn't as if there weren't plenty of people around to make sure she and her dogs got on into Duluth. That reason didn't make the idea of staying behind any more palatable, though.

The starter's voice, amplified by the bullhorn, called for any stragglers to line up, and Sandy's head swiveled toward the noise. He looked back at her, pain, uncertainty and indecisiveness in his eyes.

"Laura, I need to win this race," he said quietly. "For the money more than anything else. It's not just for me; it's for Tracie and her future. Things . . . things happened in Alaska that didn't come out at the hearing. If it weren't for Tracie, I'd stay here with you, and believe me, it's hurting me like hell to have to go on. But I have to decide."

A chorus of yaps from a team starting out onto the trail sounded, but Sandy kept his attention on her.

"If you were hurt—I'd never leave you. If I didn't have Tracie to think about—"

His concern over the tiny girl who also meant so much to Laura defused her anger. "Go, Sandy. Go. You'll miss your start."

He hesitated, then asked, "Laura, why do you want to run in the Alaskan race?"

She gave him a wobbly grin. She'd wanted so badly for him to ask her that question, for so long. "Because I have to," she murmured. "Because it's there."

"I understand," he breathed more than spoke, and she knew without a doubt he did. "I understand."

Cupping his hand behind her head, Sandy bent forward and kissed her cheek. The soft caress meant more than if he'd ravaged her mouth, and she blinked at the sudden renewed mist of tears in her eyes.

"Go," she ordered in a choked voice. "Win for Ladyslipper Landing. And win for yourself."

"Promise me you'll head straight over to the officials' tent."

She nodded. "Go."

"And save me a dance at the victory celebration tonight."

"One," she promised. "Now, go!"

After a deep look, which probed her very core, he turned and strode off. As soon as he was out of hearing, she sat back down on the sled and let the sobs have full rein. God, she never cried, but the sobs escalated into gut-wrenching shakes, and she covered her face with her mittens. Blancheur, pegged near enough to the sled to guard it, nuzzled her arm and whined.

She threw her arms around his neck, and the storm of weeping immediately subsided. Sniffing in further control, she raised her head. "Boy, this is stupid, isn't it, Blancheur? If I don't get over to the tent, the officials will be gone and we'll be stranded out here. I—"

"Miss Laura!" Buck pulled the team to a halt beside her.

"What are you doing here, Buck? You'll miss the start of the race!"

"I . . . I . . ." He stared at her for a moment, a frown

crossing his forehead as though he'd forgotten what he meant to say. "I heard Sandy tellin' them officials what had happened," he finally said, emphasizing the explanation with a funny nod of his head. "Can't believe he's just gonna go off and leave you here! An' you was cryin'!"

"There's nothing Sandy can do, Buck. The harness isn't repairable. I might piece together enough of it to have Blancheur pull the sled into Duluth, but that's about it."

Buck tossed out his snow anchor and stepped from his runners. He glanced over his shoulder toward the starting line, a look of longing on his face. Laura sniffed and wiped the back of her mitten against a lingering tear gliding down her cheek.

"Aw, Miss Laura," Buck said in a forlorn voice. "I didn't think—" He clamped his mouth shut and chewed his cheek, then said, "I mean, I don't want you to be cryin'. You take my harness. We can switch it real quick here, and you won't have to lose too much time getting back in the race."

"I couldn't do that, Buck!" she said with a gasp, but with a rising sense of excitement. "You've talked about this race from the moment my father announced it. It means the world to you to run in it."

He avoided her gaze, but that was Buck. At times she tried to figure out if it was shyness or maybe a slight infatuation he had with her, but she'd never decided.

"It don't mean as much to me as not hearing you cry again, Miss Laura," he said stoutly. "I don't never want to hear you cry like you was cryin' just now. If it means that much to you to finish this race, I want you to do it. All it means to me is havin' a little money in my pocket, so's I don't have to trap so hard next winter."

For a fleeting instant she heard some contradiction in his words, but before she could focus on it, the idea of truly being able to get back in the race blotted all other thought from her mind.

"Then I'll buy your harness," she said eagerly, jumping to her feet. "I'll give you five hundred dollars for it, the same as if you'd won second place. And you can have Snowstorm for your team when we get home. I know you've been eyeing him." Racing over to him, Laura hugged Buck's neck. "I'd give you first place money, but that's mine!"

"You don't have to—"

Laura ignored him and headed for his lead dog, which she knew well. "I'll start unharnessing your team up here. Where are your peg chains?"

Chain rattled, and by the time Laura had Buck's lead dog free of harness, Buck handed her a chain and reached for the next dog. They tied the dogs to nearby trees as they worked, and very shortly after Laura heard the last shot from the starter's pistol, she had her own team ready to go. She waited impatiently until Buck gave Blancheur a hug and told the dog to take care of Miss Laura, then reached out and hugged Buck one more time herself.

"I'll give you your money out of my winnings, Buck," she said gaily. "And Snowstorm's yours whenever you want him!"

She yelled "Mush" so loudly she imagined the officials could hear she was on her way. Blancheur took off and hit his stride of a dead run within three leaps, the rest of the team as eager as he. Laura had trouble halting the dogs at the starting line, and had to make a wide loop back round in order to satisfy the requirement of allowing the officials to be the ones to set her on the trail.

"I don't know how you did it, Miss Goodman," the official with the starting pistol said with a chuckle, "but there's no rule saying you've gotta be here when it's your turn. So all it's costing you is the place you won in the race yesterday."

"I'll make up for it," she promised both herself and the official.

He raised the pistol while the other official put a check on the list in his hand. "The deep snow gives out about a mile from here," the starter said helpfully. "We saw that on our way up here. Them little dogs of yours ought to be able to fly over the trail after that."

"I'm counting on it."

He grinned at her and fired the pistol. Laura raced after the other teams, heart pounding in excitement and her laughter blown behind her by the rushing wind. Buck's dogs were bigger than her huskies, but the harness had adjusted easily. Along with his dogs, Buck maintained his equipment in top shape. Her team flew down the trail as smoothly as always, their swift pace in time with Laura's joy at still being in the race.

No wonder men liked competition, she thought, giving in to her joy with a shout that echoed from the treetops and perked Blancheur's ears. The exhilaration she felt could only be topped if—no, *when*—she won the race.

Within the first hour, she passed four teams. A stab of worry hit her when she didn't see another team ahead of her in the next half hour. The packed snow allowed the other teams to make top speeds of their own, and she realized the race might not be won on speed alone, as Sandy had repeated over and over. While she hadn't totally ignored him, she'd counted on her dogs' fleetness and endurance. Knowing now that might not be enough, she turned her mind to the other pieces of wisdom Sandy had passed on to her.

She'd traveled between Grand Marais and Duluth many times in her life, both in summer and winter, by ship and by the shoreline trail. As far as she knew, every other man in the race, except Sandy, had been over the shore trail, too. Many of those from the Grand Marais area probably had as much experience as she did with the landscape.

Several rivers cut paths across the trail, beautiful in the summertime with water rushing over the glistening stones and boulders on its way into the huge lake. Now they were frozen, their steep banks extremely perilous for a team to traverse down one side and back up the other.

On the Gooseberry River Laura ran across her first casualty and recalled Sandy's caution that still more mushers would be forced out of the race today. The river ran through a steep and treacherously deep gorge. A sled lay scattered in pieces at the bottom of the drop, evidently having tumbled over when the driver lost his battle to hold it back on the steep slope. Her heart actually stopped for a long moment until she could tell it wasn't Sandy or Pete.

The driver and his dogs appeared all right, and her lighter team and sled navigated the descending bank successfully. She paused for a second before starting up the other side.

"I'm fine," the musher said before she could ask. "Go on, little missy. Show them there men what you can do."

"Thank you!" Laura called. "Mush, Blancheur!" She held the harness reins and climbed with the dogs, allowing them to pull the sled without her weight, but using their strength to help her up the bank.

A few hundred yards on down the trail, she found another musher out of the race, one of his sled runners broken.

"Hit a rock the wrong way," he called, waving her on. "Go get 'em, Miss Goodman! Glad to see you back in the race!"

Laura's heart swelled with his words and she waved at him. He and the other musher could have been angry and frustrated over their failures and bad luck, but instead they wished her well and cheered her on. Right then she decided to make this race an annual event, giving the mushers other chances to win.

The next silent stretch of trail gave her a chance again to plot some way to shorten the distance for herself. The upcoming river, the Encampment, didn't have as rugged a bank as some of the others but the slope was still bad enough. She remembered a picnic with some of her friends one summer at the mouth of the Encampment, though. There, it opened up into a smooth expanse of beach, where some of the young men with them had even stood and fished. Making a quick decision, she hied her team to the left of the trail. If this worked, she'd make a lot better time crossing the mouth of that river than she would negotiating the steep banks.

Alert in case she'd made a wrong decision and had to pull her team up, she scanned the river mouth as soon as she emerged from the trees. It looked exactly as she remembered, and she let the dogs keep on running. They flew across the frozen water almost without pause, then Laura headed them up an easier trail she remembered using when they carried their picnic supplies down to the shoreline. The dogs barely slowed on the upward path, and when they hit the top of the trail, she heard a shout behind her.

Looking back, she saw two teams just emerging over the river bank. She waved at them, unable to hold back a laugh of glee. A few minutes later, when she looked over her shoulder, she saw no sight of them.

Her dogs resisted the few times she tried to slow them for a rest, but she sternly made them obey. Still she passed all the teams except Sandy's, Pete's and one other within the next three hours, keeping count as she went. The closer she got to Duluth, the less steep the hills were, but then again, the less reserve strength her dogs had. She paced them, chewing on her thoughts and trying to think of a shortcut the other drivers might not know about.

Once in a while the reason she was so far behind the leaders of the race crept into her mind. She tried to banish those thoughts and concentrate on the race, but the doubts remained.

Sandy's primary interest in winning was the prize money. Even if he hadn't admitted that to her, she would have had to be blind the last few months not to notice how he watched every penny—how he bristled each time money was mentioned. How she had learned fairly quickly not to bring Tracie back from their trips to Grand Marais with any expensive bauble.

She, like everyone else in town, had noticed the Dyers' rich attire at the hearing. She'd been too caught up the last few weeks in her shattered emotions to puzzle it out, but here on the lonesome trail she had time to wonder about the story behind that. Sandy's own words about there being a lot more to the story than what came out at the hearing fired her curiosity.

The Dyers hadn't appeared to be the type of people who would stand for their daughter marrying a poor sled dog trainer, and her father had also hired Sandy to manage his shipping business, so he had to have other experience.

As sometimes happens, when Laura let her mind wander away from the problem at hand—winning the race—a sudden idea burst into her head. This one chased away her interest in Sandy's prior life.

Two more rivers lay in her path—the Knife and French—but the lakeshore also curved inward closer to Duluth. She knew exactly where the finish line was—halfway down the brick-paved expanse of Superior Street. If she headed out onto the lake, then cut back on the other side of the Knife—

Laura pulled her dogs up and dropped her snow anchor. She dug into her supplies, and within a few minutes, she had protective leather booties on all of her dogs. The dogs accepted the gear without protest, and she blessed Sandy for making her practice over the rough lakeshores on her training runs. After one final perusal and a chew of her bottom lip as she rethought her decision, she nodded and pulled her snow anchor free.

"Mush!" she called. "Haw!" The team headed toward the lake.

Near the shore, as she expected, the ice was rough and could have cut her dogs' feet to pieces without the tough moosehide booties. Yet further out the ice smoothed and slickened, covered by enough snow to give the dogs plenty of traction. They picked up speed, enjoying the run as much as Laura.

She'd spent enough winters here—all of her life—to know how far out the lake froze, so she had no fear of encountering any thin ice. She passed the mouth of the Knife, glancing aside when she heard a shout. Far along the river's path, two teams struggled up the bank. She recognized the dogs, Pete's team and a strange one. Shouting back an excited challenge of "Catch me if you can," which carried on the frozen air, she headed for the French River.

She reached it within a half hour. Beyond it the landscape was an easy grade, and she guided her dogs into shore just on the other side of the mouth. They scrambled up the bank and hit the trail, panting heavily with exertion but still as enthusiastic as ever to keep on running. Ahead of her she saw the last sled she had to pass. Sandy.

He was pacing beside his sled instead of riding the runners. And she was closing the distance between them!

Hard as she tried to keep quiet and sneak up on him, she failed. While she was still at least fifty feet behind him, she yelled her invitation for him to make this final portion of the race a sight for the spectators to enjoy.

"Hey, Montdulac! How come you're moving so slow?"

Sandy jerked and looked over his shoulder. He stumbled as he did so, and she gained another few feet on him when his team had to drag against his pull on the reins. Ahead of them she saw the first spectators lining the street and imagined she could hear a roar go up even through the wind in her ears.

She moved up beside Sandy, and he leapt onto his runners, giving her a broad grin. "Let's do it!" he shouted. "Let's make a race out of it!"

Grinning wildly, she leaned over her sled handles to offer less wind resistance and screamed at her dogs to go. Sandy did the same, and Keever and Blancheur gave each other one quick glance before they put even more muscle into the harness. The two teams raced neck and neck until they hit the edge of the spectators, and she and Sandy glanced at each other joyously at least twice.

Then her huskies began to pull ahead—inch by hard-gained inch.

The finish line streaked past Laura in a blur of flying red, white and blue ribbon, and she straightened on her runners. One hand flew over her head, her fist reaching for the sky, and she threw back her head, shouting in elation.

Her voice broke, and she realized she was on the verge of going hoarse. While she still had the ability, she called to her dogs, "whoa'ing" them and hearing Sandy's voice beside her—just behind her, she thought with a grin—doing the same. The dogs obeyed willingly, seeming to realize the fun was over.

When the sleds both stopped, she looked over at Sandy. He was already at her side, and he swung her into the air, then around and around again. She clung to his neck, and when he finally set her down, she stood on tiptoe and kissed him.

At first his lips were unyielding, but just as quickly they

softened and he kissed her back. Deeply. Satisfyingly. Hotly and thrillingly.

She broke free with a gasp and placed her hands on his chest. "I'm not apologizing for doing that," she told him. "Just consider it done in the excitement of the moment. And to thank you for teaching me what it took to win this race."

"I'm not asking for an apology, Laura," he growled. "And you're welcome. Congratulations."

"Thank you! Let's get back and collect our accolades from the crowd."

He nodded agreement, and they both got back on their sled runners. A half a minute later, they rode through the crowds lining the street again, waving and accepting the cheers. Sandy graciously allowed her to keep a few feet in front of him.

19

*T*HE DULUTH OFFICIALS held the victory celebration at the Dubuque Mansion, a fine old house set back from Lake Superior with snow-covered grounds stretching down to the rocky shore. Some of the mushers had never been in such a grand place, but Laura frequently visited the Dubuques. Their fortune had initially sprung from the fur trade, and they never forgot it. They opened their ballroom to the town officials and crusty old mushers alike, making plenty of liquor available along with the overflowing tables of food, and soon not one person stood alone against a wall.

Laura managed to slip away from the mayor finally, using the tired but workable excuse of a friend she had to greet. She cautiously glanced around before she stepped behind a large potted plant by one of the back windows. Sipping the glass of champagne the mayor had almost spilled down her dress, she gazed out over the huge back gardens of the mansion.

The moon hung low over the lake, reflecting a twin in the

open waters out in the middle. The ethereal light gave the snow a silver tone, accenting the gray and black colors on the trees, and even the dark green pines looked black in the night. She stepped closer to the floor-length window, but a chill emanated from it and goosebumps covered her bare shoulders. She moved back a step.

She'd chosen this dress with care while in Duluth over Christmas, leaving it at the Dubuques' in anticipation of tonight. Every once in a while she did like to enhance her femininity by wearing pretty clothing, and the muted elegance of the emerald green velvet, banded with black, had immediately caught her eye. She'd decided she had to have it as soon as she tried it on and saw what it did to her eyes and hair.

At the time she had tried to imagine what David would think of her in the dress, but Sandy Montdulac's blue eyes kept overriding David's brown ones in her mind. And Sandy Montdulac hadn't even shown up tonight. So much for his insistence she save him a dance!

She took another sip of champagne, grimacing when it hit her empty stomach. She was starving, but every time the mayor spied her, he hurried to her side, chattering a mile a minute. Turning, she dumped the champagne on the plant, heard the band start tuning up and pushed aside a leafy branch to peer out. If she could find Pete or Buck, one of them could run interference for her until she got a bite to eat.

She didn't see either one, but she immediately recognized the broad shoulders at the buffet table. So, he'd shown up at last. And *he* wasn't having any trouble fending off the mayor while he browsed the food. He shifted, and she caught a glimpse of the overladen plate. Her mouth watered.

Scanning the room, she saw the mayor over beside some elderly, portly lady dripping with diamonds. She looked important enough for him not to offend by walking away before she finished talking, and from the animated way she waved her hands and poked her finger now and then on his arm, that might be a while. Laura eagerly scurried out from behind the plant and headed for the table.

"Thank you," she said in a breathless voice, taking the

plate from Sandy's hand. "There's a small table over there in the corner. I'll go sit down and hold it for us, while you get another plate."

"Yes, ma'am," Sandy said with a grin and a salute. "I wouldn't want you to injure my private parts if I failed to obey."

Her skin heated in a fiery blush, but she reached out and grabbed the fork from him. It had an olive on the end of it, and she popped it in her mouth, chewing the tart morsel eagerly.

"Lord, I'm starved," she said after she swallowed. "I haven't eaten all day."

"Go sit down, Laura," Sandy said. "I'll be there in a minute with some more food and something to drink. Anything on the table that's not already on the plate strike your fancy?"

"Ummmm." She chewed on a piece of cheese and pointed the fork, her mouth too full to speak.

"Ham. All right, I'll get some of that."

She surreptitiously cast a look over her shoulder. The diamond lady still collared the mayor, and Laura headed for the table in the corner. Since another convenient plant sat by the table, she stuffed a piece of beef into her mouth and set the plate down, then tugged the table behind the plant. Grabbing one of the chairs, she pulled it to the far side of the table and sat, eyeing the plate in anticipation.

Within minutes, Sandy arrived with another heaping plate and two cups of punch. Laura took a fluffy roll from the plate he brought, something not on the other plate, and bit off a piece. It was warm and buttery, and she closed her eyes in delight.

"You keep eating like that," Sandy said, picking up a napkin and unfolding it, "and you'll split the seams on that lovely dress."

She opened her eyes and tilted her head. "Do you really like the dress?"

"What man wouldn't?" he asked with a shrug.

What had she expected? For him to say the woman inside the dress was what made it lovely, as any other halfway courteous man would say? But Sandy Montdulac wasn't any man, as she well knew. And he could easily get up from the table and leave her to finish the meal alone, if she pushed him.

Since that afternoon, they had shared an easiness, both excited over their victories. He'd never once sounded disgruntled over her beating him out of first place, and his praise rang sincere. Of course, it could be because he assumed his training had been the deciding factor in her ability to win. Which it was, she admitted.

She took a huge bite from a pickle, pursing her mouth in dismay when sourness filled it. Glancing around instinctively to see if anyone was watching—which they couldn't be with her behind the plant—she whipped her napkin to her mouth and deposited the pickle in it.

"Ohhhh," she said when her mouth was empty. "I thought that was going to be a sweet pickle!"

Sandy held out his fork, a piece of fluffy cake icing clinging to it. "Here. This will take away the sour taste."

Letting him keep hold of the fork, she licked the entire glob of icing off it, savoring the sweetness as it chased away the sour. A dab of icing didn't make it all the way into her mouth, and she flicked her tongue to her lower lip to catch it before it dropped to her dress bodice.

She missed. Ducking her head, she saw the icing in the valley between her breasts. Shrugging, since no one would see her except Sandy, she flipped her index finger down there and retrieved the icing, then put it in her mouth where it belonged.

Sandy grunted as though she'd kicked him between the legs again, and she widened her eyes and stared at him. "Did you eat something that's not agreeing with your stomach?"

"It's lower than my stomach," he growled back at her. "God, Laura, are you really so innocent, or do you know exactly what you do to a man?"

"I don't understand—"

"Ladies and gentlemen!" Laura strained to see through the plant leaves, but she recognized the mayor's voice. "It's time for the band to take a break and for us to give out the prizes from the race. Tom Goodman is very sorry he couldn't be here, but he made arrangements with our banker, Clyde Clebert, to do the honors. Will all the prize winners come up here, please? And the losers, also, since there's something for each entrant, even those who didn't make it across the finish line by themselves."

"Have you eaten enough to get you through this ceremony?" Sandy asked as he stood and stepped behind Laura's chair.

"Ummmph." She chewed the bite of ham and swallowed it as she rose. Sandy moved her chair out of the way, and she started around the table. "Oh!" She stopped, and Sandy plowed right into her, grabbing her around the waist to steady her.

"For such a thing of flowing beauty on the trail, Laura," he said with a wry laugh, "you sure do stumble around when you don't have a sled to lean on."

"Oh, hush," she said. "You ran into me, not the other way around. I just remembered, I have something for you." Reaching into the deep pocket on the gown, where she kept her handkerchief, she pulled out a small package. "Here."

"We need to go collect our prizes," he murmured, but he didn't hand the package back.

"Oh, pooh. They won't give our money to anyone else. Open it, please."

He tore the paper off and held the small scrimshaw dogsled in the palm of his hand. Laura had known it was for Sandy the minute she saw it. The detail was amazing, with some of the dogs even showing open mouths, teeth and tongues panting in their eagerness. They stretched out in a run, and the tiny driver on the sled runners wore the mandatory boots, heavy trousers and thick coat.

"You can even see the wolfskin around his hood," Sandy murmured.

"Isn't it amazing? One of John Beargrease's sons carved it. I was going to give it to you for Christmas, but . . ." She lifted a shoulder, not wishing to go into that. "Now seems a more appropriate time anyway."

"Thank you." Sandy closed his hand around the dogsled. "I'll remember you whenever I look at it."

She ignored the stab of hurt his words sent through her, fathoming at once he was referring to the time after he left Ladyslipper Landing. With a nod, she said, "We better get on up there. That mayor is a persistent man, and he'll probably come looking for us."

She led the way to where the Dubuques had placed a podium in one corner of the room and started to take her place among the crowd of mushers.

"No, no, Miss Goodman," the mayor said. "Since your father sponsored this race, you come on up here with me."

"I was a participant in the race, just like the rest of these people," she told him firmly. "I'll wait with them."

The mushers crowded around her, one of them slapping her on the back and nearly knocking her down. Sandy caught her, and she glanced up to thank him, seeing him glaring at the too enthusiastic man.

"It's all right," she whispered. "It didn't hurt, and he's just happy for me."

Sandy's fingers tightened almost imperceptibly on her waist, then he nodded and dropped his hands. They turned their attention to the mayor, who began calling names while Clyde Clebert passed out consolation prizes of a refund on the men's entry fees plus five dollars. Two prizes went unclaimed but would be held for the recipients—the one for the man who broke his arm and Buck's. Laura frowned when Buck didn't emerge from the crowd around her, knowing she had seen him earlier in the evening. She glanced toward the bar set up in the corner of the room—the most likely place to find Buck—but he wasn't there either.

Third place of two hundred and fifty dollars went to Pete, and he and Sandy shook hands before Pete went up to collect his money. Sandy followed, and a few minutes later, Laura walked up to the podium.

"Won't you say a few words on your father's behalf, Miss Goodman?" the mayor asked after he handed her a pouch of money. He reached out a sweaty hand to pull her behind the podium, but she managed to evade his grasp.

"I'll tell you what I'd rather do," she said to the people gathered around. "I'd rather celebrate my victory with a dance. Do you think we could ask the band to play again?"

Beaming, the mayor waved a hand at the band, and the strains of a waltz filled the room. He turned to offer Laura his arm to lead her onto the floor, evidently thinking she meant to dance with him. She ignored his arm and glided over to Sandy.

"I believe you asked for a dance," she said.

"I believe I did," he agreed in a quiet voice.

He took her hand and led her onto the floor. In an old-fashioned gesture, which brought a smile to her face and a wonderful warmth to her breast, he bowed to her. Then he raised one of her arms over her head.

"To the winner of the Northshore Race," he called to the crowd. As the clapping and cheers spread through the room, he folded her into his arms and began to dance.

She felt as though she were made for his arms, but she'd felt that way every time he held her. They glided across the floor, matching step for step, and it was a slower version of the wild and beautiful rides behind her dogs. On the trail she felt alone with nature and her dogs, an addictive feeling she treasured. Here in Sandy's arms she found the same type of addiction, and the rest of the room receded to the fringe of her consciousness, then completely out of her awareness.

He gazed down at her face, his eyes deep blue and caressing. His thumb stroked the tender skin on the inside of her right wrist, and she inched her other hand up on his shoulder until her fingers tangled in his hair. It was as though a cocoon surrounded her and Sandy alone, separating them from the rest of the world.

A shrieking woman's voice shattered the cocoon.

"There he is! Arrest him! Now!"

Sandy halted abruptly, and the waltz ended in a few raucous chords from the band. Laura whirled to see the woman who had been at the hearing in Grand Marais—Tracie's grandmother—standing on the edge of the crowd, her finger pointing at Sandy and her eyes gleaming ferally. Behind her stood two men in policeman uniforms.

"What's going on here?" the mayor blustered. "You're interrupting our celebration."

Elvina Dyer turned on him with a malicious glare, and her husband stepped out from behind the policemen. "We have a perfect right to be here and have the police take that man into custody," George Dyer said. "We appealed that asinine ruling the judge in Grand Marais made, and a higher court judge here in Duluth issued a warrant to take this man into custody until he examines things himself. He agreed we didn't want to take a chance on this man fleeing again with our granddaughter, as he did once already."

"And as soon as he rules in our favor, we're going up to that backwater town to get our granddaughter," Elvina snarled. "Take him to jail. Now!"

She pointed at Sandy again with one hand and shoved at one of the policemen with the other. The policeman had a pained look on his face, but he shrugged and moved forward.

"Sorry," he said in an undertone when he approached Sandy. "She's a harridan, but they do have a warrant."

Laura moved in front of Sandy, but he pushed her aside. "Don't get yourself in trouble, Laura," he said through gritted teeth, his tone of voice a contradiction to his gentleness when he moved her away from him. "There's nothing you can do."

"The hell there isn't," she muttered. "You watch me!"

"Don't," he ordered. "This isn't any of your business."

Distress flared through her, so deep she gasped with the hurt, and she searched his face in amazement. How could he hold her so close—so lovingly—just a minute ago and now tell her to stay out of his business? As if she were some stranger on the street?

Suddenly it dawned on her what he was trying to do. For one thing, he was embarrassed. Who wouldn't be? The policeman pulled out a pair of handcuffs, and Sandy closed his eyes as he held out his hands. But mostly he wanted to protect her, Laura realized. He evidently thought the Dyers were dangerous people, since they had the power and influence to get a judge to look at possibly overruling Judge Barstow's decision.

She glared across the room at Elvina and George Dyer. *Well,* she thought, feeling the anger in her eyes wave across the room and settle on the two of them, *Dyers, meet Goodman. I have a hunch you might be out-powered here, because Katie always told me good will win out over evil.*

Elvina Dyer seemed to sense Laura's glare, and their gazes locked for a second. A touch of fear or uncertainty—Laura wasn't sure which—flickered in Elvina's eyes. When the policeman started to lead Sandy away, Laura quickly moved back to his side.

"Just a minute, Officer," she said.

The policeman knew her from her many visits to town, and he nodded respectfully at her. "I need to get him out of here, Miss Goodman, but you can have about ten seconds."

She ignored Sandy's scowl and stepped in front of him, her back to the crowd and her voice low so no one could overhear. But she would make it clear to everyone watching whose side the Goodman faction favored.

"I'm not going to stay out of this, Sandy. If you can't take my assistance as that of a friend who cares about what happens to you, then take it as a boss helping an employee. Or as part of my friendship to your sister and love for your daughter."

"Laura," he said in a matching low voice, "I'll handle this somehow."

"Damn your pride, Sandy Montdulac," she snarled. "Or is it your lack of trust in anyone else?" He started to say something, but she overrode his words. "This isn't the place to talk about this, so just go on and I'll do what I can to get you out of jail as soon as possible."

"The judge won't be available until Monday, Miss Goodman," the policeman said in what she assumed was an attempt to be helpful. "But he is in town, and he lives about a block from here." He gave her the address, then continued, "But it will be an hour or two before we can even have him ready to release, what with the booking and all. You've got plenty of time to get the judge out of bed."

"Thank you," Laura said.

He nodded and took Sandy's arm again. For an intense moment, Sandy stared at her, his face devoid of emotion. Finally, he said, "Thanks. For Tracie's sake, I need someone with influence to help me out."

Laura nodded, and the policeman led him away. The crowd parted, some of the people with confused looks on their faces. Others, who had been privy to the happenings in Grand Marais, began answering questions as to what was going on. Laura knew the Grand Marais people were enjoying being the center of attention as they spread their knowledge, and she made a quick decision not to quell their doing so. Sliding to the side of the room, she listened for a few minutes, hearing the tide of opinion shift in Sandy's favor. The people were banding together against the outsiders in their midst, and on the side of a father's love for his little girl.

George and Elvina Dyer made a few attempts to plead their own case, but soon they stomped out of the room in disgust. The chatter in the room kept everyone's attention, and Laura followed them unnoticed and at a distance. She retrieved her cloak from the coatroom off the front foyer and stepped out into the cold just shortly after the Dyers. They were standing halfway down the brick walkway, and since the Dubuques' door opened silently, they didn't observe her presence.

"I told you not to pay that nasty little man until after he did what you ordered during that race," Elvina hissed. "Those people in there should have already been halfway on our side when we went in there."

"I did what I could," George snarled back. "And he did part of the job. You heard about that this afternoon, while listening to people talk about the race. But he double-crossed us, and he didn't leave the evidence that pointed to that damned son-in-law of ours, so he'd be arrested. You're lucky the judge here is a reasonable man. *And* that I was able to make you keep your mouth shut instead of trying to bribe him. I could tell right off the bat that he wasn't the type of man to take kindly to something like that."

"You still should have forced the police chief to arrest him this afternoon, right after he crossed the finish line."

"You heard the chief. The mayor would have had his ass if he'd pulled something like that and marred these festivities. I had a hell of a time getting him to agree to do it during the celebration this evening. He only gave in after I told him that I'd go to the papers and let them know how he'd refused to serve a legal warrant. I told him Sandy might sneak off tonight, if he got wind we were still in town instead of back in Alaska, and I'd make a stink heard all the way to the state capital if that happened."

Silence stretched for a moment, then Laura heard a sniff.

"I want my granddaughter, George," Elvina said.

"We'll get her, my dear. Haven't I been doing everything possible?"

"I don't know," Elvina said in a weary voice. "Sometimes I wonder what Colleen would think."

Something sparked in Laura's mind, and she moved without examining it too closely. Pulling her light-colored shawl from her cloak pocket, she wrapped it around her neck and removed the hairpins from her hair, letting it stream down her back. Then she draped the shawl across her lower face, cleared her throat to get the Dyer's attention, and stepped down from the door stoop beneath a tree limb with beams of moonlight filtering through it.

"I think you're a couple of fools, who don't deserve a wonderful granddaughter like Tracie," she growled, the shawl muffling her voice.

Elvina Dyer whirled. "Colleen!" she screamed. "No! George, it's Colleen's ghost!"

"It can't be." But George Dyer didn't step close enough to unmask Laura. Grabbing his wife's arm, he raced down the walkway and continued on down the street. The last Laura saw of the two of them, they were scrambling into a carriage parked at the end of the line waiting for the party attendees to leave. The horse took off in a clatter of hoofbeats audible even where Laura stood.

Had she not been so worried over Sandy and involved in trying to figure out who George Dyer had paid to sabotage the race—her cut harness without doubt the result—she would have laughed at them. When they gained control over their fear and had a moment to think about it, they'd come to the conclusion fairly easily that it was her and not their daughter's ghost in the moonlight. They'd seen her very clearly at the party and had to have noticed the resemblance.

They'd also be aware she'd heard every blasted word as they rehashed their atrocious plans!

Right now it was more important to get Sandy out of jail. She had no doubt he would be treated fairly, since she wasn't without influence in Duluth, and her support of him had been clear at the party. Frowning into the darkness, she chewed on her lip and tried to decide her next move.

She had a sneaking suspicion who might have cut her team's harness, and if so, his confession might help her plea to the judge. If she could prove the Dyers were dishonest people—

The door opened, and she turned to see Pete.

"The mayor's looking for you," he said, the light from the hallway illuminating his face and his wry grin. "He thinks you might be so upset over the disruption of the celebration that you found a fainting couch somewhere to lie down on. He's searching all the bedrooms."

"Slip back in and ask Mrs. Dubuque if we can borrow a carriage, Pete. I'm sure she'll accommodate us, so I'll meet you around back at the stables. Do you have any idea where Buck might be staying?"

"Probably the Superior Hotel. Your father arranged for rooms for all the race participants who wanted one."

"Let's go."

Laura headed around the side of the house on the walkway the Dubuques' servants kept clear of snow. The stable was set back a ways from the house, and electric lights burned inside. Laura still marvelled at the wonder of those lights and nagged her father every possible chance about getting electricity to Grand Marais. Stepping inside the stable door, she flipped a switch she'd seen on previous visits to the stable, where it was always possible for the young people visiting in town to borrow a horse for a ride in the country.

A wiry little man emerged from a snug room on the side. "Miss Goodman," Shaun said. "It's wonderful to see you. Can I do something for you?"

"Hello, Shaun. Yes, you could help. Pete's asking the Dubuques if we can borrow a carriage, and I'm assuming they'll be agreeable. Would you get one ready?"

"Of course."

By the time Pete got there, Shaun had the horse hitched to the carriage. Laura climbed in and Pete jumped in beside her, taking the reins from her hands. "Dogs you know how to drive," he said in a typical masculine move. "I'll handle the horses."

"Just get us there in a hurry, Pete. I have a feeling Buck is hiding from us because he knows more than he should about what the Dyers are up to."

20

*T*HE SUPERIOR HOTEL on Lake Avenue wasn't the best in town, nor the worst. Her father obviously knew the mushers wouldn't be comfortable in a luxurious setting. They'd rather have a place to relax and have a few more drinks after the celebration dinner. Rather small, the hotel was neat and clean, with electric lights, like the other businesses in town. Laughter sounded in the bar set off the lobby area, and Laura glanced at Pete questioningly.

"Knowing Buck," he said agreeably, "that's probably where he is. You stay right beside me, Laura. I don't want to end this evening fending off a drunk who wants to get his grubby paws on you."

"Oh, masterful Pete!" Laura clasped her hands together under her chin and mischievously batted her eyes at him. "I'll have nothing to worry about as long as I'm with big, strong you. And you drive a horse soooo well."

Pete snorted with laughter and shook his head. "All right, Laura, maybe I did sound overbearing. But the bars here in

Duluth aren't like Bootsie's place back home. And I'd hate for Sandy and me to end up back in jail for fighting after we get him out. He'd knock me halfway into the next county if I let some drunk lay a hand on you."

Pete suddenly looked away from her, as though embarrassed to have said that. He took a step toward the bar, but Laura grabbed his arm. "What do you mean, Pete? About Sandy?"

Pete sighed and looked back at her. "Laura, it's none of my business. Let's go find Buck."

"Are you saying that Sandy cares for me? More than just as a friend?"

"I don't want to talk about this, Laura."

Tilting her head, she pursed her lips and set a fist on one hip.

Pete shook his head. "Don't get that look, Laura. I can be just as stubborn as you, and I'm not about to turn traitor to my race. We men have a code, and it's worth my right to call myself a man to break it."

Laura caught a twinkle in his eye and tightened her grip on his arm. "We can stand here all night, if you want. Sandy's not going anywhere until we bail him out of jail."

"You forget. He's got his prize money. If they set bail, he can get out. But I think it's going to take a little influence to get the judge to even set bail this time of night. And that's where you come in."

"I might be more inclined to use my influence if you told me what you didn't want to say a minute ago," Laura lied. Nothing was going to stand in her way of getting Sandy out of jail. Nothing. And the smirk Pete gave her let her know he was fully aware she was lying through her teeth.

"I can't tell you, Laura. You heard me. I can't tell you that, when Sandy thinks no one's watching, he looks at you like a bull moose in dire need of a tender look from a cow."

"A moose?" Laura fumed. "You're comparing me to a moose?"

"That's just what comes to mind when I catch Sandy pining after you," he said with a shrug. "And remember, I'm not saying this—not breaking the man code thing. I'm also not saying that those two weeks on the trail with him when you had to stay home were hell. I couldn't do a damned thing right, from digging in my snow anchor to fixing the fire for lunch. I knew he was thinking *Laura does it better*. In fact, once I even heard him mutter—" He mimicked a prissy voice. "—'Laura would have had that fire going five minutes ago. Laura knows how to find dry wood instead of that damn damp stuff.'"

With an effort, Laura kept from preening. Suddenly the simmering emotions of the last few months boiled over and hit her like a wildfire gone out of control.

She loved him. She loved that stubborn, overbearing, independent, tender, oh-so-masculine man. That's why his barriers against her hurt so badly. Why her broken heart hadn't pieced itself back together yet.

But if Pete were right, Sandy did care for her, yet something held him back from a commitment or even a chance to explore their feelings for each other. Her heart sank again. That something might very well be insurmountable. It sure seemed to be so far.

She wasn't a quitter, but how could she fight for Sandy's love if she didn't even know what the enemy was?

"Why, Pete?" she asked in a sad voice she hardly recognized as her own. "If he cares for me, why is he so adamant about leaving Grand Marais and starting another life somewhere else?"

"I don't know," Pete said. "There are some things even men don't tell each other. I think that's going to be up to you to find out." He winked. "And remember, we haven't had this conversation."

She managed a half-hearted smile, and Pete shifted her hand to beneath his forearm, then started toward the bar again. The bartender glanced up, giving a start when he saw them. Laura lifted her chin, daring the man to make a remark about her presence in a male-dominated establishment, but then she noticed he was glaring at Pete.

"Shoot," she muttered in a low voice, but nevertheless loud enough to carry to the bartender's ears. "I forgot about the prejudice against Indians in some places, Pete. If that man gives us any trouble, I'm going to have my father buy this place and fire him."

The warning worked. The bartender studied her for an instant, fortunately taking her words to heart. He moved to her end of the bar and asked courteously, "Can I help you, ma'am? Miss Goodman, isn't it?"

"Yes," Laura replied. "And I'm looking for one of my employees. Buck Svenson."

"Haven't seen Buck tonight, Miss Goodman. Is he staying here with the other mushers from the Northshore Race?"

"That's what I understand."

"Then he might be up in his room. The hotel clerk can give you the number."

"Thank you." Laura swept out of the bar and over to the check-in desk at the far end of the lobby. The clerk sprang to attention as soon as he saw her. A minute later, she and Pete were climbing the stairs to the second floor, where the clerk informed her Buck's room was located. She knocked on two-oh-nine and Buck's shaky voice called out, asking who was there.

"It's me, Buck," she said. "Laura. And Pete's with me. May we come in?"

Barely two seconds later the door flew open. "Miss Laura!" Buck exclaimed. "You didn't have to hunt me up to pay me. I could've waited 'til we got back home."

Whiskey fumes hit her full in the face, and Laura instinctively lifted a hand to wave them away. Beyond Buck a half-full bottle sat on a table beside an overstuffed chair, but no sign of a glass. When Buck wobbled and leaned against the door jamb, she shook her head.

"I didn't come for that, Buck. Can we come in?"

Red-veined eyes gazed at her mournfully, and Laura thought for a moment he was going to cry. He sniffed and bowed his head, staggering back from the door and holding out a trembling hand.

"Please come in, Miss Laura," he said. "I ain't got but one chair, but it's yours."

Pete followed her in and shut the door.

"I don't believe I'll be here long enough to sit down and visit, Buck," she said sternly. "I want you to answer a couple questions for me. Did you know the Dyers were still in town?"

Buck crumbled, covering his face with shaking hands and reeling back against the wall. "He come back to town one night and was a'waitin' when I got home from the bar," he said in an agonized voice. "Told me he'd pay someone to kill my dogs, I didn't do what he said." Buck dropped his hands and gazed at Laura with a look that filled her with pity. "They's just about all I got, Miss Laura. My dogs. I couldn't let nothin' happen to them."

"Oh, Buck."

"He started out 'bout me doing somethin' to the dogs— yours and Sandy's dogs. But I told him that'd never go over, 'cause no one who knew Sandy would believe he made the dogs sick. So he told me I had to cut the harness so you wouldn't win. Make it look like Sandy had done it."

"He wanted people to think Sandy had done that?"

"Yeah." Buck pulled a dirty hanky from his back pocket and blew his nose. He stared longingly at the liquor bottle, but didn't move toward it. "Only thing is, I forgot to leave Sandy's glove there, like it'd dropped out of his pocket. So no one really knew who had done it."

Laura tried to muster up anger at Buck, but the pitiful sight of him leaning against the wall, tears trembling in his eyes and the dirty hanky crumpled in his hand only made her sorry for him. Pete evidently didn't have that problem.

He stepped forward, grabbing Buck by the front of his shirt and lifting him off the floor. "Do you know what happens to men who turn on their friends? My ancestors would make you pay slowly. By the time they got done with you, you'd be afraid even to tell a lie to a pretty woman to try to get her skirts up!"

"Pete!"

He glanced at her. "Well, he would, although I guess I could've picked a better comparison, huh?"

"Yes, you could have. Now put him down. We need him with us when we go to the police station."

Pete let Buck slide down the wall, then stepped back and dusted his palms on his trousers. Pete's words must have had a sobering effect on Buck, because Laura could see a gleam of rationality in his runny eyes.

"How did anyone find out what I done, Miss Laura?" he asked.

"We didn't know for sure who did it, Buck, but I had a suspicion it might be you. I overheard the Dyers talking, and what they said pointed to you. But that's not the reason they took Sandy to jail."

"They took Sandy to jail? I don't understand, Miss Laura. We need to get over there and tell them I done it—I cut your harness. It weren't Sandy. I didn't even leave the clue that made it look like Sandy. So why'd they take him to jail?"

His willingness to confess and take the blame from Sandy didn't make Laura respect Buck, but she tolerated his shortcomings a little better. "I'll explain on the way, Buck. And on the way, we're going to detour by a judge's house."

"A judge? Aw, Miss Laura," Buck whined. "I'll see the judge soon enough—when he tells me how long I gotta lay in jail."

"I told you I'd explain on the way, Buck. Get your coat."

He turned slowly and took his heavy coat from a closet behind him, giving Laura a pitiful look as he put it on. "Will you take care of my dogs, Miss Laura? I'll work for you for free to pay you back soon's I get outta jail."

Laura sighed and glanced at Pete. Simultaneously, they both burst out laughing, and the laughter alleviated Laura's worry somewhat. She shook her head and couldn't resist teasing Buck, "What makes you think you still have a job with me?"

His lower lip protruded. "I didn't think of that. But I can pay you outta that money you're gonna give me."

"Buck! That money was for a harness to replace the one you cut up! You don't think I'm still going to give that to you, do you?"

"Oh. No. No, I guess not." His face creased in a frown of concern. "I don't guess I'll get Snowstorm either, huh?"

"Snowstorm? Buck—!" A giggle caught Laura unaware

and she bit her inside cheek to keep it back. Her shoulders heaved in a sigh. She didn't have it in her to take revenge on Buck. He'd made a mistake—a bad one—but he'd been coerced by people a lot smarter than him.

"Buck, I've been meaning to give you Snowstorm for quite a while now, and you can still have him. But I want to be able to use him for stud."

A hopeful light glinted in Buck's eyes, though Laura saw he wasn't too drunk to forget the team he already had. "Thank you, Miss Laura. But I won't be able to take care of him, neither, even if he is mine."

Knowing his deep worry over his animals, Laura gave in more. "Buck, your dogs will be taken care of. Don't worry. But believe me, you're going to pay for every penny's worth of food they eat."

"I will, Miss Laura." He nodded his head vigorously. "I will. I will."

"Then let's go." Pete opened the door again.

In the carriage, they had to squeeze together, as it only had one seat. Laura could still smell liquor fumes on Buck, but as soon as the horse started moving, the breeze blew the odor away. Pete, in the middle of the seat, started explaining Sandy's situation to Buck. With nothing to distract her from her worry until they arrived at the judge's house her thoughts settled once again on Sandy.

Surely they would be able to get him out. She couldn't imagine returning to Grand Marais and telling Tracie her father was in jail. If need be, she would send for her father, she thought with an emphatic nod. Tom Goodman wouldn't take kindly to what the Dyers were trying to do. And she probably didn't have to worry about the Dyers trying to get Tracie until after Monday. They'd have to wait for a new court order overriding the one from Judge Barlow. Elvina Dyer had let that slip during her tirade at the celebration dinner.

Laura recalled the look in Sandy's eyes when she gave him the scrimshaw dogsled at dinner. Remembered how she felt when he held her for their interrupted dance. Why, oh, why didn't he want to at least try to explore their feelings for each other? Could it be he still loved his dead wife so desperately? That she reminded him of Colleen whenever he looked at her?

Something told her that wasn't the case, but if she couldn't get Sandy to talk about this, how would she ever know the truth? Was Pete completely mistaken? Had he misread Sandy's—her lips quirked—"moose-eyed looks" as interest, when it was really just a longing to be gone from her? To get her training over and start his new life far away from her?

"Laura?"

She swiveled her head. Pete stood beside the carriage, arms lifted to help her down.

"Are you going to set there all night?" Pete asked. "I don't think the judge will take too kindly to an Indian and a drunk waking him up. We need you to come with us."

She huffed and scrambled from the carriage. "He better not give us any trouble," she told Pete, gathering her skirts and striding up the walk. "I'll tell him that I'll let Buck breathe on him until he passes out and then you can scalp him."

Even Buck joined their chuckles, but when they stood on the door stoop and Laura lifted the knocker, they all fell silent. Laura took a breath for courage and knocked, repeating her action an additional three times. Almost immediately a light went on inside.

Half a minute later, a tiny, elderly lady opened the door, peering nearsightedly at them and holding a fluffy housecoat tight around her.

"We need to see the judge," Laura said imperiously. "Tell him Laura Goodman is here."

"Yes, ma'am," the lady said. "Come in, ma'am."

She held the door, and Laura could see at once that she wasn't as nearsighted as she appeared. Her eyes widened when Buck and Pete followed her inside, then they twinkled.

"I think this might be worth losing a little sleep over," she murmured, then raised her voice. "I'll get Judge Nordic. The parlor is the door on your right. You can wait there."

When the judge arrived in the parlor a while later, Laura had a feeling it was a good thing she'd given her name. He must have weighed three hundred pounds, and there wasn't an ounce of fat on him that Laura could see. She very much doubted Pete and Buck together could stop him if he decided to throw them out of the house for disturbing his exalted presence at such an ungodly hour.

"Miss Goodman," he said. He'd dressed, although his eyes were still sleepy-looking. "I assume this must be important, since a lady of your standing is involved."

"It is, Judge Nordic, sir." No sense taking a chance of him being offended if she didn't address him properly. "I understand you signed a warrant for the arrest of one of my employees, Sandy Montdulac. I believe you were led to do this under false pretenses, and if not that, at least by some dishonest people."

"Have a seat, Miss Goodman. And your escorts, too. My housekeeper is making coffee."

After Laura introduced Buck and Pete, she explained the Dyers' underhanded dealings. The judge's face grew grimmer and grimmer, and by the time the housekeeper brought the coffee, he was fairly glowering.

"I'm a student of the Old West," he told Laura as the housekeeper handed him a cup of coffee. "In case you're wondering what that has to do with anything, I'll tell you. In the Old West, messing with a man's horse was a hanging offense. We feel the same about our sled dogs here in the Northland."

He turned his glare on Buck, and the little man slid down in his chair. "I'm not saying that what you did won't be cause for punishment. And you *will* be punished. But what we have here is called mitigating circumstances."

Though Laura could tell Buck didn't understand the word, a flicker of hope fluttered in his eyes. He straightened just a hair and sipped his coffee.

"These Dyers threatened your dogs—" Judge Nordic continued. "—your way of travelling to your job to make a living. Your way of going hunting for food for yourself. Men take dire umbrage when their horses are messed with out West, just like we do with our dogs."

"Umbrage," Buck repeated. "Yeah, that's what I did." He glanced at Laura. "What's umbrage?"

"I think what Judge Nordic is saying is that you won't be punished quite as badly because the Dyers threatened you into cutting my harness. That is, if you agree to testify against them."

"That's true, Miss Goodman," Judge Nordic said. "I assume you will testify, Mr. Svenson?"

Laura didn't know whether Buck straightened his shoulders completely in response to the respectful way the judge addressed him or the chance to get back at the Dyers for threatening his dogs. But the Buck in the chair now was a far cry from the one in the hotel room a while ago.

"You can bet on it, Your Honor. Sir. Uh . . . Your . . . Whateverness," he said with a firm nod.

Laura covered her mouth, and Pete suffered a coughing fit, explaining it when he got his breath back as coffee going down the wrong way. Even the judge put his cup down on the table, the saucer full of spilled coffee from his hands, which shook with suppressed laughter.

"We need to get going," he said. "I'll get my coat."

21

THE JAIL DIDN'T bother Sandy that much. Despite his admonitions to Laura, no doubt she'd use the Goodman influence to turn the town upside down until she got him out. He figured he wouldn't be here much beyond morning, and only that long if the judge Laura woke up had more gumption than most men to stand against her. He didn't even try to sleep. Sitting on the edge of the bunk, elbows on knees, he stared at the floor.

Laura looked so lovely tonight. Felt so wonderful in his arms. And when they raced each other to the finish line that afternoon, he'd admitted to himself once again how desperately he loved her.

Her mischievous challenge to him had gone straight to his heart, and he'd almost fallen into those sparkling green eyes, diamond bright with the joy of the race. Her ringing cheer and raised fist of victory reminded him of his youth and love of life before everything crashed around him. He wanted that joy again—wanted it with Laura—wanted it so badly he ached with yearning.

But it could never be. A year and a half ago, he would have had way too much influence and been too well respected for the authorities ever to slap a pair of handcuffs on him and haul him off to jail in front of dozens of people. A year and a half ago, he wouldn't have had to depend on someone else to rescue him. To free him, so he could return home and care for his daughter.

He'd thought his pride beyond battering, but this evening it sank even lower.

Too, this probably wouldn't be the end of the Dyers' attempts to gain custody of Tracie. After the Grand Marais hearing, he'd thought he and Tracie would be safe from their attempts as long as they stayed out of Alaska. Now he knew differently. George Dyer would storm the capital of Minnesota next, and maybe even all the way to Washington, D.C. Sandy would never be free of looking over his shoulder.

He might have to go all the way overseas to keep his daughter, but if that's what it took, that's what he'd do. He would make a living somehow. He'd heard they needed trainers for some sort of rescue dogs in the Swiss Alps.

Laura Goodman could never be a part of his life. Even if she thought it somewhat romantic and begged to go with him, she would grow disillusioned very quickly. His love for her was too great to put her through something like that. He would rather never let her know how he felt than chance her returning his love, only to watch it die later on.

He had loved Colleen, but in a different way. Colleen had needed protection—needed caring for. Their love was a quiet thing, and she was a prim and proper wife, having been raised to take her appropriate place at some man's side. Their love life had been satisfying, if not earth shattering, with Colleen shyly eager for his embraces as long as he didn't try anything shocking. They'd had a good life, and Sandy could have been perfectly happy growing old with her.

Then there was Laura. She, too, came from a monied

background, but what a different woman! She could effortlessly manage a social occasion with everyone from the mayor to the core group of the town's old money. Yet the next day, she'd be ready to mush through the cold with her pack of dogs, wearing a pair of trousers, cheeks red with both the excitement of the moment and the frigid air. Life with Laura Goodman—both in bed and out—would never be dull. On the contrary, it would be exciting.

Tracie thought Laura walked on water, and Laura had the patience of a saint with his daughter. He supposed Laura would want children of her own, given her delight with Tracie. Hell, he couldn't support even one daughter, and he'd never be able to keep his hands off Laura if she were his wife. There were ways, of course, to avoid pregnancies, but you had to keep a somewhat clear head during lovemaking for those to work. He doubted very much making love with Laura would allow that. They'd have those children if some miracle ever made it possible for them to have a life together.

He shook his head. It would take more than a miracle for him and Laura to ever be together. It would take a different life, on a different planet. No chance of that.

He would never subject Laura to the life forced upon him. He could take the brunt of the bad times and keep Tracie from suffering, but it would be different with a woman at his side.

Footsteps sounded down the hallway, and Sandy looked up. The same policeman who had led him out of the Dubuques' mansion came toward him. Of the six cells in the room, two held drunks who seemed used to jail and were soundly sleeping. The policeman had placed Sandy in a far cell, so he would have a little distance from the men's buzz-saw snores.

"Judge Nordic is here," the policeman said. "He wants you in the interrogation room, so he can talk to you."

Fitting a key in the door, he unlocked it, then turned to lead Sandy away. Sandy chuckled wryly. The man didn't even think him dangerous enough to bother guarding against his escape.

The policeman looked back over his shoulder. "You won't try to run, will you, Mr. Montdulac? I know you wouldn't want to be stuck in here for a *real* charge, and not be able to get back to your daughter."

Respect for the man filled Sandy, along with gratitude for the way the policeman trusted him. "You don't have to worry," he assured him.

The interrogation room was off the main entryway, a grim, windowless room with dirty walls. Since this room wasn't wired for electricity it was lit by a small lantern, the atmosphere conducive to bringing a confession from a true criminal. At a table in the far corner, Laura, Pete and Buck sat with a huge man, who could probably break Sandy in two with one hand.

The policeman motioned for Sandy to approach the table, then retreated, leaving the door open behind him. Sandy's eyes unerringly settled on Laura, and it took a determined effort on his part to keep a poker face when she smiled at him. But he'd had plenty of practice hiding his love for Laura.

"Mr. Montdulac," the large man said. "I'm Judge Nordic. If you'll sit down here, we need to talk."

Sandy complied, taking the only empty chair, which was beside Laura. Her scent filled his nose, and he felt the caress of her gaze as she kept her eyes on him. As he recalled holding her while they danced, his palms tingled, and he curled his hands into fists, then hurriedly released them. Laura placed a hand on his forearm, and he could no more resist the pull to look at her than he could have flown to that different planet where they might have a life together.

"It's going to be all right," she said. "And if you yell at me for interfering, I'll—" She frowned, then continued, "—I'll lord it over you from now on until we have a month of Sundays about how I beat you in that race!"

He forced a half-hearted chuckle. "Heaven forbid. Besides, I knew you wouldn't pay any attention to me telling you to stay out of it. I've been expecting you for the last half hour. What took you so long?"

"Oh, you!" Laura swatted him on the arm. "I had to talk

to Buck first. I think you'll be interested in what he has to say."

"Well, I was damned interested in it," Judge Nordic said. Then, "Excuse me, Miss Goodman. That just slipped out."

"I was *damned* interested, too, Judge," Laura said with a smile.

"Don't curse, Laura," Sandy growled in a low voice.

"Yes, boss," she responded.

Buck was the only one who didn't laugh at their byplay. He was obviously about to fall off his chair with terror. He kept gnawing on a thumbnail and glancing through the open door, where you could see the bars on the front window of the jailhouse. Sandy could imagine how the little man felt. Even though he'd been sure he wouldn't be locked up for very long, the sound of that door clanging shut behind him and the key turning in the lock sent a shiver of icy fear through him. He had no idea how men stood being locked up year after year.

Laura kept her hand on his arm, and her touch burned through him. He should shake her off, but the effort was totally beyond him. He wouldn't have that many more chances to experience her touch, he thought, justifying his lack of resistance. It wouldn't hurt to add this one more memory to his cache.

Even the thrill of Laura's touch paled, however, as Judge Nordic led Buck through his confession. Sandy knew George Dyer was ruthless, but he thought the man's attempt to get him into trouble rather amateurish, compared to what he'd done before. His father-in-law was obviously feeling his lack of influence in a strange place. Otherwise he probably would have tried to pin something more serious than sabotaging a dogsled race on Sandy. Even that could have been worse, he guessed, if Buck had followed through and left the false evidence. Or hadn't broken down and confessed.

Sandy could see the judge and Laura both thought Dyer would be defeated easily now that they had the goods on him. At this point Sandy didn't want to disillusion them, since it meant his being freed from jail. He'd take his own precautions afterward to ensure Dyer didn't get him in a corner again.

"I've already signed another warrant and sent two policemen over to the hotel to pick up George Dyer," Judge Nordic said after Buck finished his story. "I won't be able to hold him without bail, but I can make myself unavailable to set bail until Monday. And I'll let it be known among the other judges that I won't take it kindly if one of them steps in and does anything against my wishes.

"For now, given what I've found out about the character of the man who requested it, I've decided to rescind my decision to look into the matter of whether that Alaskan court order might somehow be valid down here. I don't regard it the duty of my court to take time out of my busy schedule to consider a charge from a criminal against a lower court judge."

At that moment, they heard a ruckus in the outside hallway, and Sandy recognized George Dyer's voice. "You'll be sorry for this!" Dyer shouted. "I'll sue your entire police department!"

"Well, now," another voice snarled, which Sandy recognized as the desk sergeant's. "Like Judge Nordic says sometimes, messing with a man's dogs oughtta be a hangin' offense, just like messin' with a man's horse was back in the Old West. I'd sure hate for our understaffed police department not to be able to stand against a lynch mob of mushers storming our jail to try to hang a man who messed with a team of someone's dogs!"

"Why you stupid moron," Dyer snarled. "Nothing happened to those dogs."

"Could've." Sandy heard a shrug in the desk sergeant's voice. "And messin' with a racing team is just as bad as messin' with a team a man's using to help him make a livin'. We don't take kindly to anyone doing that here."

"You've got no proof! I demand you call an attorney for me, and I need to get hold of the judge who signed that earlier arrest warrant for my son-in-law!"

As Dyer spoke, Judge Nordic motioned with his head for them to join him in rising from the table and walking over to the doorway. Pete had to literally hold Buck on his feet, since the wiry man was shaking so hard at the sound of Dyer's voice his legs trembled. His face had gone utterly pale.

They stood in the doorway, looking at George Dyer's back as he continued to yell at the desk sergeant. Sandy smiled grimly when he saw George's hands handcuffed behind his back.

"Did you hear me?" Dyer yelled. "That's one of those new-fangled telephones there on your desk, isn't it? Get on that damned thing and call an attorney for me!"

"Well, now," the desk sergeant mused, rubbing at his chin. "I can't think of even one attorney who would be happy about me waking him up in the middle of the night. Guess you'll just have to wait until Monday."

"I'm not spending all day tomorrow and tomorrow night in a jail cell like some common criminal!" Dyer fumed. "Who the hell do you think I am?"

"A common criminal?" the desk sergeant said with a raised eyebrow.

"You son of a bitch!" Dyer jerked on his hands and surged toward the desk.

Two patrolmen moved in a synchronized lunge; a fist from each landed in Dyer's stomach and he doubled forward with a muffled "oomph." His head hit the sergeant's desk with a loud crack, and he crumpled to the floor.

"Hmmmmm," Judge Nordic mused. Raising his voice, he said, "Sergeant, I do believe you should add assault on a police officer to the list of charges against that man. If you'll get your patrolmen to haul him off to a cell, I'd like to talk to you about another matter."

"Yes, Your Honor," the desk sergeant said.

"And please put the names of your two patrolmen in for a commendation at the next Commissioner's meeting," Judge Nordic said. "Our streets are much safer with the two of them being so ready to protect someone from the criminal element, as they just did for you."

"Will do, Your Honor."

Both the patrolmen gave the judge a grateful look, then

each grabbed one of Dyer's feet. They dragged him down the hallway, toward the jail cells.

"We'll call a doctor for him," the desk sergeant said. "But he's gonna have to pay the bill for it himself, not the city."

The judge chuckled his agreement, then turned to Buck. "I want you to understand something, Mr. Svenson. What you did is reprehensible." When Buck frowned in confusion, he explained, "It was wicked of you, and unlawful, of course, to interfere with the race. Even though you were afraid Dyer would poison your dogs, or injure or kill them some other way, you should have gone to the authorities instead of letting him blackmail you into doing what you did—sabotaging Miss Goodman's team."

Buck bowed his head and nodded. "I know that now, Mister Judge. All I ask is that you don't put me in the same cell as him." He flicked his eyes down the hallway. "I'll do my time, but I can't ask Miss Laura to look after my dogs forever. And I probably wouldn't get out of jail without bein' crippled up, if he gets a'hold of me."

"It will be up to Miss Laura herself as to how long your time will be," the judge said, and Buck's head sprang up. "It was her harness you destroyed, and her you almost cost the race. She's the one who will be pressing charges against you."

Laura tilted her head and studied Buck. "This might take some careful deliberation, Judge Nordic."

"Take all the time you need, Miss Goodman."

Buck lifted his chin and stood at what he probably considered attention. He gazed past Laura to where the bars covered the windows, and his eyes dropped to the floor.

"Well, I did promise Buck that I'd look after his dogs," Laura said. "The problem is, Buck's one of my employees at the kennel. With one less employee and ten more dogs, I might have to worry about Pete quitting on me because he was overworked."

Pete nodded his head. "Yeah, you don't pay me enough for all the hard work I do around there now." With his head turned away from Buck, he slipped Laura a wink.

Laura laid a hand on her cheek and frowned as though in

indecision. "Dear, dear," she said with a shake of her head. "You see my problem, don't you, Judge?"

"Can't say as I do, Miss Goodman," he said seriously. "Maybe you should explain it."

"Well, it's like this. No matter what Buck is like in the evenings when he's not working, he does pull his weight at the kennels every day. Ever since that time he got drunk on the job, that is."

"I ain't never gonna let nothin' like that happen again, Miss Laura," Buck insisted. "I ain't never let you down since then, has I?"

"No, not at the kennel," Laura told him. "But destroying my harness is another matter. Let me see. How much did George Dyer pay you for that?"

"Fifty dollars," Buck admitted, hanging his head. "But he only gave me half of it, enough to pay my money so I could get in the race. He was gonna give me the rest afterwards."

"My harness cost fifty dollars and I'm donating my race winnings to the charity hospital. I think if I deduct two dollars a week out of your wages until I have the twenty-five dollars you were paid, and give that to the hospital, also, I would be satisfied. And you can either repair that harness piece by piece on your own time, or allow me to keep making that same deduction until it's paid for."

"I'll do it, Miss Laura. I will. Fix the harness, I mean." Buck nodded emphatically. "And you can keep the money out of my wages for the other. I learnt my lesson, and I won't never do nothin' like this again. If someone tries to make me, I'll come tell you 'bout it."

Laura glanced at Judge Nordic, and he patted Buck on the shoulder. "See that you remember that, Buck." Looking over at the desk sergeant, the judge said, "Make a note of this for the records, Sergeant. I doubt we'll have any trouble over Mr. Svenson not fulfilling his promises, but we'll want it down on paper just in case. He'll be on probation until Miss Goodman notifies us he's compensated her properly. And if you have a form there, I'll sign it dismissing the charges against Mr. Montdulac. I'm freeing him, also."

"Yes, sir."

Within five minutes, they left the police station. Judge Nordic offered Laura a ride back to the Dubuques', where she was spending the night. After a moment's discussion, they decided to let the other men use the Dubuques' carriage to return to the hotel and bring it back in the morning before picking up their dogs in the park, where they had been chained after the race.

Sandy desperately wanted a few minutes alone with Laura, but he resisted the urge just as strongly. For one thing, there wasn't an opportunity, and the night was so cold, standing outside and holding a conversation would be foolish. "Thank you" seemed inappropriately weak for what she had done, and "I love you" wasn't an option.

After goodnights were exchanged, he climbed into the Dubuques' carriage and the two carriages went in opposite directions. Sandy did lean out for one last sight of the other carriage, finding Laura doing the same. She lifted a hand in a silent, private good night to him.

22

*L*AURA DECIDED SHE must have gotten all of two hours sleep the rest of the night, and only because her exhausted body finally overrode her jumbled mind. Suddenly her eyes flew open and she checked the clock on her bedside table.

"Five-thirty," she mumbled.

By the time she packed, got a cup of coffee and some food for the trail, it would be daylight. She stumbled out of bed, hoping the Dubuques' cook would be on duty already, despite the late hour the celebration had strung into. There had been stragglers leaving when Judge Nordic dropped her off last night, and then she'd had to tell the Dubuques the latest developments. She'd also warned them she would probably be on her way home by the time they crawled out of bed themselves this morning. Good friends, she knew the Dubuques wouldn't be upset over her leaving so early. She'd be back to visit them many times again.

When she got to the kitchen a while later, she smelled coffee and found the cook baking.

"Miss Goodman," Cook greeted. "Your food for the trail is in the pack over there. The beefsteaks you wanted are still froze, but wrapped separate so they'll cook fine over the fire. And if you'll tell me what you'd like for breakfast, I'll fix you right up."

"I'll just have a couple of those sweet rolls cooling over there," Laura said. "Do you think Shaun's up, so he can take me over to the park to get my dogs? I'll eat the rolls on the way."

Cook walked over to a boxy telephone on the wall and stared at it reluctantly for a moment. Then she straightened her shoulders, picked up the ear piece and gave the crank a resounding turn.

"Hello!" she yelled after a second. "Stella, ring the Dubuques' stable for me, will you?" While she waited, she said, "Stupid thing, having a dadblamed tellyphone in a stables." Then, "Shaun, Miss Goodman is ready to go to the park!" A brief hesitation, then, "Well, same to you!"

She slammed the ear piece down into the hook and glared at the instrument. "Huh. Tells me he could hear me just as well if I stepped out on the back porch and hollered! New fangled contraptions, anyway." She turned to Laura. "He'll get a carriage ready by the time you get out there, Miss Goodman."

She hurried back over to her bread dough, muttering something about how the Dubuques would probably be getting rid of their horses and filling the stalls full of those noisy horseless carriages next thing anyone knew.

Laura couldn't resist saying, "You're probably right about that, Cook. In fact, Mrs. Dubuque was talking about that last evening."

Cook's eyes grew round, then she shook her head. "The day they try to send me home in one of them things, that's the day I quit!"

Giggling under her breath, Laura picked up two of the sweet rolls cooling on the counter, then the food pack. She backtracked to the hallway outside the kitchen and retrieved her coat and satchel of clothing, then went out a side door and headed for the stable. Shaun had the carriage ready by the time she got to the stable, and she climbed in.

It only took them five minutes to get to the park, and Laura scowled when Shaun pulled the carriage to a halt beside where she indicated her dogs were chained. Her dogs were there, but Pete's and Buck's were gone. Fresh paw prints and sled tracks led away, so they couldn't have left too long ago. Beyond her dogs she saw Keever, chained amid the rest of Sandy's dogs. At least Sandy was still here, so she'd have someone to travel home with.

"Did they bring the carriage back this morning, Shaun?" she asked.

"Early," he said. "That's why I was already up when Cook called and 'most broke my eardrum yelling over that tellyphone. Keep tryin' to tell her she don't have to yell for me to hear her."

"She'll get used to it eventually. But was Sandy Montdulac with Pete and Buck when they brought the carriage back?"

"No'm, he weren't. Only them two."

"Hmmmm. Would you mind going by the Superior Hotel to see if Sandy needs a ride? I'll start getting both teams harnessed."

"Yes'm."

Blancheur greeted her enthusiastically, bounding from the snow and shaking the layer of matching white from his back. She gave him a good rub behind his ears before she dug through the packs left on her sled and started feeding him and the team. After her dogs were fed, she went over to Keever and had Sandy's dogs eating by the time Shaun returned, with Sandy on the seat beside him.

"He was already walking over here, Miss Goodman," Shaun said as he pulled the carriage to a stop and Sandy climbed down. "You need anything else, Mr. Montdulac?"

"No. Thanks for the ride, Shaun."

"See you next time." He saluted with the whip and clicked to the horse.

"Good morning," she told Sandy. "I can't believe Buck

and Pete just went on and left us behind, especially when Buck didn't have a harness for his dogs."

"I doubt Buck's driving his team. I heard him and Pete discussing it last night, and they decided they'd go back together, leading Buck's dogs."

"Oh. But that still doesn't explain why they went on ahead and didn't wait for us."

"That I don't know about. All I do know is that when I got up, the desk clerk had a message for me that said they'd left for Grand Marais. I started walking over here to the park when Shaun picked me up."

"Hmmm. Well, you can harness your own dogs now. I'm ready to get on the trail, if you are. We'll still have to stay overnight somewhere, but we can get home by noon tomorrow if we get going."

He nodded and reached for the harness lying in his sled. Laura went back to her own dogs, and within ten minutes they were both ready to leave. Sandy motioned for her to go ahead and take the lead, and she mushed her team out of the park. No snow had fallen since the race ended yesterday, so they had a well-packed trail to travel, and her dogs eagerly picked up speed. Judge Nordic had explained that, on the chance George Dyer demanded a trial, she and Buck would need to return and testify. But the judge expected Dyer to pay the hefty fine he would levy and leave town. She possibly wouldn't return to Duluth again until on her way to Alaska.

As they traveled up the trail, Laura's thoughts wandered. She'd been disappointed to realize Sandy couldn't accompany her to Alaska and participate in the race. But she accepted the reality of it and knew Pete was a good second choice. What she would truly miss during that time was seeing Sandy—being with him at least part of every day.

And ever since Pete had teasingly dropped the hints that he insisted he wasn't saying at the hotel last night, she hadn't been able to get the possibility of Sandy's loving her in return out of her mind. She even let the thought of Pete and Buck deliberately leaving her and Sandy behind cross her mind. Perhaps Pete wanted her and Sandy to have this chance to be alone.

Tonight they would be alone, too. Only the two of them in the tent she would stop and retrieve at the overnight layover site. Unless Pete and Buck camped early and they caught up to them, she and Sandy would make their own camp tonight. Alone, but together.

Tonight—she had decided in the wee hours of the morning—tonight she would tell Sandy of her love for him and demand the truth from him in return. Love was too precious and too hard to find to toss away without a good fight.

They reached the layover site just before noon, and Sandy decided they would eat their noon meal there. He helped her dismantle the tent and pack it on her sled before they examined the food the hotel cook and the Dubuques' cook had prepared for the separate packs. While they shared whatever looked good with each other, Laura didn't push Sandy into conversation, following his lead when he limited his comments to the food or the fast trail.

"We'll hit Grand Marais early tomorrow, since we don't have to break trail like we did on the trip down," he said at one point.

"Um hum."

"If we had a full moon, we could probably drive on in tonight. Probably make it in by a little after midnight."

"Oh." Laura searched her mind for a reason not to agree to that. "Like you say, the moon's not full. It might be dangerous."

"I suppose," Sandy agreed with a shrug. "Well, if you're done eating, we should get moving."

She jumped up and reloaded her sled, while Sandy did the same. After they hit the trail again, she worried all afternoon about his wanting to push on into Grand Marais that night, wondering if he would chance pushing on. Finally she realized the uselessness of worry. If she didn't have a chance to talk to him tonight, she would do it after they got home. Sandy Montdulac would know she loved him before another twenty-four hours passed.

* * *

Laura stumbled one more time, then "whoa'ed" her dogs. "Sandy," she called, knowing he probably couldn't hear her since he had taken the lead a half hour ago. As she expected, he kept on going. Instead of following, she headed her dogs into a clearing she could barely see among the trees. He'd come back for her as soon as he noticed she wasn't behind him.

They'd made even better time than they'd thought, not stopping any more than necessary. From the landmarks around her, it was only about another three hour trip home. But if Sandy did decide to go on in, her dogs needed a rest first. And she needed to wait until her eyes adjusted to the full darkness, which would soon fall. Right now the shadowed half light between daylight and night made her misgauge her footfalls too often as she trotted beside the sled.

Deciding she was going to have a hot meal, she dropped her snow anchor and headed for a deadfall, where she could find dry wood in the center. She soon had a fire going and, when Sandy pulled into the camp site, she was searching in her pack for the beefsteaks she'd requested from the Dubuques' cook.

He parked his team and headed for the fire. "Sorry. My mind was wandering and I didn't pay any attention to how dark it was getting."

"Anything you want to talk about?" she asked.

"No." He glanced at her, but she couldn't make out his features in the dim light.

"We can go on, if that's what you want," she said reluctantly. "I'm going to have something to eat first, though."

"No," he repeated, and she stifled a relieved smile. "No sense taking any chances. I might even be talked into cooking those steaks if you ask me nice."

"You're afraid I'll burn them!" She put a teasingly disgusted tone into her voice. "I'll have you know, I've been practicing with Katie. And what makes you think one of these steaks is for you?"

"A little thing like you can't eat both of them." Sandy chuckled and picked up a branch to poke the fire. "We need to let the wood burn down to coals first, or those steaks will char. You want me to help you get the tent up?"

She did, and a while later, they had the dogs fed and their own food ready to eat. However, as hard as Sandy tried to keep the conversation flowing about innocuous things, he jumped away from her like a cat on a scalding hot tin roof whenever she came too close. The last straw came when she carried their plates into the tent, where he had the kerosene heater glowing with warmth, and he took his plate from her. Instead of sitting crosslegged on his bedroll to enjoy his food, as Laura did, he remained standing and picked up his steak with his fingers to take a bite.

"Good," he said. "I've got some bread in my food pack. I think I'll stick a slice on each side of this and eat it that way while I check on the dogs."

"Damn it, Sandy!" Laura yelled at him. "Sit down! I'm not going to lunge at you and try to have my way with you!"

In the lantern light his shoulders heaved and his eyes darkened. He glanced at his plate, then set it down on his bedroll and straightened.

"It's not you I'm worried about, Laura," he said in a quiet voice. "I think I'll take my bedroll and sleep on my sled tonight."

"Please don't," she said in a softer voice. She put her own plate aside. As hard as she had worked to make the steak exactly right, at the moment it looked about as appealing as a burned shoe. "Sandy, please. I want to talk to you tonight. I want to tell you—"

"Don't!" He stared at her so longingly it was all she could do not to rise and lunge at him anyway. "Don't," he said in that quiet voice again. Then he knelt in front of her and reached out to cup her cheek.

"You don't understand, Laura. If we don't say it, somehow it will be easier to make believe it never was."

"That's a lie, Sandy. Nothing will make it any easier."

He dropped his chin to his chest and shook his head, his

arm falling away from her face. Reaching down, she picked it up again, clasping his rough hand between her own.

"I love you, Sandy."

"No. No, don't."

She ignored him. "I love you, and I'll love you until the day I die. No one will ever again make me feel the way you do. I don't understand why you won't admit you love me, too, because I know you do. But as humbling as it is, I can't keep from wanting you to know I love you, even if I never hear you say it in return. I love you, Sandy."

He curled his fingers around her hand and reached his free hand up to place the index finger under her chin. Gently, very slowly, he leaned forward and kissed her. A soft kiss, a clinging kiss. A kiss with so much finality in it, it brought tears to her eyes as the last flicker of hope died inside her.

He moved back and said, "I can't, Laura. I won't. You'll find someone else someday."

She repeated his words. "I can't. I won't. But believe this, Sandy. Even though I know I'm not woman enough to make you happy, I do want that for you. I want you to find someone who has whatever it is I'm lacking and build a life with her. You're too wonderful a man to be alone the rest of your life."

He surged to his feet. Fists clenched, he glared down at her. "Damn it, you still don't understand. There will never be anyone else. I love you too much, Laura. Too damned much!"

She gasped, but he was through the tent flap before she could stop him. For just an instant she thought about going after him, but some instinct held her back. Instead she got to her feet so she could see out the tent flap. He stood at the edge of the clearing, his shadowed body almost a part of a huge pine, whose branches didn't begin to spread until high overhead.

His back was to her, hands shoved into his coat pockets and shoulders bowed. Keever was near him, and the dog strained against his chain, trying to get to his master. Sandy slowly turned toward him, then dropped into the snow and clung to the dog's neck. He was too far off for Laura to hear if he said anything, but she could have sworn she heard a sob carried on the night breeze. Or maybe it was only her own beginning tears.

She closed the tent flap and removed her coat and boots before she climbed into her bedroll with the rest of her clothing still on. Stuffed with goosedown, her bedroll would keep her warm even in the sub-zero night, but she laid her coat over her, also. The small heater didn't help much in the recesses of the tent.

She never heard Sandy come in. She thought her agony and tears would keep her sleepless, but she drifted off after her tears were only half exhausted. She knew there would be more bitter tears shed in the days—and nights—to come. Tonight her body, exhausted from too little sleep the past three nights and the hard day on the trail, overrode her mind again and she slept.

23

*N*O WORD EVER came from Duluth, so Laura assumed George Dyer had suffered whatever punishment Judge Nordic gave him without the humiliation of a trial. Sandy very effectively kept his distance during the next few weeks of final training, using Pete as a buffer between them and disappearing into his own house in the evening as soon as he cared for his dogs. Even the excitement of finally being in reach of the Alaska race couldn't bring Laura completely out of the resulting dejection.

The day before she and Pete were to leave for Alaska, David and Cristy got married at the huge log house at Ladyslipper Landing. Tom Goodman had refused to take "no" for an answer when he offered to let David and Cristy be married there and to host the reception. With Tracie for a flower girl and Laura for Cristy's maid of honor, Sandy had no choice but to rub shoulders with her the entire day. Sandy gave Cristy away, his face beaming with pride, and

Laura hadn't seen him so relaxed in weeks. But afterwards, during the reception, his moroseness reappeared.

Katie and several of her granddaughters had prepared the reception, combining it into a send-off dinner for Laura and Pete. All David's and the Goodmans' friends came out from Grand Marais, as well as some of Pete's friends and relatives. The house was crowded, and instead of enjoying the celebration, Laura had to make a huge effort to paste a smile on her face.

The first chance Laura got, she slipped unnoticed out the kitchen door. On the mud porch she jammed her feet into her boots and took her cloak from the peg. Outside she leaned her head back and stared at the velvet black sky, striving for the peace and contentment the jubilant enthusiasm inside the house made impossible.

A movement caught her attention, and she glanced toward Blancheur to see a small figure rise to its feet beside the sled dog. Tracie. What on earth was she doing out here in the frigid cold? She walked toward the child, and Tracie stood still, waiting for her.

"Tracie, aren't you cold?" she asked.

"No, Miss Laura." Her voice held a hint of tears. "I just wanted to be by myself for a minute. I'll come back in now."

"Is there something wrong, Tracie?" She knelt in front of her, tipping her chin up and trying to see the little girl's face in the darkness. "Do you want to go out to the kennel and talk instead of going back into the house right away? It's at least a little warmer there."

Tracie shrugged her small shoulders. "It doesn't matter. It won't make nothin' different."

Laura stood and took her hand. "We don't know unless we try, darling. Come on."

Tracie followed reluctantly. Inside the kennel Laura dropped her hand long enough to put a couple logs in the wood heating stove and light a lantern in the office. When she sat down in the desk chair, opened her cloak and held out her arms, Tracie ran to her, sobbing her little heart out.

For a long time Laura could only hold Tracie close and let

her cry. The child sobbed and choked so hard it scared Laura, and there was no way Tracie could talk and tell her what was wrong. Tears leaked from Laura's eyes, also, and she pushed Tracie's hood back, laying her head on the child's soft hair.

At last Tracie pulled back from the soaked collar on Laura's dress and sniffed mightily. Laura shifted her in order to reach the handkerchief in her dress pocket. She wiped the tears off, then held the hanky to Tracie's nose.

"Blow, darling."

Tracie complied, but the minute she looked up at Laura, new sobs broke free.

"Oh, darling," Laura said, hugging her close again. "Tracie, sweetheart, please try to stop crying long enough to tell me what's wrong."

She gulped, and said in a broken wail, "I . . . I don't want . . . to . . . to go awaaaaaay!" She flung her small arms around Laura's neck and buried her face again.

"Oh my God," Laura whispered. Bending her head, she held the child tighter, her heart breaking anew. She'd fought this knowledge every day while she tried to come to terms with Sandy's plans to leave, but it wouldn't be denied now. It hit her full force. She was losing this precious child from her life as well as the man she loved.

"Oh, Tracie," she moaned in a heartbroken voice as she rocked Tracie and herself in the chair. "I don't want you to go, either. Or your father. But I can't stop him."

She thought the child hadn't heard her, but after a long span of shared misery, Tracie controlled herself long enough to speak, although she wouldn't relinquish her hold on Laura's neck.

"Who *can* talk my Daddy into staying here? Aunt Cristy tries, but Daddy goes into his room and shuts the door. Then he goes out real late and takes Keever for a run all by himself. I seen him do that bunches of times, when everyone thoughts I was sleepin'. And now Aunt Cristy's married and there's nobody to even talk to Daddy."

Oh, Lord, how much sleep had this tiny child lost during the last few weeks? Why did no one ever think of how it would affect the children when they wallowed in their own misery?

She had, though, Laura thought to herself. But she hadn't had any right to interfere in Sandy's treatment of Tracie or make judgments on his decisions. Had she? A slow burn of anger began, the heat drying the tears on her cheeks.

She rocked Tracie until she felt her slacken in her arms and fall asleep. Sensing more than knowing for sure that anyone else was there, she glanced up to see Sandy in the office doorway.

"I noticed she was gone and was looking for her," he said, inclining his head toward Tracie. "I'll take her over to bed now."

"How long have you been standing there?" she demanded in a quiet yet unyielding voice.

"About ten seconds. Why?"

She studied him intensely. Only the child in her arms kept her from letting the lavalike anger inside her erupt. Finally she rose to her feet and handed Tracie to him.

"Put her to bed," she ordered.

"That's what I was going to do."

"And you always follow through on what you say you'll do, don't you, Sandy?" she hissed in a low voice. "Even when it's your own damned stubborn pride forcing you to make a wrong decision."

He stepped back as though she'd struck him. "Stay out of my business, Laura."

She cocked her head and looked at him. "No. No, I won't, Sandy. Not for my sake, either. I've learned something, Sandy. I've learned that there are more important things in my life than my own goals. David told me lots of times that I was spoiled, but he never acted like that was a bad thing. I doubt very much he would have fallen in love with Cristy so easily, however, if I'd been more like her. More giving and not so self-centered."

"I don't consider you like that, Laura," Sandy said in a voice that sounded as though he'd rather bite his tongue off than say the words.

"It's not your opinion that matters to me right now," she

said honestly. "I laid my heart at your feet once, and you rejected it. Maybe I grew up a little bit then, but it wasn't until I saw what my love for you was doing to this tiny child that I really felt a surge of maturity."

"Laura—"

"Shut up, Sandy." She backed over to the desk and leaned against it, placing her hands on either side of her. "You're leaving here because I love you, aren't you, Sandy?" He glanced away from her, but she said, "Look at me, Sandy. Now."

"Let me get Tracie to bed, then we'll talk."

"No. No, you don't even *have* to answer me, Sandy. I know it's true. If it weren't for me, you could stay here in Grand Marais and raise Tracie among the people who have come to love her."

"Damn it, Laura, you've got it wrong again!"

"Then tell me why, Sandy. I've spent the last ten minutes holding that child in my arms, listening to her sob her heart out because you were taking her away from here. Tell me why you're doing that, Sandy."

Despite her demand, he avoided her eyes again. "Because I love you, Laura," he admitted after a moment. "You're right, and I lied. I told you that our last night on the trail, on the way back from Duluth."

She let out her breath in a whoosh and shook her head. "That doesn't make sense. It didn't make sense when you said it then, and it sure as hell doesn't make sense now."

"Don't curse, Laura."

"I'll damned well curse if I want to!" she hissed. Her fingers gripped the edges of the desk until she thought it would surely break off. Suddenly she realized how cold they were, and she pulled them free, shoving her hands into her cloak pockets. Sandy turned and started out the door.

"I'm not going to Alaska tomorrow," she flung after him.

He halted as though the door had slammed in his face. Slowly he turned back around. "It won't make any difference, Laura. After the Northshore Race, I had several offers from kennel owners around Duluth. And there was one from a man up in Thunder Bay, across the Canadian border. That man also has a brother over in Russia. He said if I didn't want to come to work for him, his brother would be interested in my coming over there."

"You know," Laura said in a musing voice, "maybe I was wrong to fall in love with you. I guess I didn't know you at all. I thought the man I was falling in love with was a strong man, not a coward who runs away from problems."

"Please try to understand, Laura," he said in a tortured voice instead of the angry one she expected. "If it were only me, I'd have stayed in Alaska and fought the Dyers until the bitter end. And I'd stay here now, if I could. But with Tracie involved, I can't. I can't take a chance that they'll end up getting her away from me."

"It's breaking her heart. She wants to stay here."

"She won't stay here anyway if the Dyers win. They'd take her back to Alaska, and I'd never see her again. I know it's going to hurt her, but I'd like to think it wouldn't hurt as much as if she lost me, after losing her mother."

Her anger evaporated, along with any smidgen of hope. Tears clouded her eyes, and she bowed her head. "I understand now," she agreed. "Go ahead. Put Tracie to bed."

"Go on to Alaska, Laura. Fight for your dream. At least you'll have that."

"All right."

She didn't hear him leave, and after a few seconds she looked at the doorway. But he was gone.

Early the next day, Laura stood at her father's office window, staring out over the frozen cove. At the head of the trail to Duluth, a crowd waited to see her and Pete off. Among the crowd were Sandy and Tracie. But they had to wait. She wouldn't go until she made sure her father and David understood what she wanted done.

"I hate to tell you this, Laura," David said. "But I can't do this on your orders."

She whirled on him. "What do you mean? I told you I'd pay you."

He shrugged. "You don't have an interest in this, Laura.

You can't contact an Alaskan attorney and file a motion to appeal the court order up there. I'll admit, you've got a good idea. We can send Buck up there to testify, and also take a copy of the charges filed against George Dyer in Duluth and show them what he tried to do down here. I can't say that it will win the case for Sandy, but it will put a slur on Dyer's reputation and show his dishonesty."

"Will you at least go to Sandy, and tell him what he needs to do? Ask him to take this chance?"

The new Mrs. David Hudson walked over to Laura. With a smile on her face, Cristy said, "Laura, maybe you can't request an appeal of that order, but I believe I can. If Sandy refuses to do it, I'll do it on behalf of my niece. And since I have an attorney who will do it for free, my brother can't get his nose out of joint about that."

"Thank you, Cristy. I promise, I'll never bother Sandy if he will at least stay here with Tracie."

Her father walked over to her and wrapped an arm around Laura's waist. "You're in love with him, aren't you, sweetheart?"

"Yes, Daddy," she admitted. "But he doesn't want me. I was awake most of the night trying to figure everything out, and I don't think it's just the worry he has about losing Tracie. I think it's because we've got money and he doesn't. It's his pride, and I can't fight that."

Tom nodded his head. "He wouldn't be the man you fell in love with if you could, darling. Sometimes pride is the only thing a man has left after life deals him several hard knocks. I wish I could make it better for you, Laura, but I can't. I'm proud of you, though. You're thinking of Tracie's happiness before your own."

"How could I not, Daddy?"

Well back from the gathered crowd, Sandy wrapped his snow anchor around a tree to hold Keever and the sled in place. Lifting Tracie into his arms, he carried her toward the crowd. Suddenly she struggled, demanding to be put down.

"I don't think I want to watch Laura leave," she said when he looked down at her. "Let's go back home."

"Tracie, it wouldn't be very nice of us not to say goodbye to Laura and wish her luck."

"I don't care," his daughter said with a mutinous pout. "It's gonna make me hurt to tell her 'bye and make me cry. I don't wants to do it."

"Sometimes we have to do things that hurt us, sweetheart."

"You didn't. You left Alaska 'cause Grandma and Grandpa Dyer was doin' stuff to you that made you hurt. And you's gonna leave here 'cause we mights get hurt. I want to go now. We can go off on our own and never see nobody ever again, like you told Aunt Cristy we was gonna do. That way, we won't get to like nobody else and then gets hurt when we leaves them."

My God, what had he done? Sandy stumbled back to the sled and sat down, holding his daughter in his lap. She didn't understand, though. How could he take a chance on losing the most precious thing he had left in his life, his daughter? He'd thought he knew love when he and Colleen got married, but it hadn't been anything like the first time he held Tracie in his arms. He'd wanted to give her the world—shield her from ever being hurt or ever crying. Shelter her from life's unfairness.

He remembered once when he came in from work and heard her crying. Colleen was calmly getting up from her rocking chair and placing her needlepoint in the seat. When she saw him, she smiled and walked toward him.

"Tracie's crying," he said needlessly. "Go on to her. I'll get my welcome-home kiss later."

"She just woke up as you opened the door," Colleen had said. "I'm not neglecting our daughter, but it won't hurt her to cry for a few seconds until I greet my husband."

He hugged her and received her kiss, then said, "I can't stand to hear her cry."

Colleen patted his cheek. "If there weren't a few tears in the world, Sandy, we wouldn't appreciate the joy nearly as much."

She'd hurried off to comfort Tracie, and Sandy hadn't thought of her words once since then. He'd only been relieved to follow and find Tracie in Colleen's arms, her tears dry and a gummy smile on her face, appreciating the joy of her mother coming to comfort her.

Colleen had done what she knew was best for the baby and her husband both. And what had he done? He'd taught Tracie that running away to avoid the hurt was the best thing to do. He'd taught her it was useless to try to fight back against the hurt.

Sandy stood and started toward the main street of town.

"Where's we goin', Daddy?" Tracie asked.

"We're going to tell Laura we love her," Sandy said. "That we're going to Alaska with her, and we're going to fight your grandma and grandpa as long as we have to in order to prove to them they've got no right to try to separate us. And we're going to ask Laura if she'll marry us."

"Oh Daddy! Oh, Daddy, do you means it?"

"I means it, darling. With all my heart."

Tracie sat up in his arms, settling her rump on his forearm and throwing her little arms around his neck. The strength of her hold caught him by surprise, almost strangling him. But Sandy never slowed his steps.

Suddenly horses' hooves pounded down the street behind him, and someone shouted Sandy's name. He glanced over his shoulder to see a large sleigh, with a driver on the front seat and two people in the back. Recognizing George and Elvina Dyer in the rear seat, he halted and placed Tracie on the walkway.

"Go on to Tom Goodman's office and wait for me, darling," he said. "It's right there, just two doors away. Tell Laura I'll be along in a moment."

"No. I wants to stay here and go with you when you get ready."

He sighed as the sleigh pulled to a stop beside him. "All right. But you stay quiet and let me handle this."

"I will, Daddy."

Elvina Dyer was closest to the walkway, and she climbed out of the sleigh when the driver pulled down a set of steps. She staggered a little, catching herself on the side of the sleigh.

"Hello, Sandy," she said. "I haven't been out of that sleigh more than a couple times all night, so my legs are a little stiff."

"You might as well get back in and leave, Elvina," he said. "You're not coming near Tracie."

"Will you at least give me a chance to say what I came for, Sandy?" she asked in a pleading voice. "I'm not here to try to take Tracie away from you. On the contrary, George is going to tell you how sorry he is for everything that's happened since Colleen died." She turned to glare into the sleigh. "Aren't you, George?"

Her answer was a harumph, and Elvina sighed. Picking up her heavy skirts and cloak, she climbed the steps to the walkway. Sandy shoved Tracie behind him, and Elvina's eyes clouded with tears. She leaned a little to one side and said, "Hello, Tracie. Oh, my darling, Grandma's so sorry she hasn't been able to hold you for so long. Can I have just one hug?"

Sandy heard a door open on down the walkway, but he never took his eyes off Elvina. He felt Tracie grip his trouser leg in one hand, then she said, "I don't wants to hug you 'long as you tries to take me away from my daddy, Grandma."

"I'm not going to do that ever again, darling," Elvina said. "And neither is your grandpa. I've come to tell your daddy that we've rescinded the court order, and we'll never, ever try to do anything like that again."

When Tracie moved out from behind him, Sandy bent down and swept her into his arms. Elvina held her hands out, biting her lip and tears streaming down her face. "Oh, please, Sandy." A heart-wrenching sob escaped her, but Sandy hardened his heart.

"I'll need proof, Elvina."

"I don't think Grandma's tellin' a fib, Daddy," Tracie said. "And I really would like her to hug me."

Sandy cautiously examined Elvina's face. She met his gaze steadily, and after a moment, he glanced at the carriage in time to catch sight of George's face before he turned his head. The naked longing on the other man's face as he stared at Tracie gave him some hope that Elvina spoke the truth. Still, he'd assumed Elvina was as involved in the attempt to take Tracie away from him as George.

"I just don't trust you, Elvina."

Digging in her cloak pocket, Elvina pulled out a yellow piece of paper and thrust it at Sandy. "This is the telegram I demanded George have the Alaskan court clerk send him, confirming that we rescinded our request for sole custody. And—"

Elvina fumbled some more in her coat pockets, but came up empty. She turned to glare at George, who had something ready to hand to her. Grabbing it, she passed a black bank book on to Sandy. "That's the account in Duluth, where George deposited your money."

Sandy opened the bank book, confirming the amount and finding it even included interest. He shook his head in amazement, yet his desire for revenge burned deeply. Until he looked at Elvina's face and saw tears streaming faster and her blotting at them with a half-frozen handkerchief.

He handed Tracie to her grandma. With another sob, Elvina clasped the child to her and rocked back and forth.

"Oh, Sandy," she said over Tracie's head. "I'm so sorry. So sorry. My only excuse is that I was so heartbroken over Colleen's death, I couldn't think straight. Maybe if you'd stayed in Alaska, we could have worked things out, but I'm not making excuses for what we did. I just want you to know that I told George I'd leave him if he ever tried something like this again. And he's going to apologize for swindling you out of that money."

"I didn't swin—"

Elvina swung around and glared at her husband, who had scooted across the back seat and was gazing longingly at his wife and granddaughter. Immediately, George dropped his gaze and huddled on the seat, burying his face in his hands.

"I did," he admitted. "And I'm sorry." He raised his head. "I didn't really do anything illegal, but it was unethical."

Stunned, Sandy shook his head. In only a few minutes, his entire life had turned upside down again, this time for the better. He didn't have to worry about the Dyers' trying to separate him from his daughter ever again, and the money he'd worked all his life to make was restored to him. The only thing now that could make his happiness complete would be to have Laura Goodman for his wife and Tracie's mother.

"There's one more thing you're both going to have to accept," Sandy said. "I plan to ask Laura Goodman to be my wife. If she says—"

"Yes!" came Laura's voice from right behind him.

He turned, and she flung herself into his arms. "Yes," she repeated. "Yes, yes, yes, I'll marry you, Sandy! I love you."

Tightening his arms around her, he said, "I want you to know, I was coming here to ask you before Elvina and George showed up. Tracie's my witness. I realized that I didn't love you too much to stay with you. I love you too much to be able to leave you."

He kissed her then, kissed her for the first time without all the turmoil and trouble coming between them. Kissed her as he'd always wanted to. Kissed her as a prelude to the millions of kisses they would share in the future. Kissed her to the accompaniment of the claps, shouts and whistles from the crowd of people, who had filtered down the street when they got tired of waiting for Laura to show up at the head of the trail.

He finally broke the kiss, lifting his head to see Laura's cheeks pink with embarrassment, but a loving warmth in her eyes. He glanced at Tracie and found her now in George's arms. George gave him a tremulous look, and Sandy slowly nodded his head. His own happiness was too complete now for him to withhold his permission for George to hold his granddaughter at last after all these months.

Pete pushed his way through the crowd, with Buck on his heels. "Buck and I want to be the first ones to congratulate you, Sandy," he said, holding out a hand. Sandy reluctantly removed one of his hands from Laura's back to shake Pete's and shifted the other one to pull her close to his side. "I need to know if I'm still going to Alaska, though. I was all set to go up there and show them what a team of Minnesota dogs could do."

Sandy glanced down at Laura, but before he could speak, she said, "How do you feel about a honeymoon in Alaska, darling? If I have any say in the matter, that's what I'd like. And we can take Pete and Buck, with their dogs, too."

Tom Goodman stepped forward. "Welcome to the family, son," he said. After Sandy also shook his extended hand, he said to Laura, "Man might want to have his first few weeks alone with his wife, Laura, not with an entourage of people tagging along on his honeymoon.

"Oh," Laura said, a renewed flush staining her cheeks. "I didn't think of that."

"Laura, darling." Sandy tucked a finger under her chin and lifted her face. "I say a honeymoon in Alaska and running in that race is the most appropriate thing I can think of. What do you say?"

"I love you, Sandy Montdulac."

He cuddled her head against his shoulder. "I love you, too, Laura. And since the whole town is already here, we could get married right now if you want."

"I want. Oh, I want, Sandy."

24

TRACIE COUNTED THE number of sled dogs racing across the finish line until she got to five. None of the teams were led by Keever or Blancheur, but her friend Buck and his pretty lead dog, Snowstorm, came in second. Tracie strained to see down the trail as Buck circled his team and headed back to what Grandpa had told her was the winners' circle. She'd hope to see either mommy or daddy in that circle, but being able to count, she knew they wouldn't be now. Grandpa had said there were only places for three mushers in the winners' circle.

"Hold me higher, Grandpa," she said.

"You won't be able to see any better if I do, Tracie, honey," her grandpa said. "But don't worry. I'm sure your daddy and Laura are all right."

"She's not Laura now, Grandpa," Tracie insisted. "She's Mommy."

"Then I'm sure your mommy and daddy are all right," Grandpa corrected. "They'll be along."

"Look! Look, there's Pete's dogs!"

She bounced up and down in Grandpa's arms as Pete's dogs flew across the finish line. He whoa'ed the team on down the street and turned it to come back toward them. As soon as he settled the team and patted his lead dog, he walked over to them.

"Where's mommy and daddy?" she asked. Then she hurried on, "Oh, I's sorry, Pete. I should've said congrad'shuns for finishin' the race. Grandpa says that's a 'complish . . . 'complishment all by itself."

Pete rumpled her hair. "Thanks, Tracie. And don't worry about your mommy and daddy. They were just late getting on the trail this morning, as usual."

"Oh," Tracie said wisely. "They's more interested in honeymoonin' than winnin' the race, huh?"

Pete looked at her in surprise, and she shrugged. "I heard Grandpa tellin' Grandma he betted mommy and daddy wouldn't win, 'cause they'd rather honeymoon than race. What's honeymoonin'?"

Pete threw back his had and laughed, and when Tracie looked at her Grandpa, she saw his cheeks get red.

"You ask your Grandpa what honeymooning is, Tracie," Pete said, still snorting with laughter. Then he glanced at her Grandma, and Tracie looked at her, too. Her cheeks were red, also.

"Or maybe you better ask your Grandma," Pete said, "while me and your Grandpa go look over my dogs. Some things are for women to talk about together."

Grandpa shoved her into Grandma's arms real fast and walked away with Pete. "Thanks," she heard Grandpa mutter. "Us men gotta stick together."

"Grandma," Tracie said. "What's . . ."

"Look, darling." Grandma pointed down the trail. "That looks like Sandy and Laura coming there!"

For a second, Tracie wondered why Grandma sounded so funny, but she guessed Grandma had been a little bit worried and now she was glad to see Mommy and Daddy coming. And yes, it was Mommy and Daddy coming down the trail.

Suddenly, just like Daddy had told her it had happened back in Duluth, Mommy yelled something and bent over her sled handles. Daddy did, too, and their dogs ran even faster. A minute later, they both crossed the finish line, with Keever's head just a little bit in front of Blancheur's.

Now Mommy and Daddy were even, she guessed. They'd each beat the other one once. Wonder if they would have to race one more time to break the tie?

ROMANCE FROM THE HEART OF AMERICA
Homespun Romance

__TUMBLEWEED HEART		0-515-11944-X/$5.99
	by Tess Farraday	
__TOWN SOCIAL		0-515-11971-7/$5.99
	by Trana Mae Simmons	
__LADY'S CHOICE		0-515-11959-8/$5.99
	by Karen Lockwood	
__HOME TO STAY		0-515-11986-5/$5.99
	by Linda Shertzer	
__MEG'S GARDEN		0-515-12004-9/$5.99
	by Teresa Warfield	
__COUNTY FAIR		0-515-12021-9/$5.99
	by Ginny Aiken	
__HEARTBOUND		0-515-12034-0/$5.99
	by Rachelle Nelson	
__COURTING KATE		0-515-12048-0/$5.99
	by Mary Lou Rich	
__SPRING DREAMS		0-515-12068-5/$5.99
	by Lydia Browne	
__TENNESSE WALTZ		0-515-12135-5/$5.99
	by Trana Mae Simmons	
__FARM GIRL		0-515-12106-1/$5.99
	by Linda Shertzer	
__SWEET CHARITY		0-515-12134-7/$5.99
	by Rachel Wilson	
__BLACKBERRY WINTER		0-515-12146-0/$5.99
	by Sherrie Eddington	
__WINTER DREAMS		0-515-12164-9/$5.99
	by Trana Mae Simmons	
__SNOWFLAKE WISHES (11/97)		0-515-12181-9/$5.99
	by Lydia Browne	

Payable in U.S. funds. No cash accepted. Postage & handling: $1.75 for one book, 75¢ for each additional. Maximum postage $5.50. Prices, postage and handing charges may change without notice. Visa, Amex, MasterCard call 1-800-788-6262, ext. 1, or fax 1-201-933-2316; refer to ad #411

Or, check above books Bill my: ☐ Visa ☐ MasterCard ☐ Amex _____ (expires)
and send this order form to:
The Berkley Publishing Group Card#_____
P.O. Box 12289, Dept. B   Daytime Phone #_____ ($10 minimum)
Newark, NJ 07101-5289   Signature_____

Please allow 4-6 weeks for delivery.   Or enclosed is my: ☐ check ☐ money order
Foreign and Canadian delivery 8-12 weeks.

Ship to:

Name_____   Book Total $_____
Address_____   Applicable Sales Tax $_____
                                      (NY, NJ, PA, CA, GST Can.)
City_____   Postage & Handling $_____
State/ZIP_____   Total Amount Due $_____

Bill to: Name_____

Address_____   City_____
State/ZIP_____

Our Town

...where love is always right around the corner!

■■■■■■■■■■■■■■■■■■■■■■■■■

__ *Harbor Lights* by Linda Kreisel	0-515-11899-0/$5.99
__ *Humble Pie* by Deborah Lawrence	0-515-11900-8/$5.99
__ *Candy Kiss* by Ginny Aiken	0-515-11941-5/$5.99
__ *Cedar Creek* by Willa Hix	0-515-11958-X/$5.99
__ *Sugar and Spice* by DeWanna Pace	0-515-11970-9/$5.99
__ *Cross Roads* by Carol Card Otten	0-515-11985-7/$5.99
__ *Blue Ribbon* by Jessie Gray	0-515-12003-0/$5.99
__ *The Lighthouse* by Linda Eberhardt	0-515-12020-0/$5.99
__ *The Hat Box* by Deborah Lawrence	0-515-12033-2/$5.99
__ *Country Comforts* by Virginia Lee	0-515-12064-2/$5.99
__ *Grand River* by Kathryn Kent	0-515-12067-7/$5.99
__ *Beckoning Shore* by DeWanna Pace	0-515-12101-0/$5.99
__ *Whistle Stop* by Lisa Higdon	0-515-12085-5/$5.99
__ *Still Sweet* by Debra Marshall	0-515-12130-4/$5.99
__ *Dream Weaver* by Carol Card Otten	0-515-12141-X/$5.99
__ *Raspberry Island* by Willa Hix	0-515-12160-6/$5.99
__ *Pratt's Landing* by Martha Kirkland (11/97)	0-515-12180-0/$5.99

Payable in U.S. funds. No cash accepted. Postage & handling: $1.75 for one book, 75¢ for each additional. Maximum postage $5.50. Prices, postage and handling charges may change without notice. Visa, Amex, MasterCard call 1-800-788-6262, ext. 1, or fax 1-201-933-2316; refer to ad # 637b

Or, check above books   Bill my: ☐ Visa   ☐ MasterCard   ☐ Amex _____ (expires)
and send this order form to:
The Berkley Publishing Group   Card#_____

P.O. Box 12289, Dept. B   Daytime Phone #_____ ($10 minimum)
Newark, NJ 07101-5289   Signature_____

Please allow 4-6 weeks for delivery.   Or enclosed is my: ☐ check   ☐ money order
Foreign and Canadian delivery 8-12 weeks.

Ship to:

Name_____	Book Total	$_____
Address_____	Applicable Sales Tax (NY, NJ, PA, CA, GST Can.)	$_____
City_____	Postage & Handling	$_____
State/ZIP_____	Total Amount Due	$_____

Bill to: Name_____

Address_____ City_____
State/ZIP_____

PUTNAM ꝑ BERKLEY
online

Your Internet gateway to a virtual environment with hundreds of entertaining and enlightening books from the Putnam Berkley Group.

While you're there visit the PB Café and order up the latest buzz on the best authors and books around—Tom Clancy, Patricia Cornwell, W.E.B. Griffin, Nora Roberts, William Gibson, Robin Cook, Brian Jacques, Jan Brett, Catherine Coulter and many more!

Putnam Berkley Online is located at
http://www.putnam.com

♥ Kiss & Tell ♥

Do you Kiss and Tell? We do. Once a month get an inside look at the hottest romance authors and books around. Plus delicious recipes, revealing gossip and more!

Find Putnam Berkley's Kiss & Tell at
http://www.pbkiss-tell.com